STATE OF GENESIS

Virgil Jones: Book 7

THOMAS SCOTT

For information contact:

ThomasScottBooks.com

Linda Heaton - Editor
BluePenEdits.com

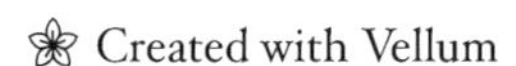

VIRGIL JONES SERIES IN ORDER

State of Anger - Book 1
State of Betrayal - Book 2
State of Control - Book 3
State of Deception - Book 4
State of Exile - Book 5
State of Freedom - Book 6
State of Genesis - Book 7
State of Humanity - Book 8
State of Impact - Book 9

Updates on future Virgil Jones novels available at:
ThomasScottBooks.com

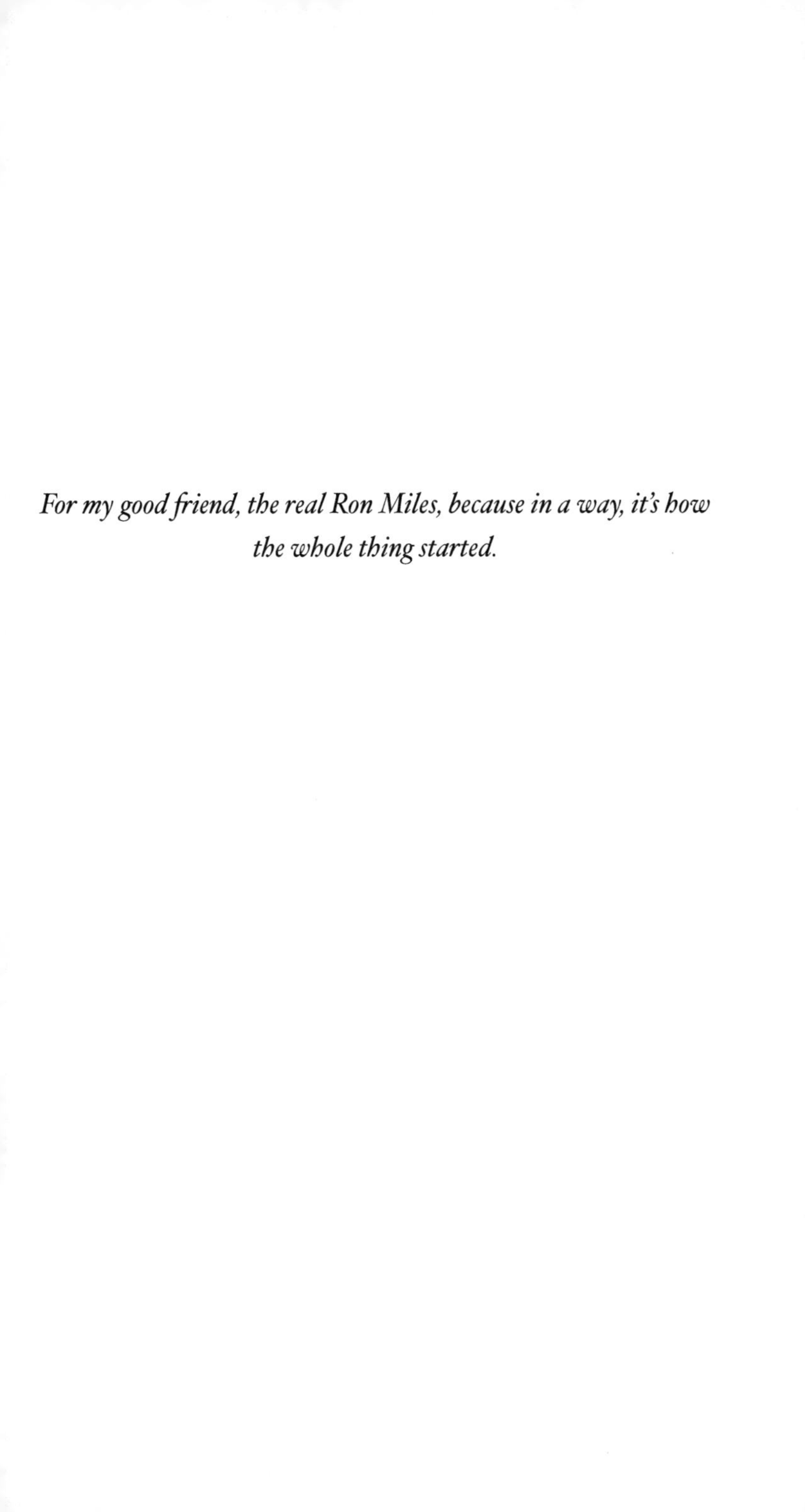

For my good friend, the real Ron Miles, because in a way, it's how the whole thing started.

gen·e·sis

/ˈjenəsəs/

noun

The origin or mode of formation of something. “This tale had its genesis in fireside stories.”

“All the crimes of history, lest we forget, have their genesis in the moral wilderness of their times.”

--Eskinder Nega

“A people without the knowledge of their past history, origin and culture is like a tree without roots.”

--Marcus Garvey

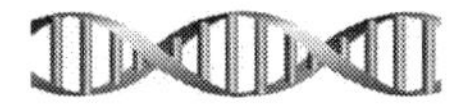

“We make our choices, and right or wrong, we have to live with the consequences.”

--Mason Jones

CHAPTER ONE

THEN

In the quiet of the past, things like honor and morality were more than just words, they were a foundation of sorts, there to stave off the storm in a time of need, no matter the type of sanctuary required. Except wants are often many, and needs almost always few. So in a perfect world it might have all gone away after Mason died. But no matter the complexity of time or the formation of things yet to come, the rich intricacy of the world—both then and now—was slowly turning, ready to show its teeth yet again.

Because the wolf...always at the door.

JOE AVERY WASN'T A BAD MAN, JUST ONE OF THOSE GUYS

who couldn't manage to catch a break. Ever. Even as an adult, he often felt like a kid in a little league game who always managed to drop the fly ball. Uneducated past the eighth grade, he'd married young, and got a job in an Indianapolis foundry as a hoist operator. The hoist carried molten brass from the blast furnace over to the casting dies. The factory made parts—brass valves and fittings—for fire trucks and city hydrants.

When he arrived home from work one afternoon, he found his wife sitting on the sofa, her flowered house dress arranged just so, her hands twisted into a knot on her lap. When she gave him the news of her pregnancy, the corner of Joe Avery's mouth twitched a fraction before he told her congratulations, his voice flat.

"If it's a boy, I'd like to name him Jacob, after my father," she said. "Would that be okay with you?"

When he walked back over to the door he'd entered only moments ago, his wife said, "Where are you going? Dinner is almost ready."

"Where else? I'm going to head down to the tavern. Thought I'd toss back a few and tell the fellas. Gonna be a father. Ain't that something?"

"Did you get paid today? Isn't this payday? The name...we don't have to talk about it right now."

He laughed through his nose and walked out the door.

HE FOUND HIS GROUP OF REGULARS AT A CORNER TABLE

near the back. They were just getting started, their pitchers of beer still half full. They'd come straight from the foundry, their faces blackened except around the eyes where the safety goggles they wore kept the soot away. They looked like a table full of raccoons getting ready to tie one on.

When Avery told them the news of his wife's pregnancy, his co-workers all hooted and hollered and poured him a glass of beer. Then one of them said something stronger was in order and waived the waitress over. "Whiskey for everyone, little darling. One of us is gonna be a father, though I thank Jesus H. his own damned self it ain't me." He gave her ass a squeeze and the waitress let him. She needed the tip money. When she returned they told her to leave the bottle. Joe Avery tried to pull out his wallet, but the others wouldn't hear of it. "Not tonight, buddy boy. For the father to be, drinks are on us."

Avery smiled a much bigger smile than the one he'd given his wife, then put his wallet away. When someone poured him a shot, they dropped it into his glass of beer and said, "Bottoms up." They all clinked glasses—the first of many—and drank the night away.

Later in the early morning hours last call came and went, most of Avery's buddies now long gone. When the only other man at the table offered him a ride home, Avery mumbled something to the effect of, "Walked here...walk back. Gotta somber up."

"You mean sober up." He checked his watch. "Better

get after it, too. Gotta punch the clock in less than three hours. C'mon, I'll help you."

Avery yanked his arm away. "M'all right."

"Suit yourself, then. See you later."

Avery didn't answer. He rested his forehead on the table until the bartender came over and nudged him with the business end of a push broom.

"Time to head home, Joe."

"Am home."

"No, you're not. You're in my bar and the bar is closed. Should have been closed to you a long time ago. Want me to call you a cab?"

"No. Walk." When Avery stood the room spun and he had to hold on to his chair for a moment. Then he felt the bile rise in the back of his throat and despite the spinning room he made it out the back door before vomiting in the alley.

The bartender followed him out, said, "Take 'er easy, Joe. Congrats on the kid." Then he stepped back inside, pulled the door shut, and locked it behind him.

AVERY WOKE FOUR HOURS LATER, STILL DRUNK IN THE alley, but not as wobbly. When he reached for his pocket watch—the only gift he'd ever received from his own father—to check the time he realized it was missing. He'd cherished that watch ever since he'd been a boy. The face of the watch was silver with gold hands and black Roman numerals. The engraving on the inside of the lid was simple and direct. *From your father, with love.* When he checked for his wallet he found that missing as well. He'd cashed his paycheck on the way home—all two weeks' worth—and now it was gone. He spat in the alley, rubbed his face with both hands, then walked out into the street. When he asked a passerby the time, he felt the blood drain from his face when answered. He was an hour late for work.

By the time he arrived he was covered in sweat, the black streaks on his face making him look more like a zebra than a raccoon. The foreman, though not pleased, had heard the news about Avery's wife being pregnant and the celebratory events of the night before. He didn't smile when he spoke, but there was kindness in his voice. "Don't let it happen again."

"It won't." He turned toward the operating cab of the hoist, the factory floor tilting slightly as he did. The foreman caught the tilt.

"You okay, Joe?"

"Yeah, I'm good. Got mugged last night. They got my watch and all my pay. Take any overtime you can give me."

"That's rough. I'll see what I can do. Better get on the hoist. You're gonna back up the line." It never occurred to the foreman to send Avery home for a sick day.

Avery nodded and climbed into the cab. The furnace was blasting out the heat and when the metallurgist was satisfied the molten brass had been properly smelted, he stepped away from the furnace, removed his fireproof helmet, wiped the sweat from his brow, and released a lever that allowed the liquid metal to flow from the furnace and into the ladle. The ladle was essentially a giant bucket made from some sort of infusible metal that could handle the heat. It was attached to the hoist by a series of cables and pulleys that allowed the hoist operator to raise, lower, and pour the metal as needed. When the ladle was full, the metallurgist made a twirling motion at Avery. A sign to raise the bucket and make the transport to the casting area.

Avery caught the twirl, but when he looked at the control levers he couldn't remember which one did what. Maybe it was the alcohol still surging through his system, or maybe it was the fact that he'd been robbed of his pay—money that was supposed to cover groceries and rent—but either way, when he reached out and grabbed the lever that would raise the bucket of molten metal in the air and carry it to the casting station, he grabbed the wrong one.

The ladle—already ten feet high because the furnace drain had to be well above the floor—didn't slowly raise as Avery had intended. Instead it tipped violently to one side in a quick massive pour that spread molten brass across the foundry floor, some of it splashing back up and hitting the metallurgist. His body was somewhat protected by the fireproof gear he wore, but his face and head were completely exposed.

Avery pushed the lever back in place, but by then it was much too late. Men were scattering out of the way of the lethal metal, alarm bells were ringing, red lights were flashing everywhere, and the metallurgist's face seemed to be melting away from his skull. Someone tried to grab him by the arm with a long rod that had a hook on one end to pull him away. But the metallurgist couldn't see, his face on fire, his vision gone, and when he felt the hook on his arm, somewhere in the bowels of his brain he imagined the hook and the attempt of his own rescue as the hand of death pulling him to a place he desperately didn't want to go. He fought the hook the way a drowning person often fights with panic against their own rescuer. He jerked his arm free, but lost any semblance of balance he may have had in the process. When he fell to the floor he landed in the puddle of molten metal. The fire suppression system kicked in, everyone ran for the exits, and the metallurgist fought against himself until his nerve endings were burned away.

Avery, sitting high above it all in the cab of the hoist watched him die, and in the midst of the noise and smell and steam and flashing lights he vomited again less than five hours from the time he was kicked out of the bar.

CHAPTER TWO

The blast furnace had an automatic shut-off valve that killed the fuel feed unit, closed the inlet ducts, and opened the chimney flues to let the heat escape. The fire suppression system knocked out the floor fire and stopped the molten brass from spreading any further than it already had. When it was safe to exit the hoist, Avery climbed down in a robotic fashion, his leg and arm movements stuttered and uncoordinated. When he walked outside he found his co-workers waiting for him, many of them the same men he drank with the previous evening. There was no mistaking their expressions or the thoughts running through their heads. When Avery glanced at the gate, he saw a police car pulling up to the scene. In the distance he could hear the firetrucks approaching.

The man who had tried to rescue the metallurgist had been at the bar last night, though Avery wasn't sure what time he'd left. He still held the long rod, its butt end resting on the ground, the hook high in the air. He spun it in his hands and the curved end of the shaft twisted like a weather vane. When he spoke, his words were packed with anger and disgust.

"I can't imagine a worse death. Can you, Joe?"

Avery held his hands out in front of himself. "I...I can't. It was an accident."

"It was ignorance, is what it was, plain and simple. Man had a family." He spun the shaft again, the hook glinting in the sunlight.

"I grabbed the wrong lever. I didn't mean to."

"How long you think it took him to die, Joe?"

"What? What kind of question is that?"

The man with the hook and shaft reached into his pants and pulled out a pocket watch, and clicked the lid open with his finger. Even though he was still drunk, his vision not right, Avery could make out the face of the watch—silver with gold hands and black Roman numerals. The man with the shaft and hook, the man who Avery thought was his friend, had robbed him of his father's watch and most likely his last two weeks worth of pay.

Suddenly Avery didn't feel drunk or even hung over. The rush of adrenaline that poured through his system blanketed the effects of the alcohol and he felt every bit as hot as the blast furnace in the foundry. That's when Avery did something that set off a chain of events, his own death guaranteed, though it would take nearly twenty years to happen.

The first officer on the scene was a Marion County Sheriff's deputy, a rookie. When he pulled up to the foundry's gate, his vision of the events about to play out were almost completely obscured by the line of men. One of them held some sort of long metal rod that was hooked on one end. It almost looked like a cane made for a giant. Smoke and steam were pouring out of the doors and windows of the foundry. When he turned around, he saw the sheriff pulling up to the gate in his squad car. With reinforcements right behind him, the rookie got brave and pushed his way through the crowd of men, his baton in one hand, the holster strap that secured his sidearm unsnapped in case things turned uglier than anticipated. The radio call had mentioned something about an accident, but with certain groups, you didn't take chances. He thought this group fell into that category. He didn't hear the sheriff telling him to wait.

He made it to the front of the line, right behind the man with the long metal rod. He was about to squeeze through and address the men from the front when all of a sudden the man with the rod did a quick side step to avoid Avery's charge. Avery collided with the rookie who wasn't prepared for the hit. The young deputy was knocked flat on his back, his head impacting the pavement with a sickening crunch. His eyes remained open and fixed, both pupils instantly enlarged almost to the edges of their irises. His sidearm had slipped its holster and was on the pavement, next to his body.

Avery scrambled up off the cop and away from the blood seeping from the back of the officer's skull. He turned in time to see the hook coming at him. He ducked and heard the whoosh of the shaft as it missed his head by less than an inch. When he glanced down he saw the cop's gun on the ground. With all logical thought process now gone, he grabbed the weapon, turned toward the man whom he thought was his friend, the man he'd been drinking with last night, the same man who had stolen his watch and money, and began firing. He kept pulling the trigger until the hammer began clicking on spent rounds, the gun now useless to him.

But it didn't matter. The man with the hook was dead. Avery had managed to hit him three times, twice in the chest, and once in the neck. Most of the other men had backed away when they saw Avery pick up the gun, and then the sheriff was right there, his own weapon out, swinging it side to side, shouting for everyone to step back.

Everyone did, except for Joe Avery, who sat down on the ground, the weapon skittering away as his butt hit the concrete and his teeth clicked together. He put his face in his hands.

He'd killed three men inside of ten minutes.

It took the rest of the day to secure and process the scene. The workers all gave their statements before being sent home...the factory shut down for repairs and cleanup. The coroner's office confirmed the cause and manner of death of the metallurgist, the sheriff's deputy, and the man who'd been shot to death.

Avery was sitting handcuffed in the back of the squad car as the sheriff informed him of his rights. "Anything you want to say?"

"My wife is pregnant," Avery said.

The sheriff tipped his head and closed one eye. His own wife had recently given birth to their first child—a boy—and he wasn't sure how to answer that statement, so he didn't. "I meant, would you like to make any sort of statement before we take you down to central booking?"

"That's what I'm trying to do," Avery said. "The man I shot...I don't know what I was thinking. I thought he was my friend. We got drunk last night and when I passed out in the alley, he robbed me of my pay and the only thing I ever cherished in my whole entire life."

You don't cherish your wife or unborn baby? "What's that?" the sheriff asked.

"It was a pocket watch my father gave me when I was a child. There's an inscription on the inside cover. I'd like to have it returned. Is that possible?"

The sheriff shook his head. "I'm afraid not. It'll have to be booked into evidence."

Avery turned his head. "I know. I meant could my family have it back, after, you know, the trial and all."

"That'll be up to the prosecutor."

"What about my money? My wife needs it. I'll bet it's in his wallet. Could you check?"

"That'd be outside the scope of what we like to call proper procedure. Even if he has any cash on his person, there'd be no way to identify it as yours."

"How about the watch? Could I at least see it before you take me to jail?"

"Why?"

"Because I want to make sure it wasn't damaged."

Yeah, that makes perfect sense. Three men are dead because of you, one of them my own deputy, and you're worried about a pocket watch. But the sheriff was a kind man, and no matter the events that had played out, he knew Avery was in shock. If he wanted to keep him cooperative, he thought maybe the best way to do that would be to show a little cooperation himself. "Hold on a minute."

He walked over to the coroner's wagon and asked one of the attendants to unzip the bag.

"Why?" The attendant asked.

"Because I'm trying to keep a bad situation from becoming any worse."

"Looks like that particular ship might have already set sail, if you take my meaning."

"How about the bag, Bub?"

The attendant let out a weary sigh and unzipped the bag. The sheriff retrieved the watch, then walked back over to his cruiser. He let it dangle from its connecting chain. "This the one?"

"Yes, that's it. Would you read me the inscription on the inside of the lid? Please?"

The sheriff placed the watch in his palm and pressed the release mechanism with his finger. When the lid popped open on its spring and he saw the inside of the cover, he looked at Avery and didn't speak.

"What is it?"

"What does the inscription read?" the sheriff asked.

"It reads: From your father, with love," Avery said. "Why?"

He turned the watch so Joe Avery could see the inside of the lid. There was no inscription of any kind. When Avery began to cry, Mason Jones, sheriff of Marion County, Indiana, shut the door of his squad car and drove his prisoner downtown.

The year was 1971.

CHAPTER THREE

Virgil Jones had the grades. Nothing spectacular, mind you—he wasn't going to be a Rhodes Scholar or anything like that—but good enough to get into any of the state schools. So did his adopted brother, Murton Wheeler. Murton had never been officially adopted...he'd grown up with the Jones family after his mother died, loved by Mason and his wife, Elizabeth, as if he were their own.

The three of them, Virgil, Murton, and Elizabeth sat on the living room sofa, the boys flanking their mother. They'd already talked it over—all through their senior year of high school and well into the summer—college or the military, so there wasn't much of anything else to say on the subject. They were scheduled to leave for basic training in less than two days. Though it hadn't yet reached the boiling point, things were beginning to simmer in the Gulf. The boys—young men really—knew their mom accepted and even respected their decision, but that didn't mean she had to like it. Half her family going off to fight a war everyone knew was coming.

Virgil glanced at the grandfather clock in the corner of the room and said, "Any time now, I guess."

Elizabeth was subconsciously twisting her wedding band, spinning it around her ring finger. She glanced up at the clock when Virgil spoke. It was five minutes until midnight. "Yes, I suppose so," she said, her voice distant and hollow.

"You okay, Mom?" Murton said.

"Yes, of course. I'm nervous is all. He's never had to do this before. Witness it, I mean."

"The way I understand it, he didn't have to do it at all," Virgil said.

"He was the arresting officer. And you boys know your father well enough. Even though it was, what? Eighteen years ago now, I suppose. Anyway, he felt it was his duty to be there."

"Not to mention Avery himself requested his presence," Murton added, a touch of sarcasm in his tone.

"He's an honorable man, doing an honorable thing, no matter how awful or barbaric it might be," Elizabeth said. "He didn't write the law. He's simply an unfortunate participant." She turned and faced Murton. "And don't think I missed the tone in your voice, young man."

Murton looked down, properly chastised, and mumbled an apology. When she patted him on the thigh, he took her hand in his own. It felt cold and thin. When

Virgil took her other hand, he must have felt the same thing because he gave Murton a sideways glance. Murton caught the glance and gave his brother a half shrug.

Virgil cleared his throat then said, "Listen, Mom, Murt and I have been talking. We know how worried you are about us leaving to join the army and all that, but is there something else going on? Something you're not telling us?"

"What do you mean?"

Virgil didn't sugarcoat it. "You're losing weight. I can see it. Look at your wedding band. It's ready to fall right off your finger. Your hands are like ice."

Elizabeth pulled her hands away from her boys, then wrapped her arms around their shoulders and pulled them both close. "It's stress, I'm sure. Certainly nothing for the two of you to worry yourselves over. I want your heads clear, focused on what you're about to do, not fretting over me, like I'm some little old lady, which, by the way, I'm not. Besides, didn't I teach you it's impolite to ask a woman her age, or take note of her weight?"

Then the clock struck midnight, and a new course was charted, the lines etched deep into a future map, driven by a current that would take them places none of them ever imagined.

MASON SAT ALONE IN THE VIEWING ROOM, HAVING arrived earlier than anyone else. The room was something like a small theater...three rows of metal folding chairs arranged in an arc that all faced a thick glass window. The window was covered with a curtain that would be opened at the last minute.

Experiments had been done in the past with the curtain. At times it was left open as the prisoner was brought in and strapped to the chair, other times it was left closed right up until they threw the switch. Focus groups were held with mock executions, and ultimately the general consensus was that it was easier on both the prisoner and the viewers if the curtain remained closed until the prisoner was in the chair and strapped down, as no one wanted to witness the humiliation, fear, and panic that invariably happened when it was time to tighten the straps.

But it was much more than that as well. Even though everyone was briefed on what they would actually see and when, the sight remained a disturbingly violent image to watch. The inmate now bald, his head shaved clean, would be forced into the chair, a wet sponge held to the top of the skull as a cap with massive electrodes was strapped on and cinched tight under the chin. Thick leather belts would hold the rest of the body immobile.

After the curtain was pulled back, a priest would enter and say a few Godly words, then once he left the room there would be a minute or so until the clock told everyone they'd moved on to a new day. Then the switch was thrown, the circuits closed, and the electricity would flow through the prisoner's body until he was dead.

When the door opened, Mason turned in his seat and saw some of the family members of the men Joe Avery had killed as they entered the room. Most knew of Mason from the time almost twenty years ago...the arrest at the foundry, the trial, and the subsequent sentencing. But everyone had aged, perhaps even softened a bit as hearts sometimes will. A few polite, almost imperceptible nods were exchanged. No one spoke.

With less than two minutes to go, the door to the outer waiting area opened again. When Joe Avery's wife and son walked into the room, Mason stood, though everyone else remained seated. When they walked past, neither of them made eye contact with the sheriff. Mason did the math in his head and decided that Avery's wife couldn't be more than forty years old, though she looked much older. The son...Jacob was his name, if Mason remembered correctly, looked like an athlete. His hair held an odd color and his face was unshaven. He was a young man now, like his own sons. As they sat down Mason thought he could hear a slight scuffle on the other side of the curtained window.

Joe Avery getting strapped down.

By law, one reporter was permitted in the room to witness the execution, though no photography was allowed. He stood at the back, his pen moving across the pages of his notebook, recording what he could for an article that would make the Star, and probably be picked up by the Associated Press.

When the curtain slid open, a few quiet gasps were

heard, but Joe Avery's wife began to scream and cry. She jumped out of her seat and beat on the thick glass window with both her fists. Mason kept his eyes forward and watched as the priest said whatever he said—the glass so thick no one could hear him. Avery looked at his wife through the glass and managed to mouth *I love you,* even though the chin strap was so tight he could barely move his lips.

Mason looked at the clock on the wall behind Avery's head. With thirty seconds left to go, he let his eyes drift down and discovered that Avery was staring at the top of the window. His face was wet with tears and the water that was dripping from the sponge under the cap. That's when Mason realized that Avery could probably see the reflection of the clock behind him in the window. With five seconds to go, Avery—who couldn't nod or move his head in any way because he was strapped in so tight—gave Mason a single slow blink. Then the lights went out, the switch was thrown, and Joe Avery, a guy who never could get a break, was executed. The glass that separated the two rooms wasn't nearly thick enough to mask the sounds that emanated from the other side.

When Mason turned and looked at Joe Avery's family, he saw the son, Jacob, staring at him. The expression on his face was suggestive of someone who might be gathering his thoughts with a leaf rake, as if the words he might possibly speak would be set alight with a douse of kerosene and the toss of a match scraped off the side of a rough-hewn chair rail. Mason looked away, not out of fear, but respect. He remained seated until almost everyone had left the room.

When Jacob Avery walked past he slowed, then stopped, but the pause was brief and no words were exchanged. Avery's wife, on the other hand, wasn't nearly as generous with her actions, the genesis of her thought processes and state of mind lost even to herself.

Mason stood, and when he did, Joe Avery's wife spat in his face, then sobbed as her son led her away.

Mason was still wiping his face with his handkerchief when the reporter approached him. "May I get a statement, Sheriff Jones?" Before Mason could say no, the reporter pressed on. "How does it feel to watch the man you arrested die in the electric chair, then get spat on by his wife?"

Mason took his time removing the spittle from his cheek and nose and brow, neatly folded his handkerchief and replaced it in his pocket. Then he looked at the reporter and said, "Probably not as bad as being paid to write about it for the passive entertainment of others who'll forget all about it within a day or two. You can quote me on that." Then he slapped him on the back hard enough that the reporter dropped his notebook.

On the other side of the glass, Joe Avery's body was placed on a gurney and wheeled away. A few seconds later a trustee pushed a cleaning cart into the chamber and began washing the urine from the floor. He kept his eyes down and didn't look at the chair.

CHAPTER FOUR

Jacob Avery joined the army the day after his father was executed. The recruiter told him—tried hard, in fact, to convince him—that there was no rush. He could attend his father's funeral and ship out to basic training after he'd had time to properly grieve. He leaned across his desk, looked around the recruiting center to make sure no one was within earshot and said, "The Gulf and the rag heads aren't going anywhere, you know. This is a war that can't be won."

"Don't matter none to me," Avery said. "Pop's gone. Standing there with TV cameras pointed at me while they toss him in a hole and cover him with dirt ain't gonna bring him back. And what do you mean when you say this is a war that can't be won?"

The recruiter's uniform was perfectly pressed, his tie tucked neatly inside his shirt between the third and fourth buttons. Above the breast pockets were tiny colorful bars, their decorative meaning lost on Avery. He had a hawked nose, a square, dimpled jaw, and a haircut and physique that would identify him as either a cop or a military man no matter the clothing he wore. He had a slight trench-like hairless groove near the base of his skull. One of his ear lobes was missing.

He leaned back in his chair, his brow slightly furrowed, like a car salesman who was trying to find the right words to close a deal. He wasn't all that surprised to hear Avery's feelings on the matter of his father's death. He'd heard the story. Everyone had. It'd been all over the news, both in Terre Haute, Indiana, and across the country. Joe Avery had been the first person executed in the state of Indiana in over twenty years.

"You can kill all the jihadis you want, but they keep making more. What you can't do is kill their ideas. It's like trying to define the shape of water."

Avery held an angry look on his face, his arms crossed over his chest. He kept a three-day beard because he thought it made him look the part, though if asked, he probably wouldn't be able to say what the part actually was...at least not yet. He was stocky and tall, solid like a middle linebacker. His hair was the color of margarine and looked to have the texture of baled straw. "I ain't here to define the shape of anything, much less water. I'm here to sign on the line and serve. If you don't want the likes of me because of what they done to my pop, I'll move on down the block and try the Marines, ooh-rah. It's your choice."

The army officer had seen almost every type of recruit come though his door over the years. Most were high school graduates who didn't make the college cut. Some were sent by the courts, their fate already decided...time in jail, or time in country. Others were brought in by their parents, doe-eyed and scared, most barely able to contain their tears when they thought about what was about to happen. The recruiter kept a box of Kleenex on his desk, visible, but discretely placed on the front corner within easy reach, poking out behind a framed picture of 41, and his vice president, Dan Quayle, who was from Indiana. "Tell me more about that, if you don't mind. What they did to your father."

"Why?" Avery said. He said it through his throat, his lips not moving when he spoke.

The recruiter lifted his shoulders a fraction and turned his palms upward. "I like to get to know my recruits."

"Why?" Avery said again. "Like to keep track of how many don't come back?" Then before the recruiter could answer, he added, "Don't you worry none. I'll be coming back. I guaran-damn-tee it."

That's what I'm afraid of, the recruiter thought. Time to change tactics. "I've had men—and women for that matter—come through here, some so patriotic they'd be willing to bleed on the flag to make sure the stripes stay red. They're easy to spot, mostly because they wear it like a badge of honor. It's like they've already received their first medal even though they haven't done anything yet. You don't strike me as that type."

This time Avery leaned forward in his chair and uncrossed his arms. "How, exactly, do I strike you?" His hands were balled into fists.

The recruiter didn't have to wonder if there might be a double meaning hidden inside Avery's question. Or maybe he was simply reading too much into the situation, though he doubted it. He pulled open his desk drawer and removed a short stack of forms. "You don't want to talk about your old man, that's your business. But I'll answer your question." The words he spoke next came from his eyes as much as his mouth. "You strike me as the type who wants to learn a skill. I'm hoping it's cook, or maybe even large engine repair. Something you can use after you muster out. I hope you're hearing me on this. See some ID?"

Avery pulled a curved wallet out of his back pocket and snapped his driver's license on the desktop, then sat back and waited while the forms were filled out. After he signed, he looked at the recruiter and said, "What happened to your ear?"

The recruiter subconsciously reached up and felt the scarred tissue where his lobe used to be, a distant look in his eyes. When he turned his attention back to Avery, he said, "As of this moment you're a part of something bigger than yourself. The bus that will take you to Fort Benning, Georgia for basic training leaves at three p.m., day after tomorrow, right out of the back lot. If you don't show, a warrant will be issued for your arrest. Welcome to the United States Army." He stared at him until Jacob Avery walked out the door.

TWO DAYS LATER, AT CLOSE TO THREE P.M. ALL THE baggage was loaded on the bus behind the recruiting center. The families stood close together, all huddled around their loved ones who were about to board and go off to basic training, then most likely to fight a war, one that would light the fuse on a sequence of events which would change the world in ways no other war ever had.

Virgil pulled his father aside for a moment, out of earshot of his mom. "I need to ask you something, Dad. It's important. And I hope you'll forgive me for what I'm about to say, but I want the truth."

Mason raised his eyebrows. "That's not a question."

"No, but this is: Is Mom okay?"

Mason had taken the day off work and was dressed in a suit instead of his sheriff's uniform. "She's saying goodbye to both her boys. So am I, by the way. I'd say she's anything but okay."

"That's not exactly what I meant."

"Then spell it out for me, Bud."

"She's lost some weight. Murt and I have been talking about it. We think she might be sick."

"I'm sure it's the stress...you boys going off to the

army and all that. It's weighing on her in ways you can't yet imagine, Virg."

"You haven't taken her to the doctor?"

Before Mason had a chance to lie—something he would have done to keep both his sons focused on their immediate task, Elizabeth and Murton walked over. She smiled and handed a camera to Mason. "I'd like a picture with these two brave men. Think we can arrange that?"

"You bet," Mason said. "Here, let's turn around this way so the sun is at my back. The light will be perfect."

They all did as Mason asked, then Virgil and Murton put their arms around their mom and smiled. When Mason pressed the shutter release mechanism, the photo he captured showed two men who would eventually fall apart, then make their way back to each other, and in her own way, the woman who would help make it happen. A single tear escaped her eye and rolled down her cheek and the camera caught it.

When the goodbyes had all been said and everyone was onboard the bus, Mason put his arm around his wife and pulled her close. He could feel the edge of her shoulder blades under his arm and hand.

"I saw you and Virgil speaking. You didn't tell him, did you?"

"No, sweetheart, I didn't, though I think maybe I should have. He has a right to know. They both do."

Elizabeth shook her head. "They will. But not yet... and certainly not now. Besides, what the doctor said...we still have time."

The bus began to pull away, and that's when Mason saw something that caused his breath to catch in his throat. Jacob Avery was on the bus. He waved to Mason, his eyes flat.

"Was that young man waving at you? Who was that?" Elizabeth asked. "Mason?"

CHAPTER FIVE

The bus ride to Fort Benning, Georgia was over twelve hours. It should have only taken ten, but the bus driver had to stop for fuel, food, and a number of bathroom breaks. They were less than an hour into the trip when Murton looked at Virgil and said, "Two rows up, on the right, window seat. Guy keeps turning around and staring at us. Know who it is?"

Virgil, who'd already done the math in his head knew if they were going to get any rest, they'd better get it now because by the time they arrived at Fort Benning, it'd be too late to get everyone squared away and into bed. This was army basic training after all, not summer camp for high school graduates. "Leave me alone. I'm trying to sleep. You better do the same or you'll be dead on your feet by the time we arrive."

"I'll be all right," Murton said. "Look at the guy, will

you? He's eyeballing us right now. I'm telling you, it's him."

Virgil re-bunched his duffle bag, pressed it against the window and kept his eyes closed. "Him who?"

"The guy whose old man got juiced the other night."

Virgil cracked an eye and saw Jacob Avery turned in his seat, staring at him. When Avery saw him looking, he stood and pushed his way into the aisle and walked back to where Virgil and Murton were seated. He stared at them both for a few seconds, then said, "Know who I am? Because I know who you guys are. Your old man was the one who sent mine to the chair."

"How about you get your facts straight, Bub?" Murton said. "Our old man didn't send anyone to the chair. He was the arresting officer. He went to the execution as a sign of respect for you and your mother. How about you show a little yourself and go back to your seat?"

"What'd you call me?"

"He didn't call you anything," Virgil said.

"He called me Bub. My name isn't Bub. It's Jacob." His hands were balled into fists and his body swayed rhythmically with the motion of the bus as it rolled down the four lane highway.

Virgil stuck out his hand and said, "I'm Virgil Jones. Everyone calls me Jonesy." When Avery didn't accept his hand, Virgil jerked his thumb at Murton and said, "This is my brother, Murton Wheeler. We're sorry for your loss."

Avery didn't know how to respond to any of that. He'd been ready for a confrontation and had been met with sympathy that seemed genuine. After a moment he said, "I don't want your pity. Stay out of my way."

Murton laughed without humor. "You came back here. You're the one blocking the aisle. We're in your way?"

Avery took a half step forward. "You know what I mean. Tell me you don't."

When neither Virgil nor Murton responded, Avery turned to go back to his seat. Then he stopped and looked back. When he spoke he had at once a genuine measure of curiosity and a modicum of kindness in his voice. "If the two of you are brothers how come you don't have the same last name?"

"There's more than one way to lose your old man," Murton said. He was looking at Virgil when he said it.

THE FIRST FEW WEEKS OF BASIC TRAINING WERE ROUGH on everyone, but as they adapted to army life their unit began to function as a whole. They were a team, the stronger, more adept recruits helping the others along until everyone was up to speed. Near the end of their basic training they all had to take aptitude tests, the army's way of figuring out—on paper anyway—who might be good candidates for any given particular skill set. Virgil's test scores showed he had strong leadership qualities and was good at helping others discover and utilize their own talents. Murton's scores were an odd combination of high-level tactical thinking along with a propensity for emergency medical care. Avery's scores showed he had an aptitude for advanced mathematics.

The three of them had managed to put any ill feelings aside regarding Mason's involvement in Joe Avery's arrest almost twenty years ago and the subsequent execution a few weeks past. Virgil and Avery were talking about it one night while on CQ duty. The Change of Quarters shifts rotated throughout the entire unit, with two recruits staying awake for each shift. Known as runners, they were essentially on guard duty to make sure no one attempted to leave or enter the barracks overnight.

"He's a hell of a good guy," Virgil said. "My dad. He can be a little stubborn sometimes, but, you know, as parents go, I got lucky."

"I wouldn't know," Avery said, his voice flat and distant.

Virgil turned and looked at him as they walked the grounds. "Ah, jeez, I'm sorry, Ave. I shouldn't be talking about it."

Avery let it go and said, "Tell me about Wheeler. How is it he came to be your brother?"

Virgil told him the story of how Murton's mother had died and the events that led up to Mason running Ralph Wheeler out of town. "Never heard from him again."

"Wish I'da had an old man," Avery said. "Even one that beat me a little. Woulda been better'n nothing, which is what I got."

"You get to see him at all? In prison, I mean?"

Avery nodded. "Few times, mostly when I was a little

kid. Don't remember much about it. I was too young. You know what I remember most?"

"What's that?"

"I never got to touch him. Ever. Not once in eighteen years. I think that bothers me more than anything. Don't know why."

They stopped for a few minutes so Avery could have a smoke. Virgil looked at him and said, "That night, when..."

"When they killed him?"

"Yeah. You were there. Why?"

"How'd you know that?"

Virgil shrugged. "My dad told me about it. Not the actual...procedure—"

"It wasn't no procedure. It was killing, plain and simple. Even the word execution seems a little...soft."

"Yeah, I guess. Anyway, he didn't tell me about any of that. But he said you and your mom were there. I don't know if I could have done that."

"I didn't go to see my old man die. He was going to get fried whether I was there or not."

"Then why'd you go?" Virgil asked.

Avery stuck his tongue in his cheek. They'd gotten their heads shaved the first day they arrived, and now their hair was growing back. Avery's looked like bristles on a toothbrush. He scratched at the back of his head when he spoke. "Went to give your dad a piece of my mind, but when the time came, I didn't have the words. My mom spit in his face though."

Virgil barked out a short laugh. "Yeah, I did hear about that part."

"Wanna know something?"

"Sure."

"I was ashamed of her for doing that...spitting on your old man. Why are you looking at me like that?"

"I don't think he took offense."

"I would have. That afternoon...when we all got on the bus? I saw him. Your dad. I was already on board. I wanted to apologize for what my mom did to him, but it was too late, so I waved. He looked at me like he'd seen a ghost or something. I don't know why, but it sorta pissed me off."

Virgil thought it might be time to change the subject. "Did you get your MOS yet?" MOS was army speak for Military Occupational Specialty. Essentially the job you'd have within the service once basic training was complete.

"Yeah, seems like I'm some sort of math whiz or something. They wanted to put me into logistics, but when the DI saw how well I could shoot, they changed their minds. Looks like I'm going to sniper school."

Virgil was impressed. "Really? That's cool."

"What about you and Wheeler?"

"Recon," Virgil said.

Avery shrugged. "You guy's will be first in, though it don't matter none. War's coming. We'll all be playing in the same sandbox." Then, "You gonna take your leave after basic?"

Virgil nodded. "Yeah. Our mom...I think she's sick.

She's been trying to hide it, but something isn't right. We're going to run back up and check in with her. You?"

"Naw. Straight to school for me. They had the opening and said if I wanted it, I better take it now or lose the chance."

"Your mom okay?"

Avery looked at Virgil, his eyes dark. "What do you think?"

VIRGIL AND MURTON DIDN'T GET TO GO HOME AFTER basic training ended. Tensions flared in the gulf, the president or the secretary of defense were on TV almost every day, Iraq was making threatening, taunting statements, and the bottom line was this: Troop build up in the gulf was no longer something the generals were talking about. It was something they were actually doing. Virgil called home and told his father about it the day before they shipped out.

"I was going to come down for your graduation ceremony," Mason said. "I thought it was next week."

"It was supposed to be. But don't bother. There isn't going to be one. Things seem to be happening pretty fast."

"It's good to hear your voice, Bud."

"You too. How's mom?"

"She's fine, Son. Worried about you and Murt. How is Murton by the way?"

"Murt's fine, Dad. So am I." Then before Mason could say anything else, "Listen Dad, I'm trying to be respectful of you and mom because that's how I was raised. With the exception of kid stuff, I've always told you the truth and I've always been left with the impression that you did the same."

"I did," Mason said. Virgil thought it sounded like his father was speaking with his jaw clenched.

"You said you were going to come down for our graduation ceremony. Not we...you. Murt and I both know something's going on with mom, so how about we stick with tradition and be truthful with each other about it?"

The silence went on for so long Virgil thought maybe they'd been disconnected. "Dad?"

"Your mother is sick, Virgil. Very sick."

No shit, Virgil thought.

"What was that?"

"I said how sick?"

"She's got breast cancer, Son. Stage two. The doctors say she's got a fight ahead of her, but the five year survival rate is good. She's got a chance, Virg. That's the thing to hang on to."

Virgil was on the barrack's payphone, and when he heard the words his father spoke he sat down on the floor, the hand piece attached to the cord barely long enough to reach his ear and mouth.

"Did you hear me, Son? I said she's got a chance. A good chance I believe. I've put in my papers with the county. I'm going to retire and we're going to fight this thing together. I'll see her through it, Virgil. She's going to make it, I promise."

For the first time in his life, Virgil didn't believe his father. "You can't promise someone else's survival." After they ended their call he remained on the floor, his knees up, his hands holding his shins tight, the receiver dangling next to his ear.

Murton came around the corner and saw his brother sitting there. He walked over, put the phone's receiver next to his ear for a moment, then hung it back in the cradle. "What's going on?"

When Virgil repeated the conversation he'd had with his father he watched Murton's eyes go dark, like something had clicked off in his brain. A week later they were in Kuwait.

So was Avery.

CHAPTER SIX

The operation was codenamed KILO. They were in the process of gearing up when Murton told Virgil that there must be an entire division tasked with nothing more than coming up with clever operational names.

"KILO stands for Kill Incoming Light Ordinance."

"I know what it stands for," Murton said. He held a tone in his voice. "But you know as well as I do it might as well stand for Kill Indigenous Land Owners. You've seen these guys we've captured. Most of them are people trying to protect themselves, their way of life, and their land from invading forces."

"Murt..."

"In case you haven't noticed, the invading forces are us, by the way."

Virgil didn't want to get into a military/political debate with his brother. They'd already had plenty in the eleven months in country. But he'd noticed something about his brother, something he couldn't pin down. Murton was changing. Or the war was changing Murton. Virgil didn't like it. "It's not only the United States. We're part of a coalition." When he didn't get a response, Virgil said, "What is it, Murt?"

"What's what?"

"You're not talking to me anymore."

"And you sound like my high school girlfriend. Give it a rest, will you?"

"You've been drinking a lot."

"It's hot out here."

"I meant alcohol. You're hitting it pretty hard."

"Who hasn't?"

"You wandered off on our last patrol. I thought I'd lost you for good."

"Except it all worked out, didn't it?"

"Don't you get it? Are you hearing me on this? I said I thought I'd lost you. Doesn't that mean anything to you anymore?"

"You know better than to ask me that," Murton said.

"You were taking a leak on a dead Republican Guard soldier."

"And it's a good thing I was, otherwise you'd be dead right now, along with the rest of the guys in that HUMVEE."

Murton had a valid point, even though he'd skewed the facts in his favor, something Virgil knew his brother had never done before. If anything, it had always been the other way around...Murton could carry his own weight better than anyone Virgil had ever known.

The mission Virgil was referring to had happened only days ago. They were headed back to base camp when Murton said he had to stop to relieve himself. The HUMVEE pulled over, Murton climbed out and walked across the road and into the darkness. When he didn't return, Virgil went into the desert to find him, his .45 in one hand, and a pair of night vision goggles over his eyes that worked only half the time.

He found him about thirty yards from the HUMVEE, sipping on a flask filled with whiskey while simultaneously urinating on the body of a dead Iraqi Republican Guard. When the armor-piercing round hit their vehicle, the explosion knocked them both to the ground. The smell of phosphorus hung in the air as the three remaining men inside the troop carrier burned to death before they could escape the twisted wreckage.

"If we wouldn't have stopped, we wouldn't have been hit," Virgil said.

Murton shook his head. "Yeah, I guess it's on me, then. Three guys dead because I had to pee."

"Murt, that's not what I'm saying—"

"Stop kidding yourself, Jonesy. That's exactly what you said."

Virgil could feel the anger boiling up inside, but he pushed it back. "Look, this is our last op before we ship out and head home. Once we're back, everything will be fine. Everything will be back to normal."

"You have no idea what's going on around here, do you? Define normal for me."

Avery stuck his head through the door before Virgil could answer. "Looks like I'm on overwatch for you guys tonight. That means you're in good hands. The rest of the unit is already on board the chopper. Let's go. It's time to rock and roll."

Murton walked past Avery without saying anything else.

"What's with him?" Avery asked Virgil.

I wish I knew, Virgil thought.

OPERATION KILO WAS SUPPOSED TO BE SIMPLE AND straightforward. The helicopter would drop the recon team at a point five klicks from their target—a light ordinance stockpile the sats had picked up—and they'd hike the rest of the way in. They'd make entry into the compound, set their charges, then retreat before blowing up the Iraqi hardware. Air support was on standby— a simple radio call away, and they had Avery who would be hiding, out in the darkness, to take out any guards ahead of them.

As missions went, the main part went off without a hitch. Avery did his job and took out eight Republican Guard soldiers before Virgil and the rest of the team advanced on the compound. Murton and the others set the charges and wired them together. Then the entire unit moved to a safe distance and took cover behind a burned out abandoned tank before the switch was thrown and the entire complex was reduced to rubble.

With Avery's job complete, he walked down to join the rest of his unit to hike back to the extraction area. That's when he saw one of the infantry soldiers walking in from the other direction, a flamethrower attached to his person, liquid fire dripping from the end of the barrel. Every time the soldier came across a downed Iraqi fighter, he'd point the nozzle and give them a little squirt. The ones who were only injured wished they'd died of other causes.

Avery stopped and brought his rifle up and watched through the scope as the other soldier got closer and closer. He heard the screams of the injured as they were set alight, and it made him think about the stories he'd heard of the foundry and his dad...about the men who died because of the mistakes his father had made. He lowered the rifle, his thoughts on the past when the soldier with the flamethrower approached him.

"What the hell do you think you're doing?" the soldier said.

"What are you talking about?" Avery said. "And where'd you get the squirt gun?"

"I'm talking about you sighting in on me. Felt like you was getting ready to park one in my brisket. I pulled this off of one of the RG's. I think it's Russian."

Avery shook his head. "Should have left it. And I wasn't sighting in on you."

"The hell you weren't. I seen it." The soldier had the barrel of his flamethrower pointed at the ground between them, and the liquid fire dripping from the nozzle formed a small pool of flickering light at their feet.

"I was only using the scope," Avery said. He turned his weapon and held it at port arms. "Look, the breech is open."

Virgil and Murton walked over, flanking the soldier who held the flamethrower. "Let's move out," Virgil said. "Time to hump it back to the LZ."

But the soldier wasn't listening. "I don't care if the breech is open or not. Don't be pointing that rifle at me or things are going to get heated, if you take my meaning."

"You threatening me now?" Except Avery's question couldn't have been timed any worse. Maybe it was the change of his expression, or the speed with which he chambered a round, or even the smooth fluid motion he used to raise his rifle and fire, but the other soldier didn't know or understand what was happening, even as Avery shouted.

"On your six!"

A lone Republican Guard had snuck around one of the abandoned vehicles and was bringing his weapon up. When Avery fired it was directly over the shoulder of his fellow soldier who panicked at the sudden threatening movement. He yanked the barrel of his flamethrower up and squeezed the trigger.

Murton saw the nozzle of the flamethrower light up

and yanked Virgil to the ground, clearing them both of the liquid fire that lit up the entire area.

But Avery wasn't that lucky. He dropped his weapon and screamed, his hands useless against the searing heat that touched the side of his head and neck. Somewhere in the deepest part of his brain he heard a voice that may or may not have been his own. Something about sins of the father.

Then Murton and Virgil were right there, Murton kicking sand and dirt on the flames, even smothering Avery with his own body to extinguish the fire. Virgil yanked the soldier with the flamethrower to the ground, closed the valves on the tanks to eliminate the threat of the weapon, then grabbed his radio. "Kilo Cover, this is Kilo Actual. We need emergency medical evac at target sight. Repeat, emergency medical evac at target, over."

"Kilo Actual, Kilo Cover. Hold position. We are ninety seconds inbound..."

A FEW DAYS LATER WHEN IT WAS TIME TO SHIP OUT AND head home, Virgil went to the infirmary to check on Avery. The nurse made him wear a paper mask over his face. Avery's head and neck and hands were heavily bandaged. Only one of his eyes was visible behind all the gauze. The rest of his body was buried under hospital sheets. "Thought I'd check in on you before I go. How you doing?"

Avery let his eye slide away. "Better than some, not as good as others."

"I spoke with the doc. He says you're going to make a full recovery, Ave."

"Yeah? I guess that depends on your definition of the word full. Half my face is burned off, I'll only have one eye, and my hands look like they've gone through the meat grinder. The doc says that once I get to Reed, they're going to graft the skin off my ass and try to fix my face up. I'll probably get a job back home in the traveling freak show."

Virgil looked down at the floor. The war had hardened him. It'd hardened them all the way war does. "Could have been worse," he said.

"No shit. That's why I said better than some." Then, a touch softer, "How's your mom?"

Virgil sucked in his cheeks and gave Avery a tight nod. "She's hanging on. Listen, have you seen Murt?"

"Hand me that cup of water with the straw, will you?"

Virgil did as Avery asked and waited until he'd taken a small sip before replacing the cup on the bedside table. He raised his eyebrows.

"You shouldn't do that."

"Do what?"

"Raise eyebrows at a guy who doesn't have any of his own."

"You'll still have one."

"Right. I'll walk around raising one eyebrow. People will love that. And yeah, Murton was here a little while ago. Came to say goodbye, same as you. Saw him talking to that spook after he left."

"What spook?"

"You know, that goon who's been hanging around... Griffin or Gibson, or whatever his name is."

"I guess I haven't seen him."

"You can tell they're spooks because they don't wear uniforms. They grow beards and wear either a Pakol or a turban. They try to blend in, but it's their tennis shoes that give them away."

"Did you hear what was said?"

"No. Murton didn't look too happy about it though. What have you heard about that idiot with the flamethrower?"

"Tim Dreyer? Not much," Virgil said. "They've got him in the brig right now. He'll probably wind up in Leavenworth."

"I wonder how much time he'll get."

"Don't know. Listen, I gotta run or I'm gonna miss my flight. Get better, will you?" Then, as if his own statement was a foregone conclusion, Virgil said, "When do you get to head back?"

"I guess once the threat of infection is gone. Speaking of gone, get the fuck out of here, okay? Go be with your mom or something. Maybe I'll see you down the road someday."

Virgil wanted to shake hands with Avery, or pat him on the shoulder, but with the bandages there was no way for that to happen. So he gave him a little half wave, like a kid, then felt like an idiot for doing so.

Thirty minutes later as the transport plane taxied across the tarmac and out to the runway, Virgil looked at the empty seat next to him where Murton should have been, but wasn't.

It would be almost two decades before they saw each other again, and their reunion wouldn't be a happy event. Instead it would be one that cast a shadow over their family, pitting brother against brother, clouded by a state of anger.

CHAPTER SEVEN

NOW

The naming of the dog turned out to be a little more difficult than everyone thought it might. After the fiasco in Freedom, Indiana, the governor and Virgil took a ride back to the small town and the governor's friend gave him the dog so he could give it to Virgil's son, Jonas, who'd been begging for a puppy for well over a year.

The dog, a Golden Retriever, was taken to the vet where he was brought up to date on all his shots, and started on a monthly regiment of flea, tick, and heart-worm prevention. And even after all of that, as a family they still hadn't come up with a name everyone could agree on. Huma stayed out of it, and Wyatt wasn't yet old enough to understand the concept, so it landed on Virgil, Sandy, and Jonas to decide. Since it was only the three of them, they'd naturally whittled it down to three possibilities: One was Mac, which Virgil thought was a great idea since the governor himself made the whole thing happen. Sandy thought it disrespectful and put her foot down, so Mac was out. Sandy then suggested Buddy, and while Virgil thought it fine, Jonas didn't seem to care for it.

"Why not?" Virgil asked Jonas. "He's your buddy, right?"

Jonas, who was sometimes a little too smart for his own good, said, "I don't think you'd go around all the time calling mom, Wife, would you?" The name Buddy was dropped like a lead balloon.

Sandy looked at Virgil. "It's his dog. Why not let him pick the name?"

Virgil, who, despite his best efforts, was a bit of a control freak, said, "Uh, I don't know. What if he comes up with...Larry, or something like that?"

Jonas jumped up and shouted, "Yes! Larry. Larry the dog!"

Virgil put his face in his hands. Sandy laughed and said, "Larry the dog, then."

RICK SAID CAUGHT VIRGIL IN HIS OFFICE CLOSE TO THE end of the work day. He was on the phone when Said stuck his head in, and Virgil gave him the wait a minute finger, then pointed to a chair. Said was one of Virgil's business partners...they'd teamed up a few years ago after

Virgil and Sandy came into a couple thousand acres of farmland down in Shelby County, the land packed with shale that held millions of dollars worth of natural gas. Said's company—one of many—held the patent and operational technology for the sonic drilling units used to extract the gas. It was the future of fracking...a safe and cost effective way to get the gas out of the ground without destroying the land or the water table.

Virgil Jones, once again head of the state's Major Crimes Unit finished his call, loosened his tie a bit, looked at Said and said, "What's up? Didn't expect to see you today."

Said needed a favor from Virgil, but he wanted to circle around it for a minute. "How's it feel to be back in charge?"

Virgil shrugged. "Ah, you know...same job, more paper, is all."

"Miles fine with the retirement?"

Another shrug. "I guess so. The recovery took some time, then it turned out he had C.O.P.D. or something, so that sort of sealed the deal."

"C.O.P.D? More like D.I.C.K. if everything I've ever heard is accurate."

"Says the guy who's first name is Richard. Besides, Miles is a good guy. The job didn't suit his style, is all."

Said pointed a finger, ignoring the latter half of Virgil's statement. "I go by Rick, which I know you know." Then, "I don't believe I've seen you in a suit at work since...well, ever. What is it, kiss the ring day or something?"

Virgil gave him a fake smile. "Not exactly. Mac doesn't care about my wardrobe. In fact, I think he likes the way I usually dress. It gives him something to make fun of. Though I don't know why."

"So what's with the fancy threads?"

"You know Emily Baker, Sandy's detail driver?" Virgil's wife, Sandy, had been hand-picked by Governor Hewitt (Mac) McConnell as his lieutenant governor after his former lieutenant had died while still in office.

"Can't say I've ever had the pleasure."

Virgil chuffed. "Pleasure is hardly the word. This woman is all business. Former military—retired fighter pilot no less—and then state trooper because she thought the airlines would be too boring. Sandy picked her for the job, she said yes, so there you go."

"None of which explains the duds."

"She's down with the flu...Baker. When Sandy found out she could pick anyone she wanted to fill in..." Virgil spread his arms and let the rest of the statement speak for itself.

Said laughed. "And you said yes?"

"Of course. And now I know why you're not married. Besides, she's been so busy lately it's kind of nice to spend some extra time together." Virgil subconsciously reached down and felt the brass medallion pinned to the lapel of his jacket. It was about the size of a half-dollar coin, and featured Indiana's state seal. To those in the know, it identified him as the only person officially allowed to transport the lieutenant governor.

Said caught him fingering the pin and said, "What's that?"

Virgil explained the pin and its meaning to Said.

"So if she doesn't see the pin..." This time he let his own statement hang.

Virgil nodded. "Yeah, it's a security thing."

"Good idea. Say, how's Larry the dog?"

Virgil laughed. "He's great. Walks around with a smile on his face all the time, had him house broke in about a day and a half. Smart little pup, though with the way he eats, I don't think he'll be little for too long."

Said nodded thoughtfully, his brain changing gears. Enough circling. "Listen, I need a favor."

Virgil didn't hesitate. Said was a loyal business partner and friend, one who'd made him rich. "Name it."

"We've got a minor problem with the sonic drilling platform."

"When you say we...?"

"Okay, I'll admit it's mostly me, but it does affect you and I need your help in a round about way."

"What's the problem?"

"The problem is I sometimes tend to move a little fast. The legal department is always after me to slow down, but you've got to strike while the iron is hot and all that. They wanted the contracts drawn up differently and I told them there wasn't time, that it didn't matter anyway because we held the patent—"

"Rick?"

"Yeah?"

"Start from the beginning."

Said puffed out his cheeks. "Okay. Right. When our engineers developed the sonic drilling technology, they hit a snag. They spent so much time and money on it I was ready to drop the entire project."

"What sort of snag?" Virgil asked.

"It's...technical."

"Then dumb it down for me," Virgil said glancing at his watch. "But make it quick because I've got to go pick up Sandy in about ten minutes."

"Okay, the way the system works is through high frequency vibrations that fracture the shale. When the shale fractures it releases the gas, which is then pulled out of the ground via low pressure vacuum pumps. I know you know all that. What you probably don't know is this: Those vibrations have to be specifically and precisely tuned, individually and all at the same time. We're talking about thousands of vibrations per second, per drill—all done via computer—based on the various strata they encounter. Without the specific tuning, the system doesn't work...and I mean at all. You may as well dig a hole, drop a loud speaker down and crank out some Ted Nugent. Nothing would happen."

"Maybe if he would have stayed with the Amboy Dukes?"

"Jonesy, this is serious."

Virgil held up his hands. "Okay, sorry. Go on."

"Anyway, our engineers—and I've got some of the best in the country, by the way—they couldn't get it to work.

It took too much computing power to operate a single unit. They would have needed an entire array of super computers all tied together on site for each drill rig. And even then they couldn't get it right. The computers...they couldn't keep up."

"But it's working now," Virgil said. "Has been from the jump. How'd they solve it?"

"By doing the only thing we could do. What do you know about artificial intelligence?"

"Only what they tell you on the news. You know, we're all doomed because robots are going to take over the world and all that."

"That may be true, but that's not the type of AI we're talking about here. The only way we could get the system to work was to let it work without the aid of human interaction. Those drill units out in your fields? Every single one of them operates because of a little black box that can read the bounce-back signals, then make micro adjustments to the frequency output."

Virgil didn't get it, and wasn't ashamed to admit it. "So what? Sounds like a little independent computer. Like the kind they use to run those robot welders in factories these days."

Said shook his head. "Not exactly, but close. The type of AI I'm talking about is extremely complex. It's like a specialized computer that learns as it works. It adapts to the working environment, rewrites its own operating code, then tells the actual drilling unit what to do and when. My people didn't know anything about AI, but we did know enough to realize it was our only solution. So we contracted that portion of the build out to a company that specializes in the technology we needed."

Virgil glanced at his watch again. Almost out of time. "And it worked, right? So what's the problem?"

"Yeah, it worked great. *Is* working great. The problem is we don't own the boxes that run the rigs...the AI boxes. The company doesn't sell them...they lease them. Why sell the boxes once when you can lease them forever? It was a win-win. They have a steady stream of income, and are responsible for the maintenance on the boxes. It's a great business model. And, it's all in the contract. A contract, I should add, that is set to expire by the end of the month. I just came from a meeting with the owner of the company and they've decided not to renew their end of the agreement, which is perfectly within their rights."

"And without their boxes..."

Said was nodding. "That's right. All extraction down in Shelby County will cease, and the plans I have to ramp up the business and lease additional units is about to go right out the window."

"Did they say why they won't renew?"

"Nope. Refused to give any reason whatsoever."

"Any other vendors out there? They can't be the only ones who do this sort of thing?"

"They're not. And we're already looking into other outfits, but these are specialty builds. It doesn't happen overnight. It took our current supplier eighteen months to integrate their system with our units."

"So what do you want from me?"

"I want you to find out why they're dumping us. Like I said, in a round about sort of way."

"You want Becky to spy on them?"

Said pointed a finger again. "No. I did not say spy. I did not use that word. You did. Corporate espionage is a severe crime, and I'm suggesting nothing of the sort. But I would like her to run some background on their key people and see what she can come up with. I need some leverage here, Jonesy. We both do."

"Gotta be careful with leverage, Rick. If you find what you need and use it the wrong way, it could be construed as bribery or extortion."

Said reached into his briefcase and pulled out a manila envelope. "I'm a businessman, Jonesy. I do things on the up and up. I know how to stay inside the lines." He put the envelope on Virgil's desk. "You'll have her take a look?"

"I'll have to run it past Murton. It's his shop too. Not to mention that he and Becky—"

Said was losing patience. "Yeah, yeah, but you'll do what you can, right?"

Virgil took the envelope and stood up. Said's cue to leave. "I'll let you know."

Said looked him right in the eye. "If you don't want to wait eighteen months or more to get the drill units operational again, you'd better let me know pretty quick. It's your money too. Don't forget that."

CHAPTER EIGHT

The pick-up game should have been a friendly one...a bunch of teenagers banging it out on a street court, killing time and working on their moves. Five young men were at one end, shooting around, and a lone player at the other practicing free throws. The court was made of asphalt laid long ago, and was now buckled with age. Weeds grew from cracks along the foul lines, and the hoops had been without netting for years. One of the backboards was cracked above the rim, making any sort of banked shot nearly impossible.

The lone player shooting free throws was a white guy, a kid named Pete Long, and he was a serious player. A high school star, he'd already accepted a full ride athletic scholarship to play basketball for Purdue University. He was scheduled to leave in less than two weeks. Long was minding his own business at the other end of the court when the black guys approached.

"You up for a little three on?" one of the black guys asked. "We're one short. Nothing serious. Thought you could join us."

Long looked at the young men who had approached him. Four had shaved heads, and one had long braids tied up on top of his head. The bald ones were shirtless, their arms and chests rippling with muscle and gang tats. Their shorts hung past their knees and were dirty and torn. The one with the braids tied up on his head, however, didn't have any ink, and his shorts and shoes looked brand new.

"Maybe some other time," Pete said. "I'm about done. Besides, I was watching you guys play. I don't think I'd be able to keep up."

"Who you fooling, white boy? We know who you is. You Pete Long. Supposed to be the next best Larry Bird."

Long shrugged, his palms turned upward in a sort of 'what can I say?' gesture. "Don't know about the last part, but you got the first part right. How'd you know who I am?"

"Shit, man. Everyone around here know who you is." He bounced the basketball on the asphalt once, and when it came back up he put both hands on the ball and threw it straight at Long's face. Long, who wasn't ready for the throw took the ball right in the center of his forehead. The ball bounced off Long and back into the hands of the young black man. "Looks like you need to work on your hand-eye coordination a little."

Long was almost six-and-a-half feet tall, and weighed

over two hundred pounds. He rubbed the spot where the ball had hit him with the heel of his hand, tipped his head first to the left and then to the right, his ears touching his shoulders with each movement. "Let me see that ball."

The black guy threw the ball at Pete again, this time even harder than the last. Pete put his arm out and when the ball slapped his hand, he clenched his fingers and palmed the ball, holding it straight out. He turned his hand and looked at the ball, then brought his arm down and let it rest on his hip. "How's that for hand-eye?" He stepped up to the group of black men and looked at each of them, one by one. He pointed with his chin. "I'll take these two."

The black guy who bounced the ball off Pete's forehead said, "Look at that. White man picking his negroes. I guess some things never change."

Pete stared him down. "You want to play, or do you want to roll around in the dirt?"

The black guy held his arms out away from his sides. "Relax fool. I'm just messing with ya. Gots to see what you're made of. C'mon lets play. Street rules."

Pete took the ball off his hip and spun it on his index finger. "Street rules, then." He dropped his finger and let the ball fall into his palm. When it did, he rammed it into the black man's stomach, doubling him over. "So check me, TopKnot."

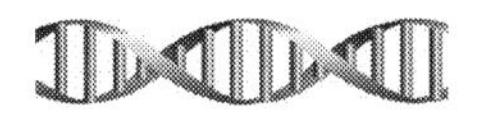

THE GAME STARTED ROUGH AND ONLY GOT ROUGHER. Calling a foul was unheard of. Trips were as common as dribbling, feet were stomped, elbows landed in the ears, knees got buckled, and a blocked shot usually meant a hand to the face. But Pete could play, street rules or not. He began to put moves on his opponents, the likes of which they'd never seen.

But it all went bad when the lane cleared and Pete juked left, spun to his right, then went in for the easy slam dunk. Except suddenly the lane wasn't clear, Pete was three feet in the air when the guy with the braids stepped underneath him and swung his arm, hard at the back of Pete's legs, knocking them out from underneath him. When he fell he landed flat on his back, his lower spine connecting solidly with a chunk of buckled asphalt right under the rim. When his back broke, there was an audible crack.

Pete screamed in pain, and one of the other players put his hand over his own mouth, as if the scream came from him.

"Help me," Pete said. "My back. I can't feel my legs."

The black men all looked at each other for a few seconds, then ran off the court and out of sight.

"Help me," Pete yelled again. When his pleas went unanswered, Pete Long began to cry. Not from the pain, but because of the future he knew he'd lost.

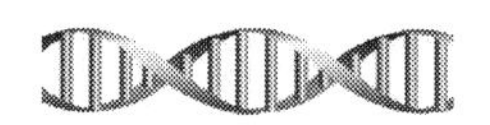

THE ARC OF MEMORY WAS LONG, WITH HIM IN LOCKSTEP like a shadow on a sunlit day. If asked how he'd managed to keep his sanity, Jacob Avery probably couldn't have answered. Mostly because he wasn't sure himself. A kaleidoscope of imagery circled his brain during the day and dominated his dreams at night. Colorful shards of cogitation...twisted, explosive images of red mist as the bullet entered the skull, then exited the other side of the head. He saw it all through the scope of his sniper rifle, the enemy combatants in their dusty white robes, turbans, and sandals so far away they shimmered in the heat like human mirages.

When he was locked on to someone, for Avery, it was almost sexual in nature. The foreplay began when he'd seat a round gently into his weapon, not ram it home like they did in the movies. No, the proper way was with a careful insertion of the cartridge, along with a soft gentle slide to lock the breech, then a slow exhale, his eye cupping the scope. There would come an awareness of the measured cadence of his own heartbeat, the rhythm slowing until he could feel the space between beats, an emptiness where for an instant his own blood didn't flow...a stillness and quiet of mind the likes of which he'd never known. When he squeezed the trigger, the bullet sometimes took so long to reach its target that when the red mist finally came it was nearly orgasmic. He'd close both eyes for a moment, clench himself tight and shudder with pleasure, then slide back away from his perch and down the slope, caught in the afterglow of the kill, the red mist so powerful he often thought he could taste it.

Yeah, try to tell that to someone when they look you in the eye and ask what's on your mind. Though with the way Avery looked these days, hardly anyone ever looked him in the eye. Not anymore.

So the killings, yes. They stayed with Avery as much as the injuries he'd suffered in the war so long ago now. Even if he somehow managed to forget for a while, all it took was a casual stroll on the street and the reminder of what happened with the flamethrower in the desert was reflected back by the rude stares of other men, or the mothers who pulled their children close and crossed to the other side of the street or ducked into the nearest storefront.

He was at the shooting range, where he often was when he had a few hours to kill. Except he wasn't shooting. He had a spotter's scope pressed to his good eye and was watching two men at the far end of the range line. It looked like one of the men might be trying to teach the other the mechanics of long range shooting. Avery normally wouldn't have paid them any attention, except he noticed they were using the exact same rifle he had, a scoped M24. The M24 was what he'd always used, and it had never let him down, home or away. He wondered if they were using the same 175 grain Sierra MatchKing boat tail bullets like he did. At five hundred yards, they probably were.

Avery wanted to check the scope on his own M24—he used a Leopold MK 4 LR/T M1 10x40mm fixed power scope—and get everything sighted in, but he liked to do it in private. He'd wait the other men out for a while, and if they didn't leave soon, he'd come back another time. There was no real rush. He'd located both targets and could get to them anytime, though the need itself was beginning to overwhelm him, and frustrate his boss. He'd have to move soon, or things could get ugly. The man he answered to didn't like excuses...he liked results. Avery lowered the scope for a moment and adjusted his head gear and scarf.

The day was calm, a bit on the cool side, the air dry. Perfect shooting weather. He put the scope back up to his eye to check the targets after the man fired again. He missed...not by much, but enough that Avery thought he might say something. Time to leave anyway.

ROSS AND ROSENCRANTZ WERE AT THE RANGE, ROSS trying to show his senior partner the finer points of long distance shooting. So far, Rosencrantz wasn't having much success.

"I understand the drop," Rosencrantz said. "I can even do the calculations in my head. It's the wind that's jacking me up."

They were both lying in the prone position, Ross acting as the spotter. He'd call out corrections to Rosencrantz after every shot, then Rosie would reach up and adjust the scope to zero in on the target five hundred yards downrange. The day was bright, sunny, and perfectly calm.

"There is no wind."

Rosencrantz pulled his eye away from the scope and looked at Ross. "Maybe not back here, but there must be a breeze or something near the target, because all I seem to be able to do is circle around it."

Ross moved his spotter's scope to the left and right and checked the flags that hung on poles at the far end of the range. The flags were bright orange, made of lightweight nylon and would flutter if a mosquito happened by. "No wind," he said. "The flags are as limp as your—"

"It's pretty bright out here. If you have one, you should use the Alumina 2.5 lens shade. Also, tell him to unlock his knees, turn his feet outward, and rotate his left shoulder back about an inch."

Both men turned and looked at the man who was standing behind and slightly to the right. His face was turned, and presented a narrow profile. He had his long gun in a case at his feet, a spotter's scope pressed to one eye. "I've been watching. You are sort of circling the target. But it's not your shooting that's bad, it's your form."

Ross looked at Rosencrantz's feet. He had his ankles crossed like he was in some sort of yoga class or something, and he hadn't noticed. "He's right. I should have caught that. Spread your legs and turn your feet out. And your shoulder *is* too far forward."

"Who are you?" Rosencrantz asked.

The man who'd spoken to them still had the scope to his eye. "I used to be an instructor for the army at sniper school. But that was a long time ago. Right now, as it happens, you do have a little breeze to deal with. Not much. Quartering crosswind downrange. Two miles per hour at the most if I'm reading the flags right. You going to shoot, or not?"

His voice was friendly, almost amused. He wore desert fatigues with a black and white checkered scarf around his neck, one end wrapped up and over the side of his face, tucked into a turban that circled his head. Thin leather gloves covered his hands. His hair was long, an odd shade of yellow, and it poked out underneath the turban like pieces of straw.

Ross looked at Rosencrantz, gave him a shrug and attached the lens shade. Then he put his own scope up to his eye. "Adjust for the quartering wind before you fire."

The yellow haired man focused on the target downrange, then said, "Find the rhythm of your own blood flow and breathing. Time your exhale to match the gap in your heartbeat. When you're in sync with your body, pull the trigger as gently as possible."

Rosencrantz adjusted his body, made a minor change on one of the scope's dials to account for the wind, focused on the smallest part of the target, then let his breathing slow. When he could feel the emptiness between beats, he matched his breath to the rhythm of his heart, then pulled the trigger.

Two seconds later Ross said, “Hit. Lower left. Adjust for drift and drop.”

Rosencrantz repeated the process, waited a beat, then fired again.

Ross said, “Hit. Center mass. Try one more.”

A few seconds later Rosencrantz fired again.

“Hit. Lower mass. Again.”

Rosencrantz made a minor adjustment on the dial, brought his shoulder back into position and pulled the trigger.

“Hit. Head shot,” Ross said. He pulled the scope away from his eye, clapped Rosencrantz on the back and said, “Nice shooting.” When they both turned around, the man who’d spoken to them was gone.

“Who the heck was that?” Rosencrantz said.

“Hell if I know. I’m out here twice a week and I’ve never seen him before. C’mon, swap out, and I’ll show you how it’s done.”

“Uh huh. Hope you can shoot better than you can teach. If that guy hadn’t come along I wouldn’t have hit anything.”

They switched positions and Rosencrantz took the spotter’s scope. “Wind’s picking up downrange. Drinks are on me if you hit anything other than dirt.”

Ross got into position and right before he put his eye to the scope said, “Deal.”

He waited a beat, then fired.

"Miss."

Ross fired again.

"Miss."

Ross waited until he got his breathing under control. He wasn't upset with himself...he was trying not to laugh. When he finally fired again, he looked up at Rosencrantz who had a giant grin on his face.

"Miss...again. Hope you brought your wallet, young man. You're buying tonight. Were you firing blanks, or what?"

"You might want to check your scope," Ross said.

Rosencrantz made a rude noise. "Yeah, like my vision is the problem. Suck it up, dude. The wind got you."

Ross stood and put his hand on Rosencrantz's shoulder. "I guess I could bone up on my teaching skills. Sometimes showing someone else how to do something is harder than doing it yourself. Whoever that guy was, he was right. Anyway, check the scope again."

"Why? You missed every shot."

Ross rolled his tongue around the inside of his cheek, then, as straight-faced as possible said, "Check the *thousand yard targets*, Rosie."

Rosencrantz narrowed his eyes, then brought the scope up and checked the targets further downrange...the ones that were twice as far away. Ross had hit every single one, center mass. "Fuck me," he said.

"C'mon, let's pack it up," Ross said. "I'm thirsty."

Then, laughing when he said it: “The way you were saying *Miss*...”

“What about it?”

“It was like you could already taste the beer.” Then, laughing again, “Like I ever miss.”

CHAPTER NINE

Virgil got in the town car and drove to the state building to find Sandy. When he stuck his head in the outer office, he saw that her chief of staff was out, so he walked past the desk, knocked on the lieutenant governor's door, waited a beat, then stepped inside. Her office was empty, but he eventually found her speaking with Mac in his office, both of them seated at a small conference table in the far corner of the room. They both turned and looked at him when he entered.

"Sorry I'm late." Virgil said. "Couldn't find anyone."

Sandy smiled at him and said, "Come on in. I think we're done here. Mac?"

The governor nodded. "For tonight, anyway. Let's circle back on this, uh...give me a moment. Let me check my schedule." The governor pulled out his phone, thumbed through his calendar, then said, "Tomorrow at two? I've got an hour."

Sandy had her own calendar open and said, "Works for me."

Virgil had no idea what they were working on, and though he loved his wife dearly and considered the governor one of his closest friends, he didn't care. Their meeting was probably something to do with a budgetary issue regarding a legislative matter that no one would ever hear about anyway.

"How's it feel to dress like a regular person?" Mac asked as he stood from the table. He gave him a toothless grin.

"It feels great," Virgil said. "So good in fact that I can't wait to get out of this suit and back to it."

The governor looked at Sandy. "His personal sense of style...it baffles me. It's like he's somewhere on the wardrobe spectrum or something. The lower end, I'd say, if I had to guess. But take Murton for example. Now there's a man who knows how to pull off a particular look. They grew up together, yet Virgil here—"

"Mac?" Virgil said.

The governor turned his head. "Yes?"

"It looks like you've got a spot of mustard on your tie."

A look of shock and horror passed over Mac's face as he looked down at his tie. There *was* a spot. He looked at Sandy. "I gave that keynote address earlier this afternoon...right after lunch. I wish someone would have said something."

"I never noticed," Sandy said. "But Virgil doesn't miss

much. Besides, that spot is about the size of a pin head. I'm sure no one else noticed."

"Let's hope not."

"Probably never come out," Virgil said. "Too bad you weren't wearing something more—"

"Disposable?"

"I was going to say bleach friendly. Besides, you've probably got Hollandaise sauce on your shoes or something."

Mac stripped the tie off and folded in neatly before placing it in his jacket pocket. He was careful not to look at his shoes, though it wasn't easy. "Okay, I know when I'm bested. Enough already."

Virgil clapped him on the back. "Sandy and I are having dinner at the bar tonight. Care to join us? You could stop at the mansion and throw on any old thing."

"I've already surrendered. There's no need to kick me when I'm down." Then, "I wish I could. But my schedule is full this evening. Probably come out to your place this weekend though if that's all right?"

"You're welcome anytime, Mac," Sandy said.

"Thank you, both." With that the governor said good night and left the room. He dropped a note on his secretary's chair so she'd see it first thing in the morning and was about to leave when he heard an unusual noise inside his office. Sort of a yelp, followed by a thud, like something or someone had fallen. He moved to the door, yanked it open, then immediately averted his eyes and said, "Uh, Jonesy?"

Virgil, so caught up in the moment hadn't heard the door open. He had Sandy backed up against the desk and they'd knocked a few heavy binders on the floor. At the sound of the governor's voice he spun around, a little red in the face, and said, "Sir?"

"For the love of God, not on my desk."

LATER, AT THE BAR, VIRGIL ASKED SANDY IF SHE KNEW when Emily Baker would be back.

"I have no idea," she said. "She hasn't mentioned anything to me."

"Huh."

Murton and Becky came over and joined them at their table. "Huh, what?" Murton asked. He was dressed in a pair of green cargo pants, a tan and black bowling shirt with the words *Spare Me* above the left pocket, and a Panama Jack hat tipped jauntily to one side.

"You look like you just came from a beach bowling tournament or something," Virgil said.

"Maybe I did."

"You wouldn't think that if you saw his wardrobe budget," Becky said. She wore jeans and a simple black V-neck T-shirt. "Everything has to be one of a kind."

"I am original, if nothing else," Murton said.

"Maybe you and Mac should get together and compare notes," Virgil said.

"And I was about to tell you how nice you look in that suit. Anyway...huh, what?"

Virgil had already lost the thread. "What?"

"When we walked over...you said, 'Huh.'"

"Oh, yeah. I was asking Sandy if she knew when Baker was going to come back."

"Soon, I hope," Murton said. "About time we got back to work. I get the feeling Mac isn't giving us much while you're on protection detail."

"He's still in withdrawal since the Freedom fiasco," Becky said.

Virgil looked at Becky. "Speaking of fiascos, I've got something for you to look at." Virgil tapped his index finger on the manila envelope that sat next to his drink. "Talk about it after dinner?"

"Sure. I'm starving, by the way. How about we all order?"

"Can't," Sandy said. "The moment we arrived Robert came out and said no menus for us tonight. Apparently he's fixing something special." Virgil and Murton co-owned the bar, called Jonesy's Rastabarian, with Delroy Rouche and Robert Whyte, their two Jamaican friends. Delroy ran the bar and front end while Robert, the head chef, took care of the kitchen.

A waitress came by and took drink orders from Murton and Becky, then headed back to the bar. "Where's Delroy, by the way?" Virgil asked.

"It's Tuesday...his day off," Murton said.

"Ah, that's right." Virgil looked around the bar. "Ever notice how quiet it is in here when he's not working?"

Murton nodded. "Yeah. It's an entirely different crowd. You end up with guys wearing suits."

Virgil ignored the comment, mostly because he noticed someone watching them. A man, sitting alone at a table near the front door. The light was dim and it was hard to see him clearly. As soon as he noticed Virgil looking back at him, he stood, dropped some cash on the table, then walked out the door.

"Excuse me for a moment," Virgil said as he stood.

"Virg?"

He glanced back at Sandy. "I'll be right back. Murt... on the rear."

Murton got up, headed for the rear exit, then circled around to the front. By the time he got there, he found Virgil standing on the sidewalk, looking back and forth and across the street.

"Anything?" Virgil said.

Murton shook his head. "Nothing, though I only caught a glimpse as he ducked out the door. Who was it, and why'd he take off so quick?"

"I might have an idea, but I'm not sure you'd believe me. Did you notice he was zeroed in on our table like he had us locked down? As soon as he knew he'd been made, he took off."

They spent a few more moments looking around, but ended up back inside. The waitress was already cleaning the table where the man had been sitting. When they approached her she looked up, smiled and said, "Hey Jonesy, Murt. What's up?"

"Do you know that man who was sitting here?"

She shook her head. "No. I've never seen him before. Left a hell of a tip, though."

"How much?"

The waitress pulled out her order pad and did the math. "He had one beer and a burger. Twelve bucks and change. Left me a fifty."

Murton looked at Virgil. "Like he was in a hurry and didn't take the time to check what he was leaving."

"Or he didn't care," Virgil said.

"Maybe he was impressed with the quality of service," the waitress said, a whiff of sarcasm in her voice.

Virgil grinned at her. "I'm sure that's it. Listen, I couldn't see him all that well. What'd he look like?"

The waitress subconsciously scratched the side of her head with her pencil. "Well, for starters, he was wearing one of those weird turban hats, like they do in the Middle East."

"They're called a Pakol," Murton said.

"Kind of weird to see that around here," the waitress said. Then she looked at Virgil. "Hey, speaking of weird, what's with the suit?"

"It's a work thing," Virgil said with a touch of impatience. "Regular guy and a head scarf isn't much of a description."

"You know how it is, guys. I see hundreds of people a day in here, but I don't really see them, see them."

"Anything at all would be helpful," Murton said, his voice soft and kind.

She closed her eyes and after a moment or two she opened them and said, "He wouldn't look straight at me. Every time I came to the table he turned his head away like he was looking at something else. And he had unusual hair. It was long and he had it tucked up under his Pack Doll, or whatever you called it—"

"Pakol," Murton said again.

"Right. Anyway, like I was saying, some of it was sticking out and it was sort of unusual."

"There you go," Virgil said. "Unusual how?"

"It might of been the lighting in here, because you guys like to keep an atmosphere or something, but it looked like it didn't have any real color. It was like he had straw for hair. I think he might have been a burn victim too. Even though he had his head turned, you could see something wasn't right with the side of his neck and face." She had the table mostly cleared, and was about to reach for the beer mug when Virgil said, "Wait. Don't touch that."

"Why not?"

"Fingerprints." He looked at Murton and said, "Let's see if we can get Mimi or Lawless down here with a kit."

"Maybe we're overreacting a little," Murton said.

"You didn't see the way this guy was looking at us."

"Who are we talking about here, Jonesy?"

"Think about it."

"You're saying it was Avery? We haven't seen him since

we were in the sandbox. But I heard something a long time ago when I was with the feds...something about contract hits out of Miami, and maybe El Sal. Only rumors, but they got my attention."

"So what's he doing here? Better yet, why show up, then run off? And why was he looking at us like that?"

"Guys?" the waitress said.

Murton held up a wait a minute finger. "Who knows? Look Jones-man, we're sitting with two of the hottest women in the whole joint. I'd be more worried if he wasn't looking."

"Guys?" the waitress said again.

They turned and said *what?* at the same time.

"Your fingerprint idea? It won't work. That's the other thing I remembered about him. He was wearing gloves... you know those thin leather driving kind. He never took them off."

Virgil looked at Murton. "Overreacting?"

"Okay, maybe not." Then, as if the whole thing had never happened he tipped his head at their own table and said, "Looks like the food's ready. Let's eat, huh?"

THEY LET THE STRAW-HAIRED, GLOVED MAN GO AND talked about Said's problem with the drill units down in Shelby County.

"That whole AI thing fascinates me," Becky said.

"It scares the hell out of me," Murton said. He looked

at Virgil and Sandy. "Your boys...by the time they're our age, the whole world is going to be run by robots." He sounded serious.

"I don't think it's all that, Murt," Virgil said.

"Think what you want. But I can tell you this, it's the guys in suits who go first. You know...guys like you and Mac."

"You're a riot, you know that?"

"I do what I can to keep the people entertained."

Becky had been thumbing through the contents of the envelope. "There's not much to go on here. I could do a basic check on the company...this, uh, Ar-Tell—not the most imaginative name, by the way—and their board, but I'm not sure I could get you anything useful without being more creative."

Virgil gave her a somewhat defeated shrug. "Well, see what you can see, I guess. One step at a time. But if you could start tomorrow morning, I'd appreciate it. Said says the contract is about up, and it'd take something like twenty years to find someone else to make what he needs."

"I thought earlier you said it was eighteen months."

"Yeah, yeah. Still...a long time. Gotta keep the gas flowing."

Becky gave him a mini eye roll. "Drill baby drill, right?"

Virgil: "Hey now."

"I'm just messing with ya," Becky said.

"One other thing," Virgil said.

"Isn't there always?"

Virgil ignored her. "See what you can find about a guy named Jacob Avery. Murt and I served with him in the army. He'd be about our age. That's all I know."

Sandy nudged Virgil under the table. Virgil had once told her the story about Mason being the arresting officer of Avery's father at the foundry.

Virgil, like any married man, knew what the nudge meant. He let out a sigh and told Becky the rest of the story, including the rumored contract hits in Miami.

When he finished, Becky said, "Next time you tell me that's all you know, how about you give me the whole story. It makes my job a lot easier." Then to Murton: "And why haven't you ever told me any of this?"

Murton opened his mouth to answer, but didn't have the words.

CHAPTER TEN

Jacob Avery drove away from the bar, cursing at himself. Sometimes he felt like he had the same bad luck as his father. How many bars and restaurants were there in the city of Indianapolis? And he picked the one where two people he didn't need to see just happened to be at the same time? Plus, he'd handled it badly. Why'd he run away? All that did was create suspicion where none existed...at least not yet. Time to fix his own mistake.

He turned around, drove back to the bar, and parked in the back lot. When he walked in the front door he saw the four of them still sitting at the same table. The blonde woman tipped her head back and laughed at something someone had said. Then she took her napkin from her lap, set it on the table, and walked toward the restroom.

No time like the present, Avery thought. As he

approached, he saw Wheeler reach down with his right hand and pretend like he was scratching his ankle.

"What's the matter, Murt? Don't recognize an old army pal when you see one?"

Murton held his .38 on his lap, under the table and out of sight. "Gotta tell you, Ave, I didn't. Virgil and I were a little concerned when you took off so quick a little while ago."

Virgil picked up on Murton's use of his given name, something he usually only did when he wanted Virgil's full attention. "Why did you take off, Ave?"

"You want the truth? I chickened out."

"But you came back," Virgil said. "And you're here now."

"I see you haven't lost your powers of perception," Avery said.

"You're not armed, are you?" Murton asked.

"It's a free country. We fought together to make sure it stayed that way."

"That's one way of looking at it. But how about you answer the question," Murton said.

"Boy, if I'd have known how paranoid a couple of cops were going to be to see an old army buddy, I wouldn't have come here in the first place. I caught you pulling your ankle piece by the way. I'm not a threat. And to answer your question, no, I'm not armed. I wanted to say hello, that's all. I chickened out when I saw you had this lovely lady with you. The way I look and all."

Becky kicked Virgil under the table. Virgil frowned at

her, then said, "Uh, sorry. Jacob Avery, this is Murton's girlfriend, Becky Taylor."

Becky said hello and Avery nodded at her. Then he looked at Virgil and said, "And your wife? Is she with you tonight?"

"Ladies' room," Virgil said. Then, "Care to join us?"

Avery shook his head. "I'm afraid I can't. I have an appointment at the VA in a little while."

Virgil glanced at his watch. "At this hour?"

Avery gave him a fake smile, the burn scars on the side of his face stretching tight as he did. "No rest for the weary, I suppose. Anyway, I simply wanted to say hello. It's been a long time. I'll say goodnight now."

Virgil stood up. "It has been a long time, Ave. What have you been up to?"

Avery let his burn scars go tight again. "Is that Jonesy the cop or Jonesy the old army buddy asking?"

Virgil raised a single eyebrow. "I heard something about Miami. It wasn't exactly flattering."

Avery winked at him with his good eye, then looked at Murton when he answered. "Probably from a former federal agent, would be my guess." He turned his attention back to Virgil. "Don't believe everything you hear, Jonesy. And stop with the brow, will you? It's not polite when you do it to a guy who only has the one." Then he turned toward the rest of the table. "Becky, a pleasure. Murt, the same. Maybe I'll see you all around some other time."

After he'd walked out the door, Virgil sat down and

said, "Becks."

Becky nodded and said, "First thing in the morning, Boss. Is this someone we need to be worried about?"

"I'm not sure," Virgil said. "Probably not."

Sandy had returned to the table and she heard what Becky had said. "Worried about what?"

"It's nothing, I'm sure. Just being cautious."

Sandy gave her husband a look. "Then why does Murton have his gun in his lap?"

AVERY DROVE AWAY FROM THE BAR AND THOUGHT ON A scale of one to ten, he'd have given himself a five. He had wanted to come across as friendly, happy to see them, but they acted paranoid. Maybe it was because they're cops. Cops are always paranoid. Of course it didn't help that he ran off as soon as they saw him. And the VA thing...he shouldn't have used that excuse. It was too late in the evening for an appointment. He'd have to somehow walk that back if it ever came up again. In the meantime, he had work to do.

He headed northwest out of the city on US 65, for a quick run up to Lebanon, Indiana. He was working on his own time, and time was short. He needed to handle the Long situation sooner rather than later. If his boss, Bob Long found out what he was doing, it wouldn't go over well...at all.

He kept an eye on his speed. Getting pulled over with

the supplies he had in the back seat of his car would not be good. The rig he was using was homemade. He'd tested it thoroughly and it worked perfectly, just like the video from the Internet said it would.

Tim Dreyer lived east of Lebanon off a quiet county road. He had a little shack he rented out in the country, which made things much easier for Avery. It'd be a shame to have to light up an entire apartment complex or something, but he still would have done it if need be. Dreyer worked as a grounds keeper for one of the cemeteries—probably the only job he could get with his military record—and Avery laughed to himself at how appropriate that was, given what he was about to do.

He killed his headlights, turned into Dreyer's drive, and coasted to a stop. Had to hurry now. He left the driver's side door open, popped the rear door, slipped into the rig, pulled the straps tight, and opened the valves on both tanks. The tanks had been converted from SCUBA gear he'd purchased on Craig's List for cash. When he felt the lines pressurize he walked up to the front door of the shack, gave a polite little knock, the way someone might if they were lost and needed directions, then put his thumb on the igniter and his finger on the trigger.

When Dreyer answered the door, Avery kicked it in, knocking Dreyer to the floor. He stepped inside, closed the door, looked at the man who'd burned him so long ago now, even as he was trying to save his life and the lives of others. When Dreyer finally recognized him, he said, "Please. It was an accident. I'm sorry. I done my time."

Avery looked him in the eye and said, "Things are about to get heated around here, if you know what I mean." He pressed the igniter and the electronic spark made a clicking noise that caused Dreyer to wet himself. Avery laughed, his face stretched tight and twisted out of shape. "Trying to put the fire out already, huh? Well, let's see if that's going to work."

He put the end of the weapon inches from Dreyer's face, pulled the trigger on the nozzle, and the liquid flame shot out and engulfed Dreyer. The fire burned away his face, neck, and hair. Avery kept the trigger pulled until the tanks ran dry, then got a little panicky when he finally noticed that half the shack was in flames. He ran out the door, slipped out of the rig, tossed it in the back seat, then hopped in the front and drove away—the flames in his rear view mirror lighting up the night.

THE NEXT DAY WHEN AVERY WOKE, HE FELT LIGHTER somehow, like a weight had been lifted. He spent an hour or so disassembling his homemade flamethrower, then put everything in his car and disposed of the various parts and pieces in different dumpsters along the back of four separate strip malls.

That done, he drove to a small studio apartment he'd rented not long ago. The apartment had a clear view eight blocks away from the court where Pete Long had been crippled. He'd paid cash in advance for a month's stay, plus a refundable security deposit if he didn't trash the place. He told the super he was in town for a few weeks on business. The super didn't care. He pocketed the cash, gave Avery a key, and was gone. Avery knew he'd never see the security deposit again because the place was already trashed. But it didn't matter. It wasn't his money anyway.

The place was like a small hotel room. A Motel Six or something like that. There was a bed, a table and a chair, and a single lamp. The lamp didn't work. No matter. He wouldn't be needing it.

Avery sat in his car for a while and waited until no one was around before he brought his gear up. He stowed the M24 sniper rifle under the bed, then pulled out his spotter's scope and a camera with a massive telephoto lens. He dragged the chair over to the window and looked outside. Closer would have been better, but he wanted to stay out of sight and this was the best location he could find. And if he had the right targets—he was fairly certain he did—he wanted to get the pictures from the same place where the shooting would happen when the time came.

He put the spotter's scope up to his good eye and scanned the court. He watched for a few minutes, then set the scope down and picked up the camera. The court was crowded, and it made it difficult to get good shots of all the players. When he finally finished, he checked the digital images on the camera's screen, decided what he had was as good as it was going to get, put his spotter's scope under the bed with the rifle and left.

Next stop...the hospital.

Avery had an affinity for hospitals. He felt like it was the one place where most of the people he encountered didn't treat him like he'd escaped from the freak show. Everyone knew what a burn victim looked like when they saw one, but medical personnel seemed to not notice the side of his face that had been burned away, or the ridiculous wig he sometimes wore to cover the top half of his scalp, or the way his left eye—the glass one—didn't track in sync with his right.

When he stepped into the doorway of the private room, he found his boss, Bob Long, sitting in the corner, facing his son's hospital bed. Pete Long hadn't yet undergone surgery—the docs were waiting, trying to get the swelling down before going in—so he was awake, but a little loopy from the pain meds. The privacy curtain was pulled mostly closed, and all Avery could see was Pete Long's feet.

Avery was chief of security for Long's company, ArTell, with Bob Long being the chairman and CEO. He was also, Avery had learned from experience, someone you did not want to cross. When Long saw Avery enter, he stood and met him at the door.

"Where have you been and what have you got? I expected you hours ago. In fact, I expected you yesterday." Long wore a rumpled business suit, like he'd slept in it, which, Avery thought, he probably had.

"It wasn't as easy as I'd hoped it might be," Avery said.

"Lots of people, and I was pretty far away. Had to wait until each individual was fairly still to get the good shots." He pulled the camera out of the bag and handed it to his boss.

Long took the camera and scrolled through the pictures. "These are the good ones? They're pretty fuzzy."

"Like I said, there was some distance involved, and quite a bit of movement. If you like, I could take them home and run them through the editor...clean them up a bit."

Long shook his head. "No, no. There's no time for that. The docs have pumped him full of steroids and they're saying the swelling is coming down. They'll be taking him in for surgery in a matter of hours. He'll be out for a few days at least afterwards...something about a medically induced coma to keep him still. They're trying to prevent any additional nerve damage. It's now or we wait. And you know how I feel about waiting."

"I'll show these to him then," Avery said. "See if he can pick the guy we're looking for."

"No, I'll do it. He's my son." Long turned to walk back to the bed, but Avery reached out and grabbed him by the arm. When Long stopped and looked at Avery's hand on his arm, Avery let go.

"Sir, let's keep you out of the rest of this. You need to stay isolated from everything. Should word get out that you were showing these pictures to your son...well, we wouldn't want that, would we? How about you go wait in the hall for a few minutes?"

Long nodded, then patted Avery on the back. "He had a full ride to Purdue. Would have made the pros."

"I know, sir, and I'm sorry. I'll get things taken care of."

"I've got caseworkers in here asking if I want to start filling out Social Security disability forms. He's only eighteen and once he gets out of here he'll be in a wheelchair for the rest of his life, pissing and shitting into a bag." He poked Avery in the chest with his index finger and spoke through his teeth. "Who's going to take care of that?"

Avery didn't know how to respond, so he didn't say anything.

"I'll be out in the hall," Long said. He moved away then stopped and turned back. "You've got to be more careful, Ave. In fact, of late, you've been downright careless."

"Excuse me?"

"How long do you think it will take the police to connect you with that burn victim?"

Avery spent a few seconds processing what his boss had said. "You had me followed?" he asked, barely able to contain his own anger now.

"I cover my ass," Long said. "I suggest you start to do the same. I've got men who could have handled Dreyer for you, and you know that. He would have simply disappeared, and with his record, I guarantee no one would be sniffing around asking questions. But instead of coming to me, the guy who writes your checks, you took a personal matter into your own hands and have put my entire operation at risk. What do you think I should do about that?"

"This was personal for me. You know the story."

"Personal or not, it was a mistake."

"We've worked together a long time, sir. Let's not forget that."

"Are you threatening me, Ave? Think you can put all my dirty secrets out in the open for everyone to see? They'd string you up right next to me."

"No. I'm not threatening you. I'm simply stating that we've had a good and profitable working relationship."

"Had might be the key word there, Ave. I think you should take some time. Getting away for a while would be a good thing. For both of us. I'll make the arrangements. Spend some time overseas or something. Cool out a little. Maybe we'll reassess in six months or a year."

"Reassess? Maybe?"

"Watch your tone with me," Long said.

Avery knew better than to argue with him. When Long's mind was made up, there was no changing it. He didn't reply.

"Remember," Long said. "I want him hurt badly. Crippled like my boy is. I don't want him killed. Show me you can handle that and maybe we can rethink this whole thing...figure out a way to get you out from under any suspicion. You're a good man, Ave. I'm sorry it's come to this."

No you're not. "Whatever you say, sir."

CHAPTER ELEVEN

Despite what he'd told the cops at the shooting range—and Avery knew they were cops simply by noting the equipment they had with them—he'd never been an instructor at sniper school, though he had taught others how to shoot, and shoot well. After he was medically discharged from the army, with the threat of infection gone, came the awful reconstructive surgeries that didn't help with his appearance. In fact, Avery thought it made him look like he was wearing half his ass on his face and neck. Or maybe that was because he knew where they'd grafted the skin from. In any case, he spent a few years in El Salvador, doing contract hits for various drug kingpins, then a few years in Miami doing the same for the larger wholesalers. The move to Miami was a no-brainer for Avery. The Miami guys were more refined, and the pay was better. Much better. One of his contacts in Miami told him about a guy named Long up in Indianapolis who needed a business partner to go away.

He checked out the businessman—you had to be careful in Avery's line of work—and Long checked out. When the business partner went away, Long payed the bill, then made Avery an offer. His official title would be chief of security. His actual job would be to take care of Bob Long's problems when they cropped up. And Long liked to deal with his problems the old fashioned way, by making them go away...permanently. Despite his past, Avery missed the Midwest and wanted to be home again.

The money was right, the jobs were few and far between, so Avery felt safe...like he didn't have to always be looking over his shoulder. Avery had a small team he worked with, and before he knew it, he and Long had developed a history, one that went so far back that Long's son, Pete, called him Uncle Ave. When he pulled the curtain back, Pete was flat on his back, staring at the ceiling. "Hey hotshot, how you feeling?"

Pete let his eyes slide over and said, "Hey Uncle Ave. I'm pretty okay. They've got me on the good stuff, so it doesn't hurt too bad. I can't feel anything below my stomach. My legs don't work at all. I guess there's some other stuff that isn't ever going to work again either."

Avery wanted to provide some comfort, but he didn't know how. Didn't want to say the wrong thing. He stepped closer to the side of the bed and turned the camera around. "I'd like you to take a look at some pictures."

"You'll have to hold the camera for me. I'm strapped down. I guess I'm supposed to stay as still as possible."

"That's no problem," Avery said. "I'm going to click through some photos and you tell me when you see the guy who hurt you. Understand?"

Pete said he did.

Avery pressed a button on the camera and waited a few seconds before pressing it again, giving Pete time to study each shot. When the photo of the black kid with the braids wrapped up on top of his head came on the screen, Pete said, "That's him."

"You're sure?"

"I'm positive. He's the one who did this to me. I'm crippled for life because of that guy. He did it on purpose because I was beating him fair and square. Either that or because I called him TopKnot, I'm not sure which. Either way..."

Avery looked at the photo then turned the camera off. "Okay, don't you worry about a thing. Uncle Ave's gonna take care of everything. All you have to work on now is getting better."

"What will they do to him? The police, I mean?"

Nothing. "How about you focus on healing up, and leave the rest to me, okay?"

"What's to heal? My life is over."

Avery reached out and stroked Pete's hair. "I know it feels that way right now, and I'm not going to try to tell you different, other than the fact that I felt the same way once. Your life has changed, but it's not over."

But Pete wasn't listening anymore. "I'm tired Uncle Ave."

Avery nodded at him. "Get some rest, then. I'll check on you when I can."

"Where's my mom?"

Avery looked away when he answered. "I think she's home, getting some rest. Your dad's here though. They've been taking turns."

"You are taking those pictures to the cops, right?"

Avery had never lied to Pete, and he didn't want to start now, not with everything the young man was going through. "Get some rest, kid. You've got a long road ahead, but you're tough and you'll make it. Are you hearing me on this?"

Pete's eyes were closed and Avery didn't know if he was asleep or simply pretending. Avery patted him gently on the thigh and walked out of the room. Pete didn't feel a thing.

When Avery went out into the hall, he gave Bob Long a single nod and kept walking.

Some things didn't need to be spoken aloud.

BECAUSE BOB LONG DIDN'T LIKE TO WAIT, AVERY WENT straight back to the room he'd rented and got everything set up. He pulled the table over to the window—he had to shim one of the legs with a pad of paper to steady it—then retrieved his rifle from under the bed. He opened the window, then pulled the curtains together leaving a small gap in the middle. That done, he attached a suppressor to his sniper rifle, unfolded the Harris bipod attached under the front of the stock, then set it on the table. He brought the chair over, took out his spotter's scope, and sat down.

The scope had a range finder readout that gave him the exact distance to his target. He made note of the reading, then began to scan the surrounding area for indications of wind direction and velocity. He spotted a flag no more than fifty yards away from the target area waving half-heartedly in the breeze. Based on the size of the flag, its height on the pole and the surrounding buildings, he estimated a direct crosswind at three to four knots. The crosswind would affect the drift, so that would have to be calculated into the shot. He put the spotter's scope away, made the necessary adjustments to the Leopold MK 4 scope on his rifle, then went to find the building's super. He couldn't afford to be recognized later.

PLAYERS WERE COMING AND GOING AT THE COURT, almost every single one of them stopping at some point to reach into a bag and hand something off to a passerby. Selling dope, probably. Almost a full hour into the wait, the target finally approached the court, a backpack slung over one shoulder, a pair of sneakers tied together over the other. He tipped his head at a few of the other players on the court as he sat down to change his shoes. He faced the court, his back to a killer who was eight blocks away with the crosshairs of the scope right in the center of the target's back. The shot would cripple him for sure.

THE ENTIRE TIME AVERY HAD BEEN TAKING CARE OF the building's super, he was thinking about the things Long had said to him. In a way, Avery knew his boss was right. He should have let someone else handle Dreyer. But the urge...it wouldn't have gone away. And this whole business about taking some time to cool out? Avery knew what Long meant by that. His boss had never been one to mince words. He'd cool out alright. He'd be sitting on a beach somewhere sipping a scotch and soda when someone would walk up behind him and stick an icepick in his ear. Cool out my ass. Avery had been through enough to know that at some point you had to make a stand...had to show them that you were not someone to be fucked with.

THE TARGET STOOD, THEN TURNED AROUND SO HE could stash his bag under the bench. He shoved it underneath, then walked onto the court. But his gait was off, like he had a pebble in his shoe or something. When the target sat back down to take care of the pebble he did so with his back to the court, which put him face-on to the crosshairs.

When he finished tying his shoe, he gave the laces a final tug to make sure they were tight, then lifted his head as he sat up. The shot caught the young man right in the center of his forehead, above the bridge of his nose. The momentum of his own movements combined with the shot that killed him jerked his upper body backwards and he rolled off the bench, landing on his back. His feet came to rest on the bench and if no one looked too closely, it looked like he might be taking an afternoon nap. Except one of the other players had dropped a three pointer from well outside the line and when he turned to high-five his partner he saw the red mist that seemed to explode from the victim's head.

THE SHOT WAS LOUDER THAN EXPECTED. THE suppressors—they were good—but they weren't as good as the movies portrayed them. The shot still created some noise...like someone dropping a heavy book on a hardwood floor. When there were no shouts or panicked shuffling about in the surrounding rooms, the weapon was put back in its case, then slid under the bed. It'd be retrieved later in the evening after dark. No one wanted to be seen carrying a rifle case down the stairs at the same time someone had been shot. The window was closed, the table and chair returned to their previous positions, and then the court was checked one more time with the spotter's scope. It was completely empty, except for TopKnot, who was thoroughly dead. Except TopKnot wasn't his name, and had anyone involved known the identity of the young man who'd been killed, they might have found a better way to get their revenge.

CHAPTER TWELVE

Early the next morning Cora called Virgil and told him to get ahold of Murton and Becky and get down to her office as soon as possible. Virgil made the calls, dropped Sandy off at the state building, and less than an hour later the three of them walked into Cora LaRue's office. She pointed to the chairs that fronted her desk and everyone took a seat. Cora was the governor's chief of staff, and their direct boss.

"You wanted to see us?" Virgil said.

"Nice threads," Cora said, by way of a greeting. "It's like I'm staring at a new and improved Virgil." There was no humor in her voice. Cora was simply stating the facts as she saw them.

Virgil threw his hands in the air, stood and turned toward the door.

"Where do you think you're going?" Cora said.

"To the pharmacy. I'm going to pick up some Thera-Flu and personally pour it down Emily Baker's throat."

"Yeah, yeah, very funny," Cora said, again without humor. She pointed at the chair. "Sit down. We've got work to do."

Virgil sat. Murton, who'd been sucking on his cheeks, said, "I heard she's pretty sick. Another couple weeks, at least."

Virgil leaned forward, put his forearms on his thighs, and stared at his shoes.

Wingtips, no less.

Becky, who was sitting between the two men, patted Virgil on the arm. "I think you look nice." She was being serious.

Virgil looked at her and said, "Thank you."

"Your welcome, and don't listen to Murt. I heard Baker will be back soon."

"Thank God," Virgil said.

Except Becky, who didn't want to be left completely out of the fun said, "But your socks don't match your tie."

WITH THE VIRGIL-WARDROBE-BASHING COMPLETE, Cora got right down to business. "Any of you know anything about blockchain?"

"Isn't that Bitcoin or something?" Virgil said.

Murton rolled his eyes. "Bitcoin uses blockchain technology. But that's not what they do. That's like saying the computer wrote all my daily reports for me."

Virgil gave Murton a dry look. "So, what then?"

Murton glanced at Cora and she gave him a go-ahead nod.

"Blockchain is basically a time-stamped series of data records managed by clusters of computers not owned or operated by any single entity. Each of these blocks—that's where the first part of the name comes from—are secured and bound to each other using high-level cryptographic connections, thus the second part of the term...the chain. Why are you guys looking at me like that? I like to read." Then he jerked his thumb at Becky. "Besides, spend enough time with this one and you learn things."

Cora was impressed. "You know what? I'm going to share something with you, Wheeler, and if you ever tell anyone I said it, I'll deny it to my grave."

"What's that?" Murton asked.

"Sometimes you impress the hell out of me."

Murton made a rude noise with his lips and said, *"Sometimes?* I think I'd like to resign now."

"Murt's description is accurate, though there's a little more to it than that," Becky said. "But why are we talking about this?"

"Because one of the state senators has introduced a bill to replace our current voting system of polling places and ballot machines with blockchain technology. If he's successful with the vote on the floor—and it looks, according to my sources, that he might be—it will put the power of voting in the palm of your hand...literally. We're talking about voting via mobile phones."

"Ah, that'll never happen," Virgil said. "Too many things to go wrong."

"Like what?" Murton asked. "The way the whole thing is designed it's practically fool-proof."

Becky tipped her head at Murton. "He's right. The system is as secure as it gets."

"Tell me more about that," Cora said.

Becky made a balloon with her cheeks before she spoke, gathering her thoughts. "Okay...where to start. First of all, blockchain networks don't have a central authority. That means, for all intents and purposes, it is the perfect definition of a democratized system."

Cora was leaning forward now, interested. "What do you mean when you say democratized? In what way?"

"It's open information...available to everyone and anyone. Look at it like this: The way it works now, when we go to vote, we walk in, show our ID, fill out a ballot, then feed it into a machine. The machine tallies the votes, then that information is combined with all the other machines for a grand total. Whoever has the most votes wins."

Virgil, who couldn't follow the thread, said, "So what?"

"I'll give you so what, mister...Once you feed your ballot into the machine, everything else is taken on faith. Humans are in charge of the machines and that means they're in charge of the numbers."

"You're saying that there's too much room for voter fraud," Murton said.

Becky tipped a finger at him. "Exactly. And who's to know? The only time any of the results ever get challenged is if there is a recount. But I'm talking about your individual vote."

"What about it?" Virgil asked.

"There's simply no way to tell if it was counted correctly, or counted at all, for that matter. It wouldn't take much corruption at the right level to simply not count a select group of votes from any given district."

Virgil was sort of shaking his head. "I don't know, Becks. That seems a little far fetched, if you ask me."

Becky pulled her elbows in and turned her palms up. "Who's to say? Maybe it is far fetched. But you've got to admit there's room for corruption and fraud. I'm not saying it's happening...I'm simply stating there's room for it to happen. Blockchain takes that room, so to speak, out of the equation."

"How exactly?" Cora asked.

"By using an immutable, shared ledger, open for anyone and everyone to see. If voting were done using blockchain, it would be completely transparent. You wouldn't feed a ballot into a machine, you'd vote on your phone and you'd be able to see your vote being counted in real time. So anything built on the blockchain—like voting—would be by its very nature, open and transparent. If you ask me, it's the wave of the future. It's coming, like it or not."

Virgil, who was in many areas of his life still a little old-school, remained skeptical. "Seems like there's too many things that could go wrong."

"Such as?" Murton said.

Virgil flapped his arms. "Well, hell, I don't know exactly. Maybe you should ask Wu and Nicky Pope. I'll bet they could crack it." Then, "What about this? Every kid in the country over the age of six these days has some sort of device that connects to the Internet—hell, Jonas has his own phone already—and that's what we're talking about, right? Voting with your phone over the Internet? I mean, you've got to be eighteen to vote. How do you keep some eight year old from voting, or worse, have mommy do it for him, then vote again on her own phone?"

"Why is mommy the bad guy in your scenario?" Becky said.

Virgil waved her off. "Figure of speech. Could be daddy, Uncle Bill, whoever. The question is valid."

"There are ways to ensure that sort of thing wouldn't be allowed to happen," Becky said. "Unique voter registration IDs, PIN numbers, social security numbers, and so on. I don't think you'd have to worry too much about any of it. That's the beauty of blockchain.

"It's nothing more than a way of passing information —in this case, your vote—from point A to point B, all in a fully automated, safe, and transparent manner. When you vote, you'd be creating a block that would be verified by hundreds of thousands of computers around the net. Your block, or vote, if you like, is added to everyone else's block, thus creating the chain. And remember, all those blocks are verified exactly like yours, creating a unique record with a unique history. If someone tried to falsify a record or even a group of records—no matter how large or small—it would mean they'd have to falsify the entire chain, which would be practically impossible."

Virgil, his eyes starting to glaze, said, "I don't know. Seems a little out there, if you ask me."

Becky sort of huffed at him. "Okay, let me ask you this: When Mac ran for office, did you vote for him?"

Virgil pointed a finger at her. "See, that's a problem right there. Voting is private. You start using blockchain and everyone is going to know who voted for whom."

Becky rolled her eyes. "No they're not. Your vote would be encrypted on the ledger, identified by a string...a long series of random numbers, letters, and special characters with literally hundreds of millions of different combinations. That's part of what makes the system work. If someone were to somehow gain access to the system with the intent of altering your vote, they wouldn't be able to do it because of the encryption. They simply wouldn't be able to identify who you voted for, or even your specific vote. So how about you answer my question. Did you vote for Mac or not?"

Virgil gave up. "Of course I did."

"So prove two things to me."

"What?"

"How do you know your vote was counted, and how do you know it was counted for Mac?"

"Well he won, didn't he?"

Murton leaned past Becky, looked at Virgil and said, "Give it up, dude. You're digging your own grave."

Virgil massaged his forehead with the tips of his fingers. "Let me go back to Becky's original question. Why—specifically—are we talking about all of this?"

"Because someone doesn't want mobile blockchain voting implemented," Cora said.

"Who?" Virgil asked.

"Great question," Cora said. "But whoever it was sent a message to the legislator pushing the bill."

"What kind of message?" Murton asked.

"They shot and killed his teenage son while he was playing basketball at one of the city's parks."

CHAPTER THIRTEEN

Before Cora could say anything else, Virgil asked, "Could Becky be excused? We've got her looking into a couple of things that really can't wait."

Cora looked like maybe she didn't fully believe him, but she waved Becky away without asking for the particulars. She'd no sooner left when Virgil's phone buzzed at him. He looked at Cora and said, "Sorry. Just a moment, please." Then into the phone: "Jones."

"Hey Boss, it's Rosie. I'm over at the office. We got a call from the Boone County Sheriff's department."

Virgil had to think for a few seconds, the change in gears grinding at his brain. "That's, uh...let me think, White, isn't it? Sheriff Dave White?"

"Yep, that's him," Rosencrantz said.

"What's he need?"

"In a word, us. Looks like they had a little fire last

night out in the countryside, up near Lebanon. Homeowner died in the house."

Virgil didn't want to sound crass, but he also didn't want to get off track in the meeting. "What's that got to do with us?"

"Maybe nothing, except the arson guy says the fire started right where the victim was found and there's heavy evidence of an accelerant. So unless the guy meant to burn himself to a crisp, it looks like murder. No evidence, by the way, of any accelerant containers at the scene."

"So what's he want with us?"

"Ah, you know how it is. They've got one detective who works homicide, of which there aren't that many in Boone County...homicides, I mean, so the sheriff wants us and our lab people to take a look."

"Okay...unless you and Ross are tied up with something, get ahold of Mimi and take a run up there. Leave Lawless behind. Looks like we're going to need him here."

"What have you got?"

"I'll explain later. Let me know what you find. Give the sheriff my best and all that."

"You got it, boss-man." And Rosencrantz was gone.

Virgil put his phone away, apologized again, and said, "Where were we?"

"The state senator's name is Michael Wright. Wife is Sharron. The victim was their son, Garrett. I want the two of you—Mac wants the two of you—to get over there and figure this thing out. He's already on record as a supporter of mobile voting, and doesn't want this to become the main issue that decides the outcome of the vote. And the vote was going to be close anyway...so close that if there ends up being a tie—"

Murton finished the thought for her. "Small will have the deciding vote." He was looking at Virgil when he said it.

THE GOVERNOR BLEW THROUGH CORA'S OFFICE LIKE HIS hair was on fire. He pointed at Virgil and Murton, but spoke to Cora. "You've got them up to speed?"

"Yes, they've been briefed on the seriousness of the matter."

"Then why are they still here?" Before Cora could answer, the governor looked at Virgil and Murton and said, "Get to it. Now." Then he yanked open his door, stepped into his office, and slammed it behind him.

Virgil was about to ask a question, but Cora already had her answer prepared. "He's under a significant amount of stress. Every lawmaker in the state is on top of him regarding the shooting."

Virgil and Murton stood. "We'll get started then," Virgil said. "Who's in charge on scene?"

"Metro homicide has a full unit out there now. Get with Brent Williams...he's running the show. It's in the heart of Haughville."

"Oh boy," Murton said.

"Oh boy is right," Cora said. Haughville was widely known as one of Indy's worst neighborhoods.

"What the hell was the Wright kid doing out there?" Virgil asked.

"That would be something to look into. But I do know the family doesn't live too far away. Other side of the river, I believe. Part of the senator's district."

Mac pulled his door open and looked at Virgil and Murton. When he spoke, his voice was soft and full of regret. "Forgive me. I just had a difficult conversation with Senator Wright and his wife. They're devastated."

"We're on it, Boss," Murton said.

Virgil looked at the governor. "A word, Mac? In private?"

The governor tipped his head toward his office and stepped inside. Virgil followed him in and closed the door. Before he could say anything, Mac turned and said, "Really, Jonesy, I'm sorry."

Virgil waved him off. "Don't worry about it. I completely understand."

"Good, good. If there's nothing else then..."

"There is," Virgil said. "I need a favor."

"Make it quick. I've got work to do, and so do you."

"That's just it. If you want my full attention on Wright, Sandy will have to find someone else to act as her detail driver for the duration. I heard Baker is coming back soon, but no one seems to know exactly when."

"Anything to get out of that suit, huh?" Then he put

his hand against his forehead and said, "Ah, Christ, what a rotten thing to say."

"It's stress, Mac."

The governor shook his head. "Still..." Then he walked to the door, pulled it open and asked Cora to let Sandy know she'd be getting a different driver other than Virgil until Baker was back on her feet.

Virgil thanked the governor and left the offices with Murton. As they were walking down the hall, Virgil noticed Murton giving him the side eye. "What?"

"It looks like you're trying not to smile," Murton said.

"I don't know what you're talking about," Virgil said as he stripped off his tie and stuffed it into his pocket.

ONCE THEY WERE ON THEIR WAY, VIRGIL CALLED Sandy and told her she'd be getting a new driver.

"I've already heard," she said. "Virgil, this is awful. He was only a kid."

"I know. Murt and I are on our way out there right now."

"Be careful."

"Always. I'll see you tonight." He killed the connection then called Chip Lawless, one of the MCU's crime scene technicians. "Chip, it's Jonesy. Get a full kit and meet us out in Haughville."

"I've been sitting here ready and waiting for the call. I'm on my way."

Virgil lowered his voice and turned away from Murton. "And listen, Chip, before you leave, go into my office. In the closet I've got a T-shirt, some jeans and boots..."

"Already got that, too, Boss."

"Atta boy." When he ended the call, he looked over at Murton and said, "What?"

Murton fed Virgil's own line back to him. "I don't know what you're talking about."

VIRGIL PARKED HIS TRUCK AS CLOSE AS HE COULD TO the crime scene, but they still had to walk about a half-block to get to the perimeter, the entire area circled with concentric rings of vehicles. The outer ring consisted of media vans, their satellite dishes pointed in various directions. The center ring was a combination of Metro Homicide vehicles, fire rescue trucks, and the coroner's van. The inner ring was all city squad cars. Virgil and Murton both scribbled their signatures on the sign-in sheet, ducked the yellow crime scene tape, and went straight to Brent Williams, the lead detective.

"Hey, Brent," Virgil said.

Williams turned around, peeled off a latex glove and shook hands with both men. "Good to see you, Jonesy. I sort of figured you'd show up. State taking the lead?"

Virgil shook his head. "No, we'll be going sideways

with you. It's your show, but we're going to do our own thing. Governor's orders."

Williams, a decent guy, didn't argue the point. If anything, he tried to go the other way. "I wouldn't mind if you guys wanted point on this. In fact, I sort of wish you'd take it. With the victim's father being who he is, it really is a state thing anyway, if you know what I mean."

Virgil gave him a toothless grin. "Nice try, and no dice. If it all goes south, we'll need someone to share the blame with."

"At least you're staying positive about it."

"How about you fill us in on what you've got so far."

Williams, a little defeated, said, "Okay. Better glove up and take a look at the victim. We'll start there."

Virgil and Murton put their gloves on and walked over to the bench where the victim was. Metro Homicide had erected a portable tent with side flaps to keep the media from getting pictures. When Williams put his hand on the tent flap, he cautioned them about the smell.

"Been here a while now. Starting to get a little ripe." He pulled the flap back and they all began breathing through their mouths. Wright was covered from head to toe with a white sheet, and the top of the cover near his head was stained red.

"Why is he still here?" Murton asked.

"We were told not to move the body until you and your people had a chance to look things over. The coroner has been here all night and he's not too happy."

"Tough shit," Virgil said. He pulled the cover away and

looked closely at the killing wound on the young man's head. He turned away and looked at Williams. "Has he been moved at all?"

Williams shook his head. "Nope. He was clearly dead by the time anyone got to him, so no one moved him."

"Who called it in?" Murton asked.

"One of the kids here at the court. We traced the call back to his cell and picked him up last night. Got him in holding downtown."

"Have one of the uniforms run him out here, will you?" Virgil asked. "I want to talk to him."

"You bet." Williams made the call and told Virgil it'd be twenty minutes or so.

"Any witnesses come forward?" Murton said.

"In this neighborhood?"

Murton nodded. "Had to ask."

"I've had uniforms doing a door-to-door on a two block radius. So far nobody knows nothing about nothing."

"Have them push it out at least another block," Virgil said. "You never know."

"They're not going to like it."

Virgil covered Wright back up and said, "Tell them to talk to me, then. Anyone recover the weapon?"

"Not yet," Williams said. "We've got the rest of the uniformed guys doing a sweep...storm drains, bushes, trash barrels, the works. Nothing so far."

Chip Lawless walked up carrying two cases and a

backpack. He handed the backpack to Virgil, who, after thanking him, made the introductions.

"Anyone search or move the body?" Lawless asked.

Virgil said, "Nope, it's your show, Chip. See what you can see."

"If you guys could leave the tent then, I'll have some room to maneuver."

They stepped out to let Lawless do his job, and the air was suddenly fresh and clean. Virgil looked at Williams and Murton and said, "I'll be right back."

As Virgil walked away, Williams turned to Murton and said, "Where's he going?"

They watched Virgil duck back under the crime scene tape and head toward a square brick building that housed a men's room and ladies' room. As soon as he was past the tape, he stripped off his jacket.

AVERY WAS BACK IN THE WINDOW, WATCHING THROUGH the gapped curtains, his spotter's scope to his eye. When he saw Virgil remove his jacket, it changed everything. He mentally marked the spot, then put the scope away. He had a little clean up to take care of, and if he didn't do it soon, the super's body was going to start to stink.

CHAPTER FOURTEEN

By the time Virgil got changed—his suit now stuffed in the backpack—a uniformed officer was holding a handcuffed young man under one of the basketball hoops. Williams and Murton were still next to the tent where Lawless was working.

Williams, who really was a decent guy, said, "Hey, Jonesy, somebody was here a little while ago impersonating you. We all played along even though we knew it wasn't you. He was wearing a suit, if you can believe that."

Virgil, who'd had enough wardrobe jokes to last a lifetime gave Williams a fake laugh, but otherwise ignored the comment. "That the kid you talked to?"

Williams looked over at the young black man and said, "Yeah, that's him. Terrance Young. He'll tell you anything you want to know. The problem is he says he doesn't know anything...like everyone else so far."

"Cooperative?"

Williams turned the corners of his mouth down. "Not exactly. Says we don't have any right to hold him, he's going to call his lawyer and sue the city...you know, the usual."

Virgil had to be careful here. A little tact was in order. "Listen, since you've already talked with him, would you mind if Murt and I spoke with him alone? Like to see if he gives us the same story he gave you."

Williams, who knew about tact, said, "Be my guest. And good luck. His story is pretty short. He's a runner too, so watch for that."

Virgil told Williams he would, and that he appreciated it. Virgil and Murton walked over and told the uniformed officer thank you, and that he could go. The officer let go of Young's arm and walked away.

Young was solidly built, his arms veined out from pumping iron. He was bald, had gang tat styled sleeves, and his eyelids looked heavy. Virgil introduced himself and Murton then told Young he wasn't in any sort of trouble. They simply needed information. "Anything at all would be helpful."

"If I ain't in any trouble, which I already knows I ain't, then how about it on the cuffs, man?"

Virgil reached for his keys and let them dangle from his hand. "Two things...you aren't in any trouble. That's thing one. Thing two is this: If I un-cuff you and you run, then you will be in trouble. I won't chase you, but see this guy here?" He pointed at Murton. "He will. He's fast, he's mean, and he'll take you down hard. No joke."

Murton gave Young a big bright toothy smile.

Young, tired and unimpressed, said, "Ooooh, yeah, boy oh boy, you put the fear of Jesus in me with that little speech." He turned around and offered his wrists. "How about it? You wants to know what I know, then turn the key, man."

Virgil removed the cuffs and as soon as Young's hands were free he spun and swung at Virgil, a long sweeping roundhouse that Virgil saw coming from about a half mile away. He took a step back and Young's fist connected solidly with the basketball hoop's support structure. There was an audible crunch as his hand broke and he doubled over in pain.

Murton stepped over and swept Young's legs out from under him, knocking him to the ground. Once he was down, Murton rolled him, then put his knee on Young's neck and held him in place. "See, now you're in trouble." He locked one end of the cuffs around the pole, and the other to Young's uninjured wrist. "Let me see your hand."

"Fuck you, man. You broke my fingers."

"Did you know that lying or making a false statement to an officer of the law is a crime? I didn't break your fingers. You did when you tried to punch my partner and run. Let's do a little math, hmm? So far we've got assault on an officer, attempting to flee, resisting arrest—that one always gets tossed in, by the way—and falsifying information relevant to the investigation of a homicide. That last one, my young friend, could very well make you an accessory after the fact. That means you'd be just as guilty as whoever pulled the trigger. I sure hope you're not on probation."

Virgil leaned down and got right in Young's face. "He's right about everything he said. You want to walk away from all this, quit digging your own hole. We don't care about you...we simply want to know what you saw. And let my partner see your hand. It's not a request."

Young looked like he didn't believe anything Virgil had told him, but he held up his injured hand. "Can't move my fingers."

Murton took hold of Young by his forearm, up near his elbow. "That's because it looks like you've shattered nearly every knuckle on your first three fingers. Don't try to move them. We'll get you some help from one of the medics."

Young snarled at him. "As soon as I talk, right?"

Murton shook his head in disgust. "No, I meant right now." He looked at Virgil and said, "What is it with people these days? I'll be right back."

Virgil nodded at him and sat down on the ground next to Young. "What the hell was that all about? The first words out of my mouth were that you weren't in any trouble."

Young was starting to sweat, the pain from his hand eating him up. "It was about no one believing me. Them other cops didn't. Said I was lying, even though I wasn't. Had me locked up all night and I ain't done nothing. They kept axing where I ditched the gun but I didn't have no gun. There wasn't anything to lie about, man. That's what

I'm trying to tell everyone who'd listen, which so far amounts to maybe you."

"Then walk me through it. From the beginning."

"How about it on the pain meds, man. My hand starting to look like a balloon."

"They're on the way. The sooner we're done here, the sooner we can get you to the hospital."

Young let out a heavy, frustrated sigh. "We was banging it out on the court, man, like we always do. Wright was sitting on the bench, lacing up, and my boy had dropped a three from way outside the line. He turned to get some respect and the next thing we know Garrett's head tipped back like he'd been hit. Blood was everywhere, man, and he rolled off the back of the bench. That's the whole story. Now what about those meds, man. I'm dying here."

Murton and a medic walked over. The medic put on a pair of gloves, looked at Young's hand, and did a little grimace. "Boy, that's gotta smart."

"Who you calling boy, man?"

"It's an expression. Not everyone is a racist, you know. Relax, already."

"I'll be relaxed when you get me something to take care of my hand."

"Uh huh." The medic reached into his bag and pulled out a cool pack and gently wrapped Young's hand. The pain was so bad that by the time he was done, Young had tears running down his cheeks.

"What the fuck is this? That all you got, man...ice cubes in a bag? Can't you give me a shot or something?"

The medic shook his head. "Are you kidding? In this neighborhood? We don't carry anything stronger than Tylenol. Too dangerous. We'll get you transported in a few minutes though, and they'll have something for you at the hospital."

"What's the holdup, man?"

"We've got to get some vehicles out of the way," Murton said. "He's all blocked in. Hang in there. We'll be back in a flash." Murton tipped his head at the medic. The medic gave him an odd look, but followed Murton as they walked away, back toward the ambulance.

Virgil looked at Young and said, "Who had the gun?"

Young shook his head. "That's what I been trying to tell everyone. There ain't no gun. We was here to play ball, man."

"Yet one of your buddies got shot to death. How does that happen with no gun?"

"Don't know. But I'm telling you, none of us had a gun. We didn't even hear the shot."

"What was that? Say that again."

"I said there weren't no gunshot sounds. Loudest thing out here was our feet slapping the asphalt."

"Did you have any music playing?" Virgil asked.

"We weren't here to dance, motherfucker."

"Don't call me that," Virgil said.

"Why not?"

"Because I haven't earned it."

Young screwed his face into a question mark and said, "What's that supposed to mean?"

"You wouldn't understand. Now answer the question."

"I did. There weren't no music. Hell, we weren't even talking trash. Beat of our feet and the ball hitting the ground was the loudest things, and even that wasn't very loud. I'm telling you, there wasn't any gunfire."

"Maybe something that could have been a shot, but you didn't recognize it at the time?" Virgil said. "A car backfiring...something like that?"

Young shook his head like he was trying to explain Calculus to a kindergartner. "Grow up around here and you know the difference between a backfire and a gunshot. Don't matter though. There wasn't any of it. I'm telling you, it was quiet."

"You know what a slide sounds like?" Virgil was speaking of the ratcheting noise a semi-automatic handgun makes after it's fired, or when a round gets seated in the chamber.

"What you think?"

"I think I don't want to offend you by making any false assumptions based on race, your prison tats, or the area in which you live. I'm trying to be respectful here."

"Yeah...I know what it sound like."

"Think about this. And think hard. Hear anything like that?"

Despite his injured hand and the obvious pain, Young did think about it. He closed his eyes as if he might be replaying the scene in his head. When he opened his eyes, he said, "You're axing if the shot was silenced."

"I am. The ratcheting noise the slide makes is often the loudest thing you'll hear."

Young simply shook his head. "Wasn't no silencer, because there wasn't no gun."

"What about other people? Was there anyone around that looked out of place? Like maybe they didn't belong... or even someone you'd never seen before?"

"No man. That's part of why it was so quiet."

"You or any of your buddies have any sort of beef with Wright?"

"No, man. We was tight. Wright was our boy. Best shooter out here."

Virgil stared at Young long and hard. He wasn't sure if it was the look on his face or the tears still running down his cheeks, but he believed him. They sat quietly for a few minutes, then Virgil said, "Okay, here comes the gurney. I'm going to un-cuff you from this pole and reattach the restraint to the side rail of the gurney once we've got you loaded up. I think we can overlook everything that's happened here. You've suffered enough. But if you try anything when I unhook you again—"

Young shook his head. "Couldn't if I wanted to. Hurts too bad. I think I might puke."

Virgil believed him on that account too. He unlocked the cuff, and together, he, Murton, and the medic got him on the gurney, then attached the cuff to the rail.

The medic reached into his bag and pulled out a

syringe. He wiped the side of Young's uninjured arm with an alcohol swab, then gave him a shot.

"What's that?" Young asked.

"Steroid injection," he lied. "It'll help keep the swelling down."

They wheeled him over to the ambulance, and once Young was inside with the door closed, Murton looked at the medic and said, "What'd you give him?"

"Morphine," the medic said, matter of factly. "But only enough to take the edge off. If these guys knew what we really carried around out here, we'd be a constant moving target."

Virgil looked around at the other vehicles in the area. "You don't look blocked in."

The medic grinned at him. "I wasn't. Your partner here told me to take my time."

CHAPTER FIFTEEN

Mimi Phillips drove one of the MCU's crime scene vans and followed Ross and Rosencrantz up to Boone County. They'd check in with Sheriff Dave White before going out to the scene. On the way there, Rosencrantz was quizzing Ross about various long range shooting techniques. "So let's say you're in a position where you've got varying conditions, like maybe you're in an urban environment and you've got wind coming from different directions between the taller buildings. That happens all the time, right? What do you do then? How do you account for that?"

Ross was driving, and when he didn't answer, Rosencrantz waved his hand in front of his partner's face. "Hey, anybody in there, or is this one of those self-driving squad cars?"

"You trying to get us killed?" Ross said as he tipped his head away from his partner's hand.

"No. I'm trying to get you to answer my questions. Maybe I should start with getting you to listen first."

"Sorry," Ross said. "My mind was elsewhere."

Rosencrantz laughed. "Would elsewhere happen to be the sweet sound of Mimi's voice?" Mimi Phillips had a voice that was so hot most people agreed she could hard-boil an egg by speaking to it.

Ross let his eyes slide over without moving his head. "No, that's not at all what I was thinking about."

"Uh huh. What then?"

Ross's shoulders started bouncing up and down as he tried not to laugh. A few seconds later he was laughing so hard Rosencrantz had to put his hand on the wheel to keep them on the road.

"Okay, you got me," Ross said, a little red-faced. "I mean, Jesus, that voice of hers. It's unbelievable. I haven't had much interaction with her, but every time I hear her speak, especially if it's to me, I get this urge to—"

"Stop right there," Rosencrantz said. "I absolutely do not want to hear whatever was about to come out of your mouth. If I do, I might have to file a report with HR."

"I think she might have something going with Lawless," Ross said. "You ever notice how he's always following her around?"

"They work together. She's his boss."

"Still."

"Whatever. They're probably saying the same thing about you...always following me around."

"We work together," Ross said. "You're my partner."

Rosencrantz laughed. “Wrong again. I’m your boss.”

“No you’re not.”

“Yeah, I am.”

“Think what you want then.”

“So what about my question? The urban environment, tall buildings, varying wind conditions...how do you handle that sort of thing?”

“Move closer.”

“What if you can’t?”

“Do you golf?” Ross asked.

“God no.”

“How about mini golf?”

“I’ve been known. What’s that got to do with anything?”

“It’s like a wavy putting green. If you’ve got wind coming from two different directions you line your shot up the same as if you’re putting on a surface where you know the ball is going to move in two different directions.”

“Huh. What if you can’t get a good read? On the wind.”

“Then you do the next logical thing any advanced shooter would do in that particular situation.”

“What’s that?”

“You move closer.”

Like that...all the way to Boone County.

When they turned into the Boone County Sheriff's department, they caught White exiting the building. He had a napkin in one hand and ham and cheese with lettuce and mayo in the other. Rosencrantz introduced everyone and the sheriff told them he was getting ready to go back out to the scene if they wanted to follow him.

"Sounds good to me," Mimi said. Then she looked at the sheriff. "It's a pleasure to meet you. See you out there."

White had a mouthful of sandwich, so he simply nodded and tried not to choke when he heard the sound of Mimi's voice. Once she was in the van, White turned and threw the remainder of his sandwich in the trash receptacle next to the doorway.

"What's the matter?" Ross asked. "It looked like you'd just started on that sandwich."

"I did," White said. "But I think your little crime scene gal might have wilted the lettuce and spoiled the mayo. Holy cow, have you guys ever noticed the voice on her?"

Ross and Rosencrantz looked at each other straight-faced, then they both shook their heads at him. "I've never noticed," Ross said. "She always sounds like that. Maybe you need to get down to the big city more often."

"He's right," Rosencrantz said. "She sounds perfectly normal to me." Then, "Looks like you've got a little mayo on your chin there, Dave."

THE CRIME SCENE WAS SLIGHTLY NORTH AND EAST OF the sheriff's department on a county road called East 75 North.

"You guys have trouble coming up with road names around here or something?" Ross asked once they'd arrived. "East 75 North sounds like something you'd tell a pilot if they asked where to land."

White gave him a lazy look. "I don't name the roads, I simply patrol them and pay my taxes, which helps keep them in proper repair. You city guys are a hoot. Anyone ever tell you that?"

"All the time," Rosencrantz said. "We were scheduled to be on the Bob and Tom show this morning, except you called, so here we are. How about you run it down for us?"

White pointed with his chin. "There's our homicide detective. Name's Frank Quayle. I'll let him fill you in." They walked over and White made the introductions.

"Quayle? That's cool." Rosencrantz said. "Any relation to—"

"None," Quayle said, like it'd been the tenth time he'd been asked already that day.

"Gotcha," Rosencrantz said. "Must be sort of a pain in the ass, then, huh?"

"You have no idea."

"Victim still inside?"

"Yeah. If it's the occupant, his name was Tim Dreyer. But he's burned so bad no one can tell who it was."

Mimi walked over with her kit and asked to be shown where the body was. Quayle swallowed noisily, then introduced himself and shook hands with Mimi...sort of a long slow shake.

He was still holding her hand when she smiled and said, "Quayle, huh? Any relation to our former Vice President?"

Quayle nodded. "Yes, he's my uncle, though sometimes I'm loath to admit it. The potato gaff, and all."

Mimi nodded. "I get it. He could have saved himself if he'd kept going and added the letter *s* at the end, there."

Quayle nodded and reluctantly let go of her hand. "Oh I know. It still comes up at family gatherings. Someone will say, 'Pass the potatoes please,' and everyone sort of snickers about it."

"I'll bet. So...show me the spot?"

"Sure." Quayle led her over to the burned out shell of the house.

Ross and Rosencrantz looked at the sheriff. "So which is it?" Ross asked. "Is he related or not?"

White shook his head. "No one is sure. His story keeps changing...you know, depending on who's doing the asking. Clearly you're not his type."

Ross looked at Rosencrantz. "Why are we even here?"

"Is that a philosophical question?"

"What difference does that make?" Ross said.

"Well, as your boss, I don't want to give you bad information."

Ross looked at the sheriff. “He’s not my boss. We’re partners.”

White shook his head and followed Quayle inside.

ROSENCRANTZ AND ROSS SPENT SOME TIME COVERING the outside of the residence, looking for anything of evidentiary value. They found absolutely nothing. The lawn was a combination of cracked hardpan and weeds, which meant footprints were nonexistent, and the drive was gravel—with almost as many weeds as the yard—so tire impressions were out of the question. They took a quick look around inside, but Mimi wouldn’t let them touch anything—Quayle and White were standing near the door, barely inside, and that was just in case Mimi happened to speak.

Rosencrantz asked Quayle if he’d spoken to any of the neighbors regarding the fire.

“Yeah, both of them. They each live about a mile away in opposite directions. They didn’t see or hear anything.”

“Who called the fire in?” Ross asked.

“Passerby. Saw the flames and called the fire department.”

“Any chance he might have been involved? The passerby?”

Sheriff White shook his head. “I sure as hell hope not.”

“Why’s that?”

"First, it wasn't a he, it was a she. And the she in this instance happens to be my aunt, who is about one hundred and eighty years old. She was on her way back from her book club meeting."

"Huh," Rosencrantz said. He liked to read. "What are they reading?"

"Would that be germane to the investigative process?"

"No, I'm simply curious."

"I'm not sure. Some sort of mystery or something like that. Burke, I think. He's their favorite. I can ask her if you like."

Rosencrantz gave him a dry look. "That's okay. Just making conversation." They were all sort of kicking the tires, waiting for Mimi to do her thing. The inside of the house was a mess. The curtains had either burned away or melted to the walls, the carpet was mostly gone, and what was left was still squishy from all the water the fire department had used to knock down the flames. The ceiling was black, the smell was terrible, and most of the body was burned so badly it was difficult to tell if it was male or female.

"Any chance you'll be able to positively ID the victim?" Ross asked Mimi.

"Not unless we can find some dental records on him."

"You're sure it's a he?"

"Positive. I checked the genitalia. Most of it was burned away, but you could still see a bit of...well, let me just say, he was a he."

"I've already checked with all the local dentists,"

Quayle said. "None of them had a patient by the name of Tim Dreyer."

"How long has he lived here?"

The sheriff shook his head. "Not long. A few months maybe. He showed up one day, kept to himself, never really saw him around town or anything like that."

"Where's he work?" Rosencrantz asked. "Anyone know?"

"Groundskeeper out at the cemetery," Quayle said. "I was going to head out there next. Wanted to see what your tech could find here first."

"We'll handle that," Ross said. "Where's it located?"

The sheriff gave them directions to the cemetery and Ross told Mimi they'd check back with her when they were finished. He looked at Rosencrantz and said, "You ready?"

Rosencrantz looked at him and said, "What, you're the boss now?"

Ross shook his head. "Of course not. We're partners."

THEY GOT LOST ON THE WAY TO THE CEMETERY AND Rosencrantz was giving Ross a little grief about it. "I think you've missed two turns so far."

"Says the guy who let a three-speed manual transmission get the better of him not that long ago."

"The clutch was bad. How many times are you going to keep bringing that up?"

"Probably every time you tell me I missed a turn. Apparently they've spent so much money coming up with cryptic road names they can't afford signs. Either that or they don't want to spend the money to make them. They'd be the size of billboards. It's probably located on some road called Southwest 375th and One Eighth by Three Quarters North-By-Northeast South 23rd and a Half, or something like that."

Rosencrantz looked past Ross, out the driver's side window, and said, "Or, it could be right over there, on the left."

Ross looked out the window and said, "Yeah, I know. I'm looking for the entrance."

"Uh huh."

"You always sound like you never believe me."

"I do?" Rosencrantz said.

Ross turned and looked directly at his partner. "Never mind. And why are you laughing at me?"

"Because you missed the entrance. We're on Cemetery Road, by the way. There was a sign about a mile back."

ROSS GOT THEM TURNED AROUND, THEN THEY SPENT the next five minutes creeping along the twisted one lane asphalt drive, looking for the maintenance building. They found it near the back, a pale yellow, windowless pole barn with a metal roof that may have been white at some point in the distant past. Rust streaks ran down the seams of the roof where the nail holes were and the entire building seemed slightly off-kilter, like it had been in a wreck on the highway and had its frame straightened. The overhead door was open, and two men in coveralls were sitting on a picnic table. A riding mower with an almost flat front tire sat next to the table and one of the men appeared to be struggling to get a new spool of line installed on a weed eater.

They parked, got out of the car, and as they were walking up, one of the men leaned over to the other and said, "Cops."

ROSENCRANTZ HEARD ONE OF THE MEN SAY COPS, BUT he pulled out his badge anyway and identified himself and Ross as detectives with the state's Major Crimes Unit. A faint smell of marijuana hung in the air.

"Well, hell," one of the men said. "We ain't done nothing."

"No one said you did," Ross said. "Though it's been my experience that the statement you made is often untruthful."

"You calling me a liar?"

"Are either of you Tim Dreyer?"

The two men looked at each other as if they weren't sure themselves. Then, the one with the weed eater said, "No, but if you happen to see that sum bitch you can tell him that I got called in today because he didn't show, so now he owes me one."

"We'll be sure to pass that along," Rosencrantz said. "See some ID?"

"Why?"

"So you can prove to us that neither of you are Tim Dreyer."

"We already said we wasn't."

"Can you prove it?" Ross said.

"Well how in the hell are we supposed to do that?"

Ross rolled his eyes and spoke slowly, enunciating each word. "By. Showing. Us. Your. Identification."

The two men looked at each other and they both tipped their heads back slightly, like they finally understood. They reached for their wallets and held out their IDs. Ross looked them over, then handed them to Rosencrantz.

"Either of you have any warrants out?"

"Out where?"

Ross was getting pissed, the huckleberry routine wearing thin. "In the ether, you moron. Are either of you out on bail, done time, or not shown in court when you were supposed to?"

The weed eater guy said, "I done my time. Showed up in court too, though not necessarily in that order, if you're picking up what I'm laying down."

Ross thought, *God help me, I am.* He looked at the other man. "What about you?"

"Unlike this one here, I'm an abider. Can't say the same for Dreyer, though."

"He did time?" Rosencrantz asked.

Weed eater nodded. "He not only did time, he did military time."

"For what?"

"He didn't talk about it much."

"How about you tell us the parts he did talk about," Ross said. When neither man answered, he prompted them with, "Or the alternative would be me and my partner here put you in handcuffs, stuff you in the back seat of our squad car, then search your maintenance building. I'm getting a contact high just standing here."

The two men gave each other a quick glance, then looked back at Ross. "Okay, okay," weed eater said. "There ain't no need to get all official, like. I got me a little Glaucoma and I'm trying to stay on top of it is all, you know, so I can keep working and paying my taxes. Taxes which, by the way, help pay your salary, if I'm not mistaken."

"Uh huh." Ross rolled his wrist.

"Dreyer was in the military. Army I think, though I ain't sure about that. Anyways, it was during the first Gulf War and I guess he got in trouble for something he done during one of their operations or missions or whatever they're called."

"What'd he do?" Rosencrantz asked.

"I ain't exactly sure. We only got bits and pieces of it. He didn't like to talk about it unless we was smoke—"

The abider smacked his buddy on the leg.

"Unless you were helping the pain and suffering associated with the sudden onset of your debilitative Glaucoma?" Ross said.

Weed eater bobbed his head around in a manner that could have meant yes or no. "Them's your words, not mine." Then before anything else could be said about the smoking, he added, "Anyways, I guess they was supposed to blow up some ammo hut or bunker or something that them rag heads was using. But after they was done, someone got their signals crossed or something and Dreyer ended up frying one of his own guys."

"What do you mean?" Rosencrantz said. "He shot one of his own men?"

Weed eater shook his head. "No, he didn't shoot him, he fried him, man. Said he found one of them old flamethrowers the sand nigg—uh, I mean, Middle Eastern A-rabs or whatever had, and he was lighting up a few of their soldiers. Somehow he fried one of his own guys. Said it was an accident. Never did say exactly how it actually happened beyond that."

"Never did," the abider added.

Ross and Rosencrantz asked a few more questions, but it didn't get them anywhere. They copied down the information from the worker's driver's licenses, and told them they'd be back in touch if they needed anything else.

"We ain't in trouble for the weed, are we? I really do have the Glaucoma."

"We don't care about that," Ross said. Then he looked

at the abider. "What about you? Any aches or pains that Mother Nature helps you out with?"

The abider nodded. "Yeah, got me a bad back."

"And the weed helps?"

He shook his head. "Not really. But if it gets too bad I usually swipe a few Oxy off mom. She's got a bad hip. She's sort of my Mother Nature, if you know what I mean." Then he slapped his own thigh, tipped his head back, and laughed like it was the funniest thing he'd ever said.

Rosencrantz looked at Ross and said, "We may have met our match."

"That might be the most self-deprecating thing I've ever heard you say. And, it's sort of mean."

CHAPTER SIXTEEN

Murton called Becky to see if she had anything for them yet. She didn't.

"What's the hold up?" he asked her.

"These things take time, Murt. You know that. I've got everything in place, and now I'm waiting for some results."

Virgil interrupted and told Murton to have her find the home address for the Wright's residence. He'd tried to Google it, but came up empty.

Murton repeated what Virgil said, listened for a moment, then said, "Okay," before ending the call.

"She have anything yet?" Virgil said.

Murton shook his head. "These things take time, Jonesy. You know that."

Virgil gave him a dry look. "So I've heard."

A few moments later Murton's phone buzzed at him. When he checked the screen he laughed then put his phone away. "The Wright's live in a subdivision about five minutes from here."

"What's so funny about that?"

"She called Lawless and asked him to read her the address from Garrett's ID."

"I was going to do that, but I didn't want to disturb him."

"Uh huh. You going to tell him we're going over there?"

"Yeah, I guess I better."

"Try not to disturb him too much," Murton said.

VIRGIL WALKED OVER TO THE TENT AND WHEN HE pulled the flap open, the smell slapped him in the face. Lawless was wearing a mask, so they both stepped outside, away from the tent.

"I've got everything I need," Lawless told Virgil after he pulled his mask down. "Pictures, measurements, all that. If you could have them take the deceased away now, I can get this tent down and get everything else set up."

Virgil told him he would, and that he and Murton would be leaving.

"Anybody find the weapon yet?" Lawless asked.

Virgil shook his head. "I've had them push the perimeter out to three blocks, but nothing so far."

Lawless looked around. "I'm not surprised."

"Why's that?"

"I can show you on the body, or I can show you with the pictures, whichever you prefer."

Virgil didn't want to go back in the tent. The smell...it not only hung in the air, but it seemed to stick to clothing as well. He could smell it on Lawless. "The pictures will do."

"Okay, hang tight. Let me get the digital." Lawless went back into the tent, then reemerged with his camera. He fiddled around with one of the buttons for a few minutes, found what he wanted, then turned the camera around so Virgil could see the digital images on the camera's display screen.

"I'm going to show you three pictures—"

Virgil cut him off. "Hold on a second, Chip." He waved Murton over. "I want Murt to see this too."

When Murton walked up his nose wrinkled at the smell, but he didn't say anything. "What have you got?"

Virgil looked at Lawless. "Chip?"

Lawless started over. "Okay, I'm going to show you three pictures. Here's the first. This is the victim's head, front facing, and you can clearly see the entry wound. Since it's his only injury, it's clear this was the killing shot. And there was only one, by the way. Not saying there weren't more shots fired or anything, I'm simply stating he was hit only one time."

"Any idea of the caliber?" Virgil said.

Lawless held up a wait a minute finger. "I'll get to that in a second. The second image here..." He pressed a button and the first image was replaced by one that showed the back of Long's head. "This is the back of the victim's head. As you can see, there is clear evidence of an exit wound."

"That's a bit of an understatement," Murton said.

"The third image is harder to see, but if you look closely, you can see the blood spatter pattern on the asphalt behind the bench."

Virgil and Murton both looked. Lawless was right. It was hard to see, but it was there if you knew where to look.

"So what are you trying to tell us?" Virgil asked. "A minute ago you said you weren't surprised that no one has found the gun."

"That's right." He clicked a button on the camera and went back to the first picture. Once there, he pressed another button that allowed him to zoom in on the digital image. "I'm zooming in here on the entry wound. I can only get so close before it starts to pixilate, but look at the wound itself."

Virgil and Murton both looked for a moment, then they looked at Lawless. "What about it?" Virgil said.

"Three things: One, there's no starring or powder burns like you'd expect to see if the shot was up close and personal. The other two things sort of go together." He glanced up at Virgil. "You asked about caliber. This looks like a high velocity rifle shot. I'm guessing it's probably a 308, but we won't know that until we do more testing. But with the size of the exit wound, I'm fairly certain about it."

"You said three things?" Murton prompted him.

Lawless nodded. "Yes. Look closely at the entry wound itself, particularly the skin around the edge. See how the lower part is curled inward slightly? Also, if you look closely enough, you can see a slight creasing of the skin at the top of the entry point."

"What about it?" Virgil said.

"One thing at a time, Jonesy. Now look at the hole as a whole. Notice anything?"

Murton caught it right away. "It's out of shape."

Lawless tipped a finger at him. "Exactly." He handed the camera to Murton and said, "Here, hold this for a second. And don't drop it. It cost a fortune." He reached into his kit and pulled out a sharp metal pointer that looked like a nail punch—a tool a carpenter uses to bury finishing nails without damaging the woodwork. Along with the punch, he removed a handball and an ink pen. He slipped the punch in his breast pocket, then drew two faces on the ball with his pen, one on either side. Satisfied with his artwork, he put the pen in his pocket and removed the punch.

"What the heck are you doing?" Virgil asked.

"A demonstration," Lawless said. "A crude one, I'll give you that, but it should make my point." He held the ball in one hand and the punch in the other. "Pretend this is the victim's head." He punctured the ball with the punch nice and straight, in the same spot where Wright had been shot. When he pulled the punch out, there was a perfectly round hole. He held it out for Virgil and Murton to see. When they didn't say anything, Lawless said, "Now watch this." He turned the ball around to the other side and punctured it again, this time at a severe angle, coming down from the top, but still in the same location where the bullet had entered the victim's head. When he pulled the punch, the hole was round, but there was a slight rip at the top and if you held the ball at the right angle, it was clear that the hole had come from above as opposed to straight on.

"You're saying he was shot from above." Virgil said. It wasn't a question.

"Almost positive," Lawless said. "The spatter pattern, exit wound, and measurements back up the theory. Once we get the body out and the tent down, I can set up the laser trajectory equipment and tell you for sure, but my guess is your shooter was well above his target's head. And based on the size of the entry and exit wounds, I'd say you're looking at a 30 caliber rifle shot."

"Probably with a suppressor, as well," Virgil said. "No one heard the shot. You've covered the vertical angle. Any idea what sort of horizontal angles we should be focusing on?"

Lawless stepped over to the tent and positioned himself in front of where the body was. He took a piece of chalk and drew two short lines in a V shape. "This is only an approximation until I get the lasers set up, but extend these lines out and I'd say anywhere within this area."

"What about a bullet...or at least fragments?" Murton asked.

Lawless shook his head. "No chance whatsoever. Given the damage done to the victim you're not going to find anything. I could spend two weeks out here with a metal detector and a magnifying glass and find everything but the bullet...or what's left of it."

"Okay," Virgil said. He looked at Murton. "Go find Williams will you?"

Murton nodded and headed over to the Metro Homicide mobile command center. A few minutes later they were back.

"Brent," Virgil said, pointing at the lines Lawless had drawn, "Tell the coroner to remove the body, have your men get this tent down and pull all the uniforms outside of these lines back in." He pointed in the direction between the lines and said, "Have everyone work outward, staying inside this arc."

"You got it, Jonesy." Williams walked away, barking orders into his hand-held radio.

Virgil stood in the center of the arc and scanned the buildings off in the distance. The shooter's perch was out there, somewhere. If they could find it, they might be able to get some good forensics that could help them find out who had killed Garrett Wright, and why. The why part of the equation was tickling at the back of his brain.

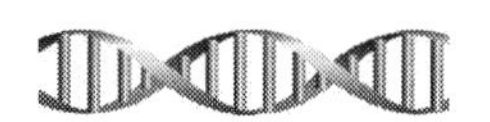

THE MEDIC WALKED BACK OVER TO VIRGIL AND Murton. “Thought you’d be gone by now,” Virgil said.

“I would have been, but your banger with the hand says he has something to tell you before we go.”

“What is it?”

The medic shook his head. “He wouldn’t say. Said he’d only tell you because you were the only one who listened to him in the first place. When I pressed him on the issue he told me to go pleasure myself.”

Virgil puffed out his cheeks. “Okay.” He walked over to the ambulance and pulled the back door open. “You wanted to tell me something?”

“Yeah. That medic lied to me. Wasn’t no steroid shot.”

“Thanks for the update. I’ll be sure and read him the riot act.” He turned to leave.

“No, wait, man, that ain’t what I wanted to tell you.” Young opened his mouth wide, like he was popping his ears, then licked his lips. The morphine was drying him out. Virgil knew about drugs. “I said Wright was our boy.”

“I know you did. Are you changing that statement?”

“No, man. I’m adding to it. Wright was our boy for sure. I also said he was the best shooter out there, and he usually was.”

“What do you mean by usually?” Virgil asked.

“That white boy was out at the court not long ago. He shows up once in a while. Keeps to himself usually, but we was one short for a three-on, so Wright axes him if he wanted to bang out with us.”

“What white boy?” Virgil said.

"That superstar everyone's been talking about for months. Got him a full ride up to West Lafayette."

"You're talking about Pete Long. He was going to play at Purdue. What about him?"

Young nodded. "Yeah, that's him. My boy, Wright sorta got in his face."

"Got in his face how?"

"Axed him if he wanted to play. Long says something like he couldn't keep up with us and Wright didn't want to hear it. He bounced the ball right off of Long's forehead. When he tried to do it a second time Long caught the ball with one hand and palmed it."

"You're saying he disrespected Wright?"

"No...I'm saying he agreed to play, then shoved that ball so hard into Garrett's gut it doubled him over."

"Did they end up in a fight?"

"Not exactly, man."

"What's that supposed to mean?"

"We was playing street rules. That means no fouls, anything goes."

"I know what street rules are," Virgil said. "What happened?"

"There was a lot of contact, if you get my drift. But even with all the pushing and shoving, that Long kid was kicking Garrett's ass. I guess he'd finally had enough."

"What'd he do...Wright?"

"He give us the look, man. We all backed out of the lane and when Long went in for the slam, Wright took his legs out from under him. He went down hard, flat on his back. You could hear his spine snap. It was louder than when my hand hit that pole."

"And then what?"

"What you mean, then what? We took off is then what. I don't think Long is gonna ever play ball again, man. Wright...he finished him off."

"And you're saying Wright was killed because of what he did to Long?"

"I ain't saying that. Maybe you is, but I ain't. I think my meds are starting to wear off. Can you get that nurse in here for me? Hey man, where you going? I'm trying to help you out here."

Virgil walked back to where Murton and the medic were waiting. "He's all yours," he said to the medic.

"Roger that."

When the medic left, Murton looked at Virgil and said, "Get what you need?"

Virgil looked at the tent where Garrett Wright, the son of a state senator was cold and dead. Then he turned a full circle and scanned the area. "I don't know, Murt. I really don't. Let's take a run over to the victim's house. Speak with his parents."

When they got in the truck, Murton gave Virgil a sniff. "The suit smelled better."

CHAPTER SEVENTEEN

The Wright family lived in a modest house at the front edge of a large subdivision. The home appeared well-tended, although it was starting to show its age. The roof looked like it might be good for a few more years, and the driveway held a smattering of small cracks, but the lawn was deep green and weed-free, the flowering plants around the landscaped sections looked colorful and bright. All in all, Virgil thought it looked like the kind of place where a happy family might live, though the reality of any visual appearances would be a stark contrast to the misery inside the home.

Virgil and Murton walked to the front door and were about to knock when the door opened and a minister greeted them with a kind, yet firm voice. "I'm sorry gentlemen, but Senator Wright and his wife are not receiving any visitors." Then in a not so kind voice, "Especially any members of the media."

Murton reached inside his shirt and pulled out his state badge that hung from a chain around his neck. Virgil did the same. "We're not with the media, Reverend. We're with the state's Major Crimes Unit. We're the ones in charge of the investigation. Would you please inform Senator and Mrs. Wright that we'd like to speak with them?"

The minister looked at their badges closely for a few seconds then said, "Wait here," before he closed the door.

"Media?" Murton said. "I think that's the first time I've ever been insulted by a member of the clergy."

Virgil, still staring at the door, said, "I don't know. You sort of look like the media type. I think it's your dimpled jawline, the sharp angle of your nose, the little bits of gray starting to show at your temples...like that. I'll bet if you had a pair of those Scott Pelley glasses and held them in your hand all the time you could anchor the evening news."

Murton turned his whole body and looked at Virgil. "How many times do I have to tell you to please leave the jokes to the professionals?"

"Who's joking? It wasn't me. I'm saying—"

The door opened again, cutting Virgil off. The minister invited them in and asked that they follow him to the kitchen.

"I don't believe we got your name," Virgil said.

"I don't believe you did," the minister answered without breaking stride.

"Have I offended you somehow, sir?"

This time the minister stopped and turned. He kept his voice neutral, his words measured and without inflection. "Your type offends me, though not you personally, Detective. People of color are getting shot down in this city and all across the country, yet little seems to change with regard to any of it."

"The sole focus of my job as we stand here today is to find out who killed Garrett Wright, and why," Virgil said. "In addition, we are doing everything in our power to ensure that not only is this person or persons caught, but prosecuted to the fullest extent of the law."

The minister waved Virgil's statement away like it was a bothersome fly. "Yes, yes, of course. Of that I have no doubt. But such interest in the son of a black state's senator only drives my point home further, don't you think? What if young Garrett's father were a simple delivery man, or bus driver, or store manager? Answer honestly Detective, would you be working the case?"

Virgil didn't want to be disrespectful, but he didn't sugarcoat his answer. "No. I wouldn't. I work directly for the governor. My team and I were tasked with solving this crime as quickly and efficiently as possible. I don't make the rules any more than you do, Reverend. I go where I'm told, do what's been asked, and I do it to the best of my abilities. We all do. Though I recognize one when I see it, I'm not here to solve a larger social injustice. I'm simply trying to do my job. How about you stand down and let me do that?"

The minister turned and led them to the kitchen

without another word. Once there, he introduced them to Garrett's parents, Michael and Sharron Wright. After the introductions were complete, he left the room.

Michael Wright waved at the two empty chairs with the back of his hand, and Virgil and Murton both sat down. "The governor told us to expect you," Wright said. "It was kind of him to stop by. You'll have to forgive the reverend. He's lost more than one young member of his congregation over the years."

"We didn't take offense, sir."

"Perhaps you should have," Sharron Wright said, her face shrunken and drawn in on itself. "I heard what he said and I think he's correct."

Virgil looked straight at her. "Then I hope you heard what I said as well, ma'am. We're here to help you get the justice you deserve by bringing your son's killer in. Would you have us focus on that, or a larger issue?"

Sharron Wright stood from the table so quickly she knocked her chair over. She put her finger in Virgil's face when she spoke, her voice no more than a whisper. "There is no justice. A larger issue is exactly why Garrett ended up dead. Capturing the person who killed him doesn't bring him back, does it?"

"No, ma'am, it does not. And with respect, please remove your finger from in front of my face. I know how upset you must be—"

"Mom?"

The four of them turned and looked toward the

kitchen entrance. A young woman—perhaps a year or two younger than Garrett stood in the doorway.

"Our daughter, Melissa," Michael Wright said. "She's our only child now."

Virgil didn't think Wright recognized the hurt his words had inflicted on his own daughter...as if she weren't enough now that their son was gone. If he didn't, he was about to.

"Thanks a lot, Dad. I'll try to make up for everything."

Wright stood from the table. "That's not what I meant, sweetheart. I'm sorry."

Sharron Wright looked at her husband. "Save it, Mike. I think you've caused this family enough grief already, don't you?"

Wright looked away, his jaw clenched tight.

"Mom, let me get you upstairs. You need to get some rest."

Sharron Wright walked past her daughter without saying a word. The front staircase creaked under her weight as she walked up to her bedroom. Melissa Wright remained standing in the doorway for a few seconds, her eyes locked solidly on Murton. Then she looked away and followed her mother up the stairs.

After a few moments, Wright said, "I'm sorry about all that. We're a happy family. We really are. Or maybe I should say we used to be. Now, with everything...I'm not so sure."

"There are places where you can get help, sir," Virgil

said. "Even outside the church if you'd like. I could have someone reach out if you think that might help."

Wright didn't answer him, and Virgil wasn't even sure if he'd heard his words. "Detective Wheeler and I would like to ask you some questions regarding your son. Would that be all right with you, sir?"

If Wright didn't hear Virgil before, he heard him now. "I don't have a son, Detective."

Virgil knew Wright was upset, but he and Murton needed to ask their questions, regardless. "Our working theory right now is that Garrett was killed as a way to send you a message."

Wright looked away as a tear escaped the corner of his eye. "Message delivered."

When he didn't say anything else, Virgil pressed on. "You're the one pushing the mobile voting bill through the senate. Is that correct?"

Wright nodded. "Yes. What about it?"

"Can you tell us about the type of resistance you're getting? Senator? Where are you going? We're trying to help you, sir."

Virgil and Murton sat alone at the kitchen table for a few minutes. When it was clear that the Wright family wasn't going to cooperate in the moment, they stood and left.

"It felt like there might be more to the story back there," Murton said once they were outside.

"It sure did. We'll give them a day or so and try again. Maybe Mac can say something to him...Wright."

"Did you notice the way their daughter was looking at me?" Murton said.

"No."

"It felt like she was trying to send me a message. I couldn't tell if she had some info for us, or if she wanted us out of the house."

"Based on what I saw, maybe both."

CHAPTER EIGHTEEN

That evening Virgil and Sandy had dinner at home with Huma and Delroy. Huma, their live-in nanny and housekeeper watched over their sons, Jonas, who was in the first grade, and Wyatt, their little miracle boy, now coming into his terrible two stage. Virgil brought everyone up to speed on the case he was working, leaving the more graphic parts out of the conversation because of the boys, even though they didn't appear to be interested.

After the meal, Virgil got down on the floor and spent some time playing and rolling around with his two sons, and Larry the dog, but no matter the way he laughed or talked with his kids, there was no joy in the sound of his voice. Huma, who seemed to have a sixth sense, picked up on the sadness Virgil was carrying around with him. When she'd finished cleaning the kitchen, she went into the family room and said, "How about you let me get these little guys ready for bed?"

"I guess that'd be okay," Virgil said. "Want some help?"

Sandy came out of the kitchen as well, and said, "We've got this, Virgil. Go relax with Delroy. I think he's out on the back deck with Larry the dog."

"Have you ever noticed that everyone calls him that?"

"That's because it's his name," Huma said.

"Yeah, yeah," Virgil said. "But why not just Larry?"

Huma turned the corners of her mouth down. "I don't know...it doesn't have the same ring to it. Larry the dog works...it sounds sweet." She tipped a finger at Virgil. "I'll tell you this: Delroy often calls me by my full name. I adore it."

Virgil grabbed two Red Stripes from the fridge, and went outside. Delroy and Larry the dog weren't on the deck...they were down by the cross Virgil had carved out of a downed willow tree as a memorial to his father. The tree had been a gift from Sandy, Murton, Delroy, and Robert after his father had been shot and killed on one of Virgil's previous cases. The shirt Mason was wearing had been buried under the tree. When a small tornado snapped the young tree in half, Virgil carved it into a cross...it was the only thing he could do to save what was one of the best gifts he'd ever received.

He pulled a chair over, handed one of the beers to Delroy, and stared out at the pond water that was as black as the night. They sat quietly for a long time, neither man speaking. Then Delroy set his beer on the table between them and said, "I hear you laughing with your boys, you, but I didn't hear the happiness dat go with it, mon."

Virgil took a long slow drink of his beer. "Rough day."

"Dat you let it make for a rough night only on you, den."

Virgil peeled his eyes away from the pond water and looked at his friend, the tone of his voice not quite civil. "I spent the morning looking at a dead teenager who'd been shot in the head, then part of the afternoon speaking with his father about it."

Delroy nodded thoughtfully. "Yeah, mon, dat sound like a hard ting to do. Delroy understand, maybe more than you know, mon, but it makes you wonder if your boys do, no?"

"I don't think they noticed anything, Delroy."

"That's because you're not paying attention, you."

"Meaning what, exactly?"

"It mean you here, physically, with your family, but your head and your heart, they somewhere else all night."

Virgil looked back out at the pond. "It's not exactly the sort of thing that you can turn off."

"For the man dat lost his child, no. But for the man who still has his entire family, yes. You're not trying hard enough, mon."

Virgil turned his head back, his voice getting loud. "Really? I'm not trying hard enough? Who made you the high-minded moral authority on the subject?"

Delroy suddenly looked as sad as Virgil had ever seen. He picked up his beer bottle and stood from his chair. "I tink I go now. But to answer your question, nobody. Delroy self-made in that regard, me. Tink about dat for a while and see what you come up with."

Virgil stood as well. "Delroy wait. I'm sorry. I didn't mean to raise my voice with you. Please stay for a while longer. It's...good for me."

Delroy put his hand on Virgil's shoulder. "Everyting irie, but not everyting about you, Virgil Jones. I'm going to go and say goodnight to Huma Moon, now. Dat woman, she the love of my life, mon. I tink I stay at my own place tonight, though."

"Delroy, you don't have to do that."

"Yeah, I tink maybe I do."

Virgil knew he was missing something, but he didn't know what it was. "Delroy, I'm sorry. I don't understand."

Delroy looked at the ground when he spoke. "I know you don't, you. Maybe somebody else explain it to you sometime. I don't tink I have the words, me." He turned and walked toward the house.

Virgil called out to him. "Delroy..."

But it was no use. He walked away, and Virgil was alone.

EXCEPT, OF COURSE, HE WASN'T.

"Mind if I ask you a question, Son?" Mason said.

Larry the dog looked at the cross and let out a small bark. A friendly woof.

Virgil turned and looked at the cross. His father was standing there, shirtless as always, a bar towel thrown over his shoulder. The scar on his chest where the bullet had entered his body was clearly visible. After he'd been pronounced dead, the doctors had told Virgil that the bullet bounced around inside Mason's chest cavity and destroyed any chance of survival.

Virgil turned his chair toward the cross and sat back down. "Of course not. What is it?"

"Do you remember the conversation we had when I told you that time isn't real?"

Virgil chuckled. "Yeah, I remember. Can't say I understand the statement though...then or now."

Mason pulled the towel off his shoulder and swatted at a mosquito before flipping it back in place.

"Are you allowed to do that?"

"I'm allowed anything I want, Virg. What I need right now is for you to hear me."

"I can't get my mind around that, Dad. Time is real. I woke up this morning. That was earlier, so now it's in the past. In a little while I'll go to bed. That's in the future because it hasn't happened yet."

"I guess that's one way of looking at it. Except your thinking is too linear, Son. Things are happening all around you, all at once. Everything that has ever happened to you, and everything that ever will is happening right now."

"Maybe for you."

Mason nodded thoughtfully. "I suppose so. Let me ask

you something else: Do you think I did Delroy a disservice?"

"In what regard?"

"I'm speaking of before my body died. By making him a party to my attempt to get you off the streets and into the bar?"

"I don't know, Dad. Why don't you ask him?"

"I'm asking you." When Virgil didn't respond, Mason changed course, if only slightly. "It's not like you need the money."

"I might. There's a good chance we may have to shut down the drilling operation for a while. But even if that's the case, it's not about money. I like what I do. I'm fairly good at it, too."

Mason grinned at him. "Better than fair, I'd say. But if you don't find a way to leave your work where it belongs, which is at work, it'll eat you up inside, no different than that bullet did to me."

"It's not exactly a common occurrence."

Mason, still grinning, said, "We lying to each other now?"

"*What?*"

"Look at every major case you've ever worked. In one way or another your family and friends have either been peripherally involved, or in direct grave danger. Your eldest son might understand that better than you."

"Can't we ever have a normal conversation?"

"What do you call this?"

"A sales pitch, if nothing else. Look, Dad, I'm not

ready to hang it up. Working the bar with Murt and Delroy and Robert would be great, but I need more than that. It's not very exciting...the bar."

"Check yourself, Virg. You're telling it to the guy who was shot there. It wasn't exactly what anyone would call a dull moment."

"That's a rotten thing to say. I carry that guilt around with me every day."

"It's time to let that go. I've told you that before. I'm simply saying a person gets their excitement where they make it, not from where they work, or what they do for a living. In either case, they shouldn't bring it home with them, and neither should you."

"So I've been told."

"He's right you know...Delroy, that is."

"About what?"

"What he told you. A man who loses a child will carry that with him for the rest of his natural life."

"I know that, Dad. I see it more often than I care to." Virgil turned and looked at the water again, his own thoughts swimming through his head.

"I'm sure you have," Mason said. "But who do you think knows it better, or feels it in their own heart more? You, or the man who has experienced it?"

"I'm having trouble understanding how it is that you or Delroy don't seem to realize why it's so hard for me to let it go, if only for one night. I'm sure Senator Wright's experience is much worse than mine, if that's what you mean. The man was absolutely devastated."

"I wasn't speaking of Mr. Wright, Virg."

Virgil snapped his head over at the cross, but his father was gone. When he turned in his chair he saw Delroy's car pulling away.

Larry the dog put his head in Virgil's lap and let out a soft moan.

AVERY WAITED PATIENTLY FOR MOST OF THE EVENING AS the police and crime scene people finished their work. He'd watched from a distance earlier in the day as the body was removed, the tent taken down, the lasers set up...all of it. Then the police seemed to zero in on the building where he'd rented the room. No matter. He wouldn't be identified. The super who'd rented him the room was on a vacation...the kind you don't come back from.

The basketball court didn't have any lights, so there weren't any players out this late in the evening. Avery parked on the far side of the court, near the restrooms and sat for a few minutes, waiting and watching. When he felt it was safe, he got out of the car, grabbed the metal detector, and moved in on the location he'd earlier marked in his mind. He began to scan the area and after ten minutes or so started to wonder if maybe someone else had already found what he was looking for. Then, as he was about to give up, he heard the beep. It was faint, like he'd barely missed the mark. He swept over the area again and the beeping was stronger this time. He zeroed in on the spot, then took a pen light from his pocket, and began fingering through the grass.

It was difficult with the gloves he always wore. That and the fact that the nerve endings in his hands always sent him erratic signals. But after a few more minutes, he found what he was looking for. He held it up in front of his pen light and smiled, then put the item in his pocket, clicked off the light, and walked away. Five minutes later he was back in his car, driving carefully, obeying all the traffic laws. He knew where he wanted to dump the super's body. It was simply all a matter of timing.

CHAPTER NINETEEN

Early the next morning Virgil had everyone in the MCU's conference room to go over what they had.

"Cora coming over?" Murton asked.

Virgil checked the clock on the wall. "Said she was going to. Probably any minute now. Let's get going and we can catch her up when she gets here." He looked at Lawless. "Chip? Want to start us off?"

"Sure."

Then Cora walked into the room. She glanced at the same clock Virgil had checked, said, "Sorry I'm late," and grabbed a seat at the head of the table next to Virgil. She removed a pen and pad of paper from her case, then rolled her wrist.

Lawless cleared his throat—Cora made him a little nervous—then informed everyone that after a careful analysis of the position of the body, the angle of the entry and exit wounds, and the blood spatter patterns, he felt the shooter had been in a fifth floor room eight blocks away. "I went over to the building with the SWAT team and waited until they made entry, but no one was there."

"What about the building manager?" Virgil asked.

Lawless shrugged. "No one could find him. His car was there, but he wasn't in the building. The SWAT commander, John Mok, made the decision to force entry into his apartment as a safety check. The place was messy, but not messed up, if you know what I mean. His wallet, cash, credit cards, and car keys were all sitting on the bedroom dresser. The watch commander told me they've had a car there all night in case he returned. I checked right before I came up this morning, which was like, five minutes ago, and he still hasn't shown."

Murton looked at Virgil and shook his head.

Lawless caught the shake and said, "What?"

Murton explained it to him. "If you had the right spot, the building manager probably rented the room to the shooter. That means the shooter couldn't take the chance that he might be identified later. He's probably dead, Chip."

Lawless wasn't sure how to respond to that, so he didn't say anything.

Virgil looked at the young crime scene tech and said, "Have the watch commander keep a car out there for another twenty-four hours."

Lawless said he would and left the room. Virgil looked

at Ross and Rosencrantz and said, "What's the story up in Boone County?"

"Guy got torched in his house," Ross said.

"Any chance you could be a little more specific?" Virgil said.

"Those were the specifics," Ross said.

Cora rubbed her forehead. "Ross, please. I'm not in the mood."

Ross, who could be somewhat direct at times, especially with his superiors, said, "Are you ever?"

Cora shot him a look, one they all knew well. If the look had any effect on Ross, he didn't let it show.

Rosencrantz took over for his partner. "Okay, okay. I think Ross was simply stating the basic facts. It looks like an accelerant was used, but there weren't any containers at the scene...not even remnants of plastic ones that may have melted away, so whoever fried this guy took everything with him. Mimi is doing an analysis on the accelerant as we speak...said she'd have something for us shortly, but I don't know how much good it'll do us."

Cora was scribbling notes on her pad, and didn't look up when she spoke. "Did you get an ID on the victim?"

Ross shrugged. "We're not sure. If the victim was the occupant of the home, then yes. But he was burned so badly it'll take dental records for a positive ID. The county homicide guy said he'd already checked with all the local dentists and none of them had him listed as a current or former patient. And get this: the homicide guy? His last name is Quayle, and he's supposedly related to our former Vice President and spelling bee champion."

Despite Cora's former statement of not being in the mood, she laughed out loud at the spelling bee comment. "You know, if he'd have simply put an S on the end there, right after the E..."

Everyone nodded...sort of a well, what can you do? nod.

"Who was the registered occupant of the home?" Murton asked.

"Guy named Tim Dreyer," Ross said.

Virgil turned and looked at nothing for a few seconds. Murton saw it and said, "What?"

"That name ring a bell?"

"Not particularly," Murton said. "Why?"

"It should," Virgil said. Then to Ross and Rosencrantz: "Where'd he work?"

"Local cemetery," Ross said. "His co-workers, if that's what you want to call them—they didn't appear to be working all that much—said he'd done some time. And we're not talking about a weekend stint for a D&D, either. We're talking about—"

Murton pointed a finger at Ross and said, "Military time."

Ross nodded. "Yeah, how'd you know that?"

"Because Jonesy and I were unfortunate enough to serve with him when we were in the sandbox."

Cora clicked her pen a few times, pointed it at Ross and Rosencrantz, but looked at Virgil and Murton when she spoke. "These two think the victim is a man who served with you in the military?"

"It looks that way," Murton said.

"In what capacity?"

"We were all part of a Recon unit," Virgil said. Then he took out his phone and called the forensics lab downstairs. He put the phone on speaker so everyone could hear. "Mimi, Jonesy. On that accelerant...did you find a gelling compound of any kind?"

"How'd you know that?"

"Lucky guess," Murton said. "We'll come down and get the full report when we're finished here. Later Meems." He pressed the end button on Virgil's phone.

"What does that mean?" Ross asked.

Virgil looked at Murton. "Avery?"

"Who else?" Murton said.

"Who's Avery?" Cora asked.

"I wonder if Avery himself could even answer that question," Virgil said. Then he told her the story.

Cora looked at Virgil and Murton. "So a former army pal of yours, this Avery guy—a suspected contract hitter out of Miami, no less—shows up at your bar right out of the blue, then the same night the guy who had previously disfigured him for life gets burned to death in his own home by what sounds very much like a flamethrower...the same weapon used against Avery."

"That's pretty much the gist of it," Murton said.

"Where is he now?"

"We've got Becky looking into that," Virgil said.

"This seems like something you might have mentioned earlier."

"There was no way to make the connection, Cora," Virgil said. "The only reason we had Becky checking on him was because he showed up at the bar."

"A contract hitter...in our city," she said, her voice strained.

"Your taking it out of context," Virgil said. "This meeting is the first time a few of the facts have come together. You know as well as I do that he's not the only bad guy out there."

Cora nodded stiffly, conceding the point. Then she looked at Ross and Rosencrantz. "Get any intel you can from Becky. Find this Avery guy and get him in here before—"

Virgil cleared his throat. "Uh, Maybe Murton and I should take the lead on that. We know who he is, and even though the facts suggest—"

"Don't even think about it, Jonesy," Cora said. "You two are on the Wright case. Period. End of discussion. This mobile voting thing is picking up traction on the floor and Mac wants the death of the son of one of our state's senators dealt with in the most expeditious manner possible. Are we clear on that?"

"Crystal," Virgil said, his voice dry and caustic.

If Cora caught Virgil's tone, she ignored it. She looked

at Ross and Rosencrantz. "Get to it. Now." Then she looked at Virgil and Murton. "You two know what needs to be done. Make it happen." With that she stood and left the room.

Murton told Ross and Rosencrantz he'd let Becky know who had point on what. They thanked him and followed Cora out. Virgil started to say something, but Murton held up his hand. "Hold on. Let's give it a minute."

"Why?"

"To make sure everyone is out of earshot."

"Earshot of what?" Virgil said.

"I'll tell you something, Jonesy...you've got a lot of great qualities, but sometimes you can be pretty impatient." Murton stood, moved to the conference room door and checked the hallways. They were empty. He closed the door anyway. When he sat back down, he turned his phone over, screen up, on the table. He pressed the speaker button and said, "Did you get all that?"

"Every word," Becky said.

Virgil looked down and grinned.

"Give Ross and Rosencrantz anything they ask for," Murton told her. Becky said she would.

"But Becks?" Virgil said.

"Yeah?"

"Make sure we get it too."

"Of course." Then, "Hey, Murton?"

"Yes, dear?"

"You called her Meems..."

"Yeah, she sort of digs me, is all."

"I get it. But, if you want me to keep digging you, start calling her by her real name. I don't like the sound of her voice."

"My heart belongs to you and you alone."

"Uh huh. Well, if you want your heart to keep beating, you'd better do as I ask." There was an audible click and Becky was gone.

"Jealous?" Virgil asked.

Murton shook his head. "No...she's been trying for months to get that throaty sound right. Hasn't been able to pull it off. I think she's mad about it."

Virgil and Murton drove over to the building where Wright's killer had taken the shot. They checked in with the patrol officer who was still waiting for the building's manager to return. "Anything?" Virgil asked.

The city cop shook his head. "Not yet. And not likely if you ask me, based on what I've heard."

"You're probably right," Murton said.

"How much longer do I have to sit here? This neighborhood...I feel like a sitting duck." It was a legitimate concern. A lone officer sitting in his squad car in a bad neighborhood was dangerous.

"I'll get with the watch commander and have some units do continuous passes," Virgil said. "If he hasn't shown by the end of the day, you can wrap it up."

"How about by the end of the shift?"

"Don't want the overtime?"

"Don't want one parked in my squash, is what I don't want."

"What time is the shift change?"

"Three."

Virgil nodded. "Good enough. We'll be upstairs for a little while. Be safe."

They climbed the five flights of stairs and when they got to the room where Lawless said the shot had originated, Virgil removed the crime scene seal and they stepped inside. The room was small...like a studio apartment or a hotel room. One window, a bed, table, chair, and lamp. There was no TV or any artwork on the walls. There wasn't, in fact, even a bathroom.

"Must be a community restroom on the floor somewhere," Murton said.

Virgil went to the window and looked down at the street, then out in the direction of the basketball court. The court itself was so far away it was difficult to tell if anyone was playing ball or not. He took out his phone and called Ross. "Where are you guys right now?"

"Getting ready to leave the MCU. Another run up to Boone County. Gonna sniff around a little."

"Think it'll do any good?"

"No, but unless you've got other ideas..."

"I don't," Virgil said. "But I could use your help with something. Won't take long."

"Sure. What's up?"

Virgil told him what he wanted.

"Can Rosie come? He's asking."

"Yeah. Do you have your long gun with you?"

"What do you think?"

"Okay. And Ross? Keep this to yourself. I don't want Cora crawling up my butt over allocation of resources, even though technically, that's my job anyway."

"You got it, Boss. See you in twenty or so."

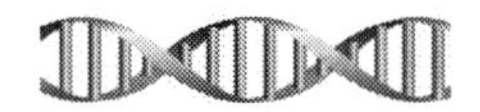

THEY MADE IT IN FIFTEEN. ROSS HAD HIS SNIPER RIFLE in its carrying case with him, along with a spotter's scope. He set his gear on the bed, looked at Virgil and said, "I see the crime scene techs printed the hell out of this room." Ross was right. Finger print powder was everywhere. "I hate the damned stuff. It gets on your clothes, your shoes, in your hair. It's a mess."

"Suck it up, dude," Rosencrantz said. Then to Virgil, "They get any usable prints?"

"A ton of latents, but so far no hits from AFIS. Doesn't matter anyway," Virgil said. "Avery wears gloves to protect his hands. Pretty sure he has ever since he got burned." He looked at Ross and said, "Show me."

They walked to the window and Ross looked it over, checking the way it opened, how far, the size of the sill, and the height above the floor. Then he looked for a long time in the direction of the basketball court. When he was finished, he said, "Huh."

"Huh, what?" Virgil said.

"Hold on a second." Ross took his spotter's scope out of the bag, opened the window, and scanned the park eight blocks away. He wrote a number down on the side of his wrist.

Then he looked around the room and pulled the table over to the window, setting it long ways, so the narrow end butted up against the sill. That done, he re-opened the window, then removed his rifle from the case, unfolded the bipod from the stock, and carefully set the rifle on the table. Next he dragged the chair over, sat down, uncapped the scope and took aim at the players on the court. The table was a bit wobbly and, worried that it might knock the rifle over, he looked around for something to shim one of the legs with. When he saw the pad of paper lying on the floor with a dent that matched up with the table's legs, he set it aside and used one of the scope's caps instead. After a few seconds he turned to Virgil and said, take a look.

Virgil sat in the chair and put his eye up to the scope. The court suddenly didn't look eight blocks away. It looked more like fifty feet.

When he stood, Rosencrantz sat down and looked as well.

Virgil turned to Ross who had the spotter's scope up to his eye again, rechecking the distance. "Could you make that shot?"

Rosencrantz who still had his eye to the scope said, "Range."

"Seven hundred and four yards," Ross said.

Rosencrantz stood from the chair and said, "Yeah, he could make it. Not sure I could. Well, that's not right...I could hit the court, but Ross here could make the shot, no problem."

Virgil looked at Ross for confirmation.

"I've been working with Rosie at the range. He's about fifty percent at five hundred yards, which is about the limit for a typical casual shooter with minimal training, optimal conditions...little to no wind, stationary target, that sort of thing. I practice at one thousand yards, varying conditions, wind, rain, snow, shifting targets, the works. I don't miss. So yeah, I could make that shot."

"Who else could?" Murton asked.

Ross sort of shrugged. "That's pretty hard to answer. I've seen self-taught guys—and girls, for that matter—who shoot as well as I do, and I was trained by some of the best instructors out there...all ex-military snipers. So if you put in the time at the range, which most people don't because it's so expensive..."

"But if you're not one of those people?"

"Then you're looking at guys like me, who have to stay sharp for a living, or the type of guys who've been properly trained, and that'd be military snipers."

Virgil and Murton glanced at each other, and they both understood what the other was thinking.

"Okay, thanks, kid," Virgil said. "You guys get back up to Boone and see what you can see."

Ross removed the shim, capped his scope, disassembled his rifle, and put it back in the case along with his spotter's scope. "I can tell you this," Ross said. "That Lawless kid and his lasers pinpointed this room and he was exactly right."

"How do you know?" Murton asked. "No physical evidence ties any shooter to this room."

"Maybe not, but this table here?" He jiggled the table to make his point. "The shooter was set up exactly the same way I was."

"How do you know that?" Virgil said.

Ross reached down and picked up the pad of paper that was on the floor. "See this indentation? Watch this." He slid it under the table leg and not only was it a perfect match, the table no longer wobbled.

Virgil clapped him on the back. "Nice work. Take off, guys. We've got it from here. And guys?"

"Yeah, yeah," Rosie said. "Don't tell Cora."

Murton was staring out the window. When he turned around he looked at Virgil and said, "Avery."

Virgil bit into his lower lip and looked down at the floor. "He had our backs in sand-land, Murt. That last mission, the one where he got burned? That Iraqi Republican Guard had an AK-47 set to full auto, and he wasn't there to surrender. Avery saved our lives."

"Then he became a contract hitter, Jonesy. El Sal and Miami both."

"You said those were rumors."

"A rumor is what the feds call something when they know it to be true but can't prove it."

"So we have to find and arrest the guy who, if not for him, we wouldn't be standing here right now."

"That about says it."

Virgil shook his head.

"What?"

"Nothing. Except I need to quit telling everyone how much I like my job."

CHAPTER TWENTY

Rick Said called Virgil and this time he skipped the circling and got right to the point. He asked if Becky had come up with any useful information for him.

"Uh, listen Rick, about that, it's sort of on the back burner at the moment. I'm not saying she can't do it, but it might be a while before she can put her focus into it for you."

Said was not pleased and the tone of his voice didn't match the polite language he used in his next question. "Would you mind if I ask why?"

Virgil could hear the frustration sneaking through. "I'm sorry, Rick, but we've got a killer on the loose and all of our efforts are going into finding this guy and shutting him down. That has to come first. I know you know that. I also know you understand that I want you to succeed for my own selfish reasons as well. When she has the time, we'll get her on it. You've got my word on that."

Said, who knew when enough was enough, let out a weary sigh. "Okay. I get it. Any leads on who your guy is?"

"Yeah, but you know how it works, buddy. I can't comment regarding an ongoing investigation."

"Well Christ, it's not like I'm a reporter or anything."

"It is what it is, pal. Maybe you should start looking into those other companies. I'll get with you when I can." Virgil ended the call.

SAID WANTED TO LOOK INTO OTHER COMPANIES ABOUT as much as he wanted another hole in his head. But Virgil's suggestion had sparked an idea, one that Said was almost ashamed to admit he should have thought of himself. He'd take one more run at the AI company he was currently using—the one about to cancel his contracts—and if that didn't work, he'd go to plan B.

Then he thought, plan B would take some doing...and some fast action. He pulled out his phone and called his assistant. "Set up an emergency meeting with the board's executive committee."

"Where and when?" The assistant asked.

"Hold on a minute." Said had to do a little math in his head. He was in Indy, but the executive committee members were all in Louisville, where Said's main offices were located.

"I won't be back until about nine tonight. Let's have a dinner catered in for everyone. You pick the menu. Make it something good. I'm going to need everyone fat and happy."

"What are you up to, Rick? You may as well tell me, because everyone is going to ask anyway."

Said chuckled into the phone. "You're right about that."

When he told her, she said, "Think they'll go for it?"

After another chuckle he said, "Pull out the articles of incorporation and read the charter, specifically the subsection in the bylaws regarding board seat assignments and compensation. They'll go for it. If they don't, I'll replace them with people who will."

NEXT HE CALLED AR-TELL, AND THE RECEPTIONIST PUT him through to the executive offices where he was promptly informed that the CEO wasn't available. Said, a CEO himself knew how to navigate the narrow pathways of well-insulated people. "I understand," he told the executive assistant. "I'm wondering, when he's done with his meeting, would you drop him a note and ask that he return my call? It's urgent."

"I'm sorry Mr. Said, but he's not in a meeting. We don't expect him back for a few more days."

"Oh that's right," Said said. "I forgot...the golf outing in West Palm. My mistake."

The assistant was suddenly confused. "I wasn't aware of any golf outing. It's not on the schedule."

Said chuckled. "I'm not surprised. It was all very last minute. Maybe it was some sort of mixup. Anyway, I was invited, except the problem was, I couldn't get away. I hated that I'd have to miss it, but you know how it is...sometimes duty calls."

The executive assistant had no idea what he was talking about, so she simply said, "I'll be sure to let him know you'd like a call back when I see him again."

Said was losing her, and he knew it. *Keep her talking,* he told himself. "That will be fine, uh, I'm sorry, I didn't get your name."

"Karen."

"Oh yes, of course. I wasn't sure if it was you or not. Listen, Karen, about that outing, could you check one more time? That's not the reason I'm calling...well, not the main reason anyway, but as it turns out, my schedule opened back up almost as quick as it closed and now I'm free. I know I'd be a day or two late, but West Palm, this time of year..."

"I'm sorry Mr. Said, but there isn't anything on the schedule. Even if there had been, he wouldn't be there anyway...his son and all."

Said, nobody's idiot, thought, *Bingo.* "Oh my God, yes. What's wrong with me? I heard. How is he?"

Karen heard the concern in Said's voice and started to open up. "It's not looking good at this point, I'm afraid. They say the surgery went well, but he's been placed in an induced coma to keep him still and all that."

"I can't believe the tragedy of it all. Listen, I'm going to call my executive assistant and have her send some flowers over. Do you think that would be okay?"

"I'm sure Mr. Long would appreciate the gesture."

"Wonderful. If I could have the hospital name and room number..."

SAID DIDN'T CALL HIS ASSISTANT. HE DROVE TO THE hospital and bought the largest, most expensive bouquet he could find in the gift shop. When he arrived at Pete Long's room, he didn't see Bob Long, the CEO of Ar-Tell. What he saw was Long's son lying in a hospital bed with every sort of tube and wire known to modern medicine poking out of his body. A machine seemed to be breathing for him, or at the least, helping him breathe on his own. Bob Long's wife, Julie, was at the bedside, holding her son's hand. When she looked up, Said thought she'd aged twenty years since he'd last seen her, even though it'd only been one time, a few months ago at a party she'd held at her home.

"I'm sorry to interrupt," Said said. "It's Julie, isn't it?"

Julie Long looked up, first at the massive bouquet of flowers Said was holding, then at Said himself. "Yes, uh, you'll have to forgive me..."

Said stepped forward and set the flowers down on a

table near the window. "No, no, not at all. I'm Rick Said. Bob and I...our companies work together. I was at the party in your wonderful home a number of weeks ago."

Julie didn't remember Said, but she knew her status and her station in life, so she pretended like she did. "Of course, Rick. It's lovely to see you again, though given everything that's happened, I wish the circumstances were different."

Said had no idea what the circumstances were, so he played along as well. He visibly swallowed. "I'm so sorry. What are they saying, if you don't mind? Is there a prognosis? I don't mean to be so forward."

She waved her hand in front of her face, almost like she was trying to erase his words from the air. "The doctors...they're not like they used to be. Remember when they would take the time to answer your questions and address any concerns you might have? Now they breeze in and out of here like factory workers who are paid piece-rate, speak to you like you're a child, then race off to the next room." She let her shoulders sag. "Perhaps that's not fair. Maybe they're simply busy people working in a disorganized system. Whatever the case, they don't tell you much and when they do, you're left to connect the dots yourself."

She was rambling, and Said let her. The fact was, he didn't want or need to hear any of it. Said wasn't cruel. He was just being a businessman. When Julie Long looked up at him, a shaft of light cut across her face and it made her look like two photos that had been stitched together in a darkroom. "He'll never walk again. The surgery was done to prevent more damage down the road. I don't think I've ever been so tired."

Said moved closer and put his hand on her shoulder. "I can only imagine. How is Bob holding up?"

"Oh, you know...Bob is Bob. He puts on a brave face, but this is tearing him up inside. I finally got him to go home and get some rest, though I'd bet you a thousand dollars he's at the office right now."

And you'd lose that bet. "I'll leave you to tend to your son, Julie. I wanted to stop by and let you guys know that I've got you in my thoughts. No, no, don't get up. That's not necessary. Give Bob my best, will you?"

"Of course. Thank you so much, Rick."

"Anything at all, just let me know." Said pulled the door closed gently, then practically ran to the elevator. He took out his phone and called his assistant back. "Forget nine tonight," he told her. "I'm staying put. We'll do the whole thing via video conference. I'll be in the satellite office up here in Indy. Get the catering going and make sure everyone is there ASAP. We'll still have time to get started before the markets close. As soon as I'm back in the office up here—that'll be thirty minutes tops—I'm going to call back and I want everything ready with both the committee and the finance team. Make it happen."

She told him she would.

Bob Long was at his home in the country, well outside the city, speaking to his entire security team, minus Avery, of course. There were only three of them now, all former Army Rangers, who, after leaving the military, spent a number of years with Blackwater, then left when the company started getting a little too much media attention a few years ago.

"I don't care how you do it," Long said to his men. "Just don't get caught and don't let it come back on me. Is everyone hearing me on this?"

The three men nodded at their boss. They all had military style haircuts, wore black clothing from head to toe, and as former Rangers had been trained by some of the best tactical fighters the military had at its disposal.

One of the men, Jensen, the natural leader of the group, cleared his throat, looked at Long and said, "If you'd be willing to hear some suggestions, sir..."

Long waved him away. "No, no, I said I don't care how you do it—"

"That's not what I mean, sir. We can get rid of Avery for you. That won't be a problem. He's good, but only from a distance. Up close and personal, it wouldn't be a contest for any of us. But there are other things to be considered. You have to stay protected until the objective has been met and the target neutralized. That means one of us is by your side at all times. Your son should be under watch as well, along with Mrs. Long."

"Are you saying we need more men?"

"No, sir. We can handle Avery and take care of your family until he's been eliminated."

Long nodded thoughtfully. "Very well. I'll let the three of you work it out amongst yourselves. I've got to run down to the office, then back over to the hospital. They're going to wake up Pete later and I need to be there when they do."

"Before you leave, sir, if you could outline the nature of your last conversation with Avery...perhaps a little insight regarding his state of mind."

"His state of mind is in question. His actions have become erratic. He's operating on his own wavelength all while putting me, my business, and my future at risk. He found and torched the man who burned him years ago and instead of letting us handle it on his behalf, he decided to take matters into his own hands. In addition, I made it perfectly clear that I did not want that Wright boy killed. I only wanted him injured. Instead, he took half his head off with one shot. So I told him to cool out for six months and we'd reassess. I'm certain he didn't believe me. If you're asking if he knows he's been labeled as persona non grata, I'd say the answer is a definite yes."

"Perhaps that should change, sir," Jensen said.

"Why?" Long snapped the question at him.

"A simple lure, sir. You said yourself he knows he's been put out, so to speak. He could be anywhere. However, if you called him back and told him you've had a change of heart—that your emotions got the better of you and there is no need to reassess—we could pull him in to us. It'd make things much easier, not to mention quicker in the long run. We'd have complete control of the situation."

Long looked away and stared at nothing for a few seconds. When he turned back, he said, "That could work. Where do you propose I send him?"

Jensen let his face show a hint of grimace. "That's the most unfortunate part of the plan, sir."

"You're saying you want it to happen here, in my home?"

Jensen tipped his head. "Yes, sir. But it wouldn't be in your home. You're well isolated out here. You've got twenty acres, most of it surrounded by woods. If we could get him close, we could wrap this up in no time."

Long looked away again. "Let me think about that. I wouldn't want it in or even near the house."

"I understand, sir. I assure you, he won't get anywhere near the residence."

Long checked his watch. "I do have to go. For now, Jensen, you're with me." He looked at the other two men, and said, "You two get down to the hospital and keep watch on the room. And for Pete's sake, make sure those room curtains remain closed. He's out there, and I get the feeling he'll be watching."

CHAPTER TWENTY-ONE

Virgil and Murton went back to the court where Garrett Wright was shot and killed. No longer a crime scene, the court was once again in use, with players banging around, showing off their skills to anyone who happened by. Virgil and Murton sat on the bench near the spot where Wright was shot and looked at the building, eight blocks away.

"Hell of a shot," Murton said.

"Avery was a hell of a shooter," Virgil said.

"What are we going to do?"

"Find him."

"That's not what I meant, Jonesy."

Virgil watched the game that was going on for a few seconds, then said, "You know dad was the one who arrested Ave's father."

"Of course I know. What of it?"

"I'm not exactly sure. The whole thing seems sort of

circular to me. Ave's old man made a mistake, ended up killing three guys, then got sent to the chair. Now here we are, trying to find his son, a former friend of ours...a guy who saved our lives when we were in the box, no less, and if we do, then what? Let history repeat itself?" When Murton didn't respond, Virgil said, "Are you even listening to me?"

"Yes, I'm listening, but we've got to find a way to back up Young's story. A street banger isn't exactly the most credible witness. You know that." Then, "Hey, take a look at your two o'clock. See that girl over there? Is that who I think it is?"

Virgil turned and looked where Murton had indicated and saw a young girl standing by herself. She wasn't watching the game. She was watching them. "It sure looks like it."

"Think she's got something on her mind?"

"Let's go find out," Virgil said.

MELISSA WRIGHT SAW THE TWO COPS HEADED TOWARD her and in a momentary flood of panic turned to run away. She took exactly three steps before she stopped, turned back, sat down in the grass, and began to cry.

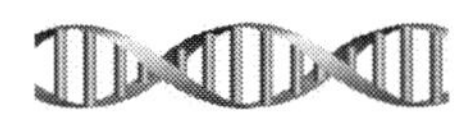

VIRGIL AND MURTON SAT DOWN WITH HER AND LET

her cry herself out. When she was finished, she rubbed at her eyes with the heels of her hands and took a big sniff to clear her nose.

"We're police officers," Virgil said. "We've been to your home. Do you remember us?"

Melissa nodded. "Yeah, I remember. That's why I'm here. I was hoping to talk to you both."

"Then why did you start to run away when—"

Murton interrupted Virgil with a backhand to his thigh. "Why did you want to talk to us, Melissa? You can answer honestly. You're not in any sort of trouble at all. I saw the way you were looking at me when we were at your house. It's clear you've got something you need to get off your chest. What is it, sweetheart?"

"My mom and dad are fighting. A lot. They don't think I can hear them because most of the time they send me to my room, but all I ever do is go to the top of the stairs and listen."

"What are they fighting about?" Virgil asked.

"What you think? They fighting about my dead brother...among other things."

Virgil nodded thoughtfully. "It's not uncommon for parents to argue when a tragedy of this magnitude takes place."

Wright shook her head. "That's not what I'm talking about. They doing that kind of arguing too, but that ain't it."

"What do you mean?" Murton said.

"I mean they ain't arguing about who killed him, or

even how. They arguing about the why of it. About what started everything."

"We already know why, Melissa," Virgil said. "One of the other ball players that day told us your brother flattened Pete Long out on the court. He's paralyzed for life. We're almost certain who did it and why. We're looking for the man right now. He's wanted for other crimes as well."

"Let me axe you something, Mr. Policeman..."

"You can call me Jonesy."

"Okay, let me axe you something, Jonesy. If a man run another man over with his car, that man gets arrested right?"

"That's right."

"Then what happens to the car?"

"I'm not sure I understand your question."

"The car don't get arrested, do it?"

Despite the gravity of the conversation, Virgil smiled at the young girl. "No, the car doesn't get arrested. It wouldn't do any good. The car would be nothing more than an instrument of—" Virgil stopped himself.

Murton looked at Virgil for a few seconds, then said, "Hey, Jonesy, what's the matter? You look like you're stroking out or something."

"He ain't stroking out," Melissa said. "He putting the pieces together." Then Melissa told them how it all started.

She cried off and on as she told them the story. "It didn't mean nothing...that's what he kept saying over and over to my mom. It was a one night fling. He begged her over and over to stay. Me and Garrett, we thought our family was falling apart. See, Garrett, he used to listen to the arguments with me from the top of the stairs before that day he got killed."

She told Virgil and Murton about the affair her father had, and how it turned out to be a setup, all of it done at the direction of Bob Long because her father had refused Long's request to push a bill that would enable mobile voting. Long's company had the technology to make it happen and he said they'd be rich. When Wright refused, Long showed him the photographs he had, photographs that showed Senator Wright and a prostitute—a young girl who was only fifteen at the time—in a motel room up in Kokomo.

"So your father never wanted the bill he's pushing to go through?" Murton said.

"The mobile thing? No. He was against it from the start. He thought it would disenfranchise the black voters in the state. I'm not even sure what that word means, but it doesn't sound good."

Virgil noticed that as she told her story, she'd taken most of the street out of her voice. "It means he felt that the people he represented in the state would lose some of their rights...especially and specifically their privilege to vote."

"Yeah, that sounds right, I guess. But Mr. Long, he came to our house one night and he and my dad got into a big argument. The next day there was an envelope in the mailbox. It was addressed to my mom. When she saw those pictures, it changed everything. It took weeks... months for her to finally come around and forgive him, though if you ask me, she still hasn't done it...forgive him, I mean, even though she says she has. But he kept telling her that if those pictures were ever made public, it'd ruin his political career and he'd end up in jail. My mom, she was as mad and as hurt as I've ever seen her...before Garrett was killed, that is, but she understood the bigger picture. She didn't have any real education past high school, which meant she wouldn't be able to get a good enough job to support us and keep the house. So I guess she sort of went along to get along, even though getting along looks a lot different now than it used to...even before Garrett died.

"So me and Garrett, we were talking about it one night, trying to figure out what we could do to help, but there didn't seem to be anything. We were just the kids, you know? Then the next day Garrett comes home and I could tell something wasn't right. He was acting strange, and he looked...tired. Not sleepy tired...more like tired on the inside. I don't know if this will sound right or not, but he almost looked like an old man, even though he was only a year older than I am right now. I kept asking him what was wrong but he wouldn't answer me. Told me to mind my place."

"I take it you didn't," Murton said.

"No, sir, I did not. Just because he didn't want to talk to me didn't mean I was going to give up trying. Since I was his little sister I kept pestering him until he finally blurt it out. Mom and Dad weren't home at the time and when he told me he screamed it right in my face, like maybe I was the one done something wrong. He said he took revenge out on Pete Long for what his dad done to ours. He said he took Pete Long's life away. Then he went into his room and cried himself to sleep. I spent the whole night thinking he'd killed him, but the next day I heard what happened because it was on the news shows. Next thing we know, Garrett is dead. Now my mom and dad have started in on each other again and she's blaming him for everything that's happened because he got with that young girl that Mr. Long fixed him up with. It's like everything keeps going around in a circle."

Virgil and Murton sat quietly for a few minutes, neither of them sure what to say to the young girl who'd opened the aperture on her family's secrets and shared her misery with them, as if the darkroom of her young life had developed a crack so wide it might never be properly sealed.

VIRGIL AND MURTON ASKED MELISSA IF SHE WANTED A ride home. When she declined, they got back in Virgil's truck and headed into the city. It was time to have a word with Bob Long. Murton gave Becky a call and asked for the address of Long's company, and he punched it into the nav system.

Virgil looked at Murton and said, "Probably should have talked with him first."

"Based on what? We're getting information on this case in bits and pieces."

Virgil's phone buzzed and the nav display went away for a moment as the screen displayed Becky's name. Virgil pushed the button on his steering wheel and said, "Did you forget something?"

"No, but something came in and you guys are going to want to hear it."

"What is it?"

"Bob Long's company? Ar-Tell? You know they're the ones with the blockchain tech for the mobile voting, right?"

"Yeah, what about it?"

"I'll give you what about it...Did Rick Said ever mention the name of the company who leases the AI boxes to him for those sonic drill units?"

Even though Virgil was driving, he closed his eyes momentarily. When he spoke, the disbelief in his voice was palpable. "You're saying that Bob Long and his company are responsible for canceling the contracts with Said in favor of shifting his operation over to mobile voting for the state?"

"That's exactly what I'm saying."

Virgil turned his truck off the road and into an empty lot. He threw the transmission into park and let his head come to rest on the steering wheel. The horn made a little beep when he did.

"What was that?" Becky said.

"That, my dear, was the sound of dismay," Murton said.

"Anyway, I got the intel back on Jacob Avery. He's wanted for questioning in Miami on a number of unsolved homicides."

"That's not exactly breaking news, Becks," Virgil said.

"No, but this is: I had a little time to kill, so I started digging around in Ar-Tell's system. It wasn't easy, but I gained access through their Human Resources department. I'll give you three guesses who's listed as chief of security for Long's company, and the first two don't count."

"Jesus Christ," Virgil said.

Murton shook his head. "That wasn't our guess. Our guess was Jacob Avery."

"You got it, baby, but I'm afraid there's more."

"There usually is," Virgil said without lifting his head. "Let's hear it."

"So, the whole mobile voting platform is built on the blockchain. Ar-Tell has designed the app that the users can download on their mobile phones. I got a look at the code."

"And..." Virgil said.

When Becky told them what else she'd found, Virgil and Murton looked at each other and didn't say a word. Neither of them knew how to respond.

"Guys, hey guys? Are you still there?"

"Yeah, we're still here," Murton said. "It's a little hard to believe is all."

"So what are you guys going to do?"

"Good question," Virgil said.

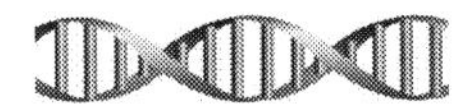

THEY WERE STILL SITTING IN THE EMPTY LOT WHEN Murton looked at Virgil and said, "Why did you say 'good question' when Becky asked what we're going to do? The answer seems obvious."

"Is it?"

"Sure. We go and find Bob Long—which shouldn't be too awfully difficult given that his son is in the hospital right now—show him a set a shiny locking bracelets, and haul his ass downtown for questioning."

Virgil shook his head. "That won't work, and you know it Murt. He'd lawyer up before we ever got him in the car. All we'd be doing is tipping our hand."

"So what then?"

"Avery is the key to all this. He has been from the start. He works for Long as his security chief and when Long's son get's crippled for life, almost immediately after that, the son of the man Long was trying to blackmail gets shot and killed. He also killed Dreyer in the same manner that Dreyer injured him all those years ago."

"You're talking about trying to get a deal for Avery in exchange for taking down Long?"

"We'd be doing him a favor."

"You think he'll see it that way?" Murton asked.

"I don't know, Murt, but the fact remains that he saved our lives. If we can get him a deal, we'll be saving his."

Murton shook his head. "Yeah, that'd be great. Let's risk our lives again to try to save the life of a former contract hitter, and current suspect in two homicides."

"I think you can frame it any way you'd like, but you're right about one thing: We do need to speak with Bob Long...not to cuff him up and haul him downtown, but to have him help us find Avery."

Murton shook his head. "That won't work. Avery leads back to Long. He'd be putting his own head on the chopping block."

"Got any better ideas?" Virgil asked.

Murton didn't. "What about the app and the rest of what she found?"

"We'll have to figure that out as we go."

"If we keep it to ourselves it could be construed as us taking part in a criminal conspiracy to cover up a crime."

"There hasn't been any crime committed as a result of the app or the mobile voting. You're assuming there will be."

"And you're assuming there won't?" Murton said.

CHAPTER TWENTY-TWO

When Virgil and Murton arrived at Bob Long's company, Ar-Tell, the receptionist in the main lobby politely informed them that they'd just missed him. Murton, who had a certain charm about him, looked at the receptionist, let his eyes go soft, and said, "His son...I guess that's where I'd want to be too."

The receptionist nodded, her eyes as soft as Murton's. "Yes, it's such a tragedy. Did you know that he had a full athletic scholarship to attend Purdue to play basketball?"

"Who didn't?" Murton said. "Even before he was hurt, it was all over the news."

The receptionist looked around to make sure no one was listening, which they weren't because no one else was in the lobby at the moment. She lowered her voice anyway and said, "But here's something no one knows, and it's a pretty big secret so you didn't hear it from me..."

Murton leaned close and lowered his voice as well. "What's that?"

"He turned it down. The scholarship."

Murton leaned back a pinch and tucked his chin into his chest. "He did?"

"Yeah. Pete and Mr. Long decided that since he could afford to pay for Pete's tuition on their own, they wanted the scholarship to go to someone who not only deserved it—like Pete—but to someone who needed it. The Long's sure don't."

"Huh," Murton said. "Pretty nice gesture."

"Oh I know," the receptionist said. "Mr. Long...he takes good care of his people. He's one of the best bosses I've ever had."

Murton had his hands resting on the counter as he spoke with the young woman, and he caught her furtive glance at his left hand, which was free of a wedding band. "I'm not busy tonight if you'd like to talk more about it," she said, her face reddening slightly as she spoke.

Murton turned on a smile, the kind that looked like it could only be removed by a surgical team, and said, "Ah, thank you. If only I could. But my heart belongs to another."

Virgil, who was standing quietly and listening, was starting to get impatient. "Time to hit the road, Murt."

The receptionist shot Virgil a dirty look, then turned back to Murton. "I hope your heart doesn't belong to this one here," she said, jerking her thumb at Virgil.

Murton puffed out his cheeks and let his shoulders sag. "Yeah, it sort of does."

The receptionist shook her head. "Isn't that the way it always goes? The good ones are never available."

"Murt..." Virgil said.

Murton turned and gave Virgil a look. "In a minute, darling," he said. Then back to the receptionist, "Thanks so much for the invite. We do have to run. My partner here, he can get a little impatient sometimes. We'll head over to St. Vincent's and catch Bob there...maybe say hello to Pete if he's up to it."

The receptionist put a question on her face. "Well don't go to St Vincent's. You'd never see him. Pete's at Methodist."

Murton smacked his forehead. "Of course, that's what I meant. Methodist. Say, listen, one more thing, I've got an old army buddy, haven't seen him in years but I'd like to say hello. Heard he's the security chief here at Ar-Tell. Jacob Avery? Is he in?"

The receptionist shook her head. "That poor man..."

"What does that mean?" Virgil said.

"With everything he's been through...first those awful burns from the war, and now this."

"This what?" Murton said.

"The memo came through earlier today. He was let go. There was no mention of why."

"He was fired?" Virgil said.

"Yes. Why are you looking at me like that?"

Back in the truck: "Darling?" Virgil said. They were headed to the hospital.

Murton shrugged. "It's a term of endearment. Besides, you do what you can to keep them talking, right?"

"You're a riot, you know that?"

Murton had to bite the inside of his cheek to keep himself from laughing. "Of course I do." Then, after a few seconds, "Got anymore Scott Pelley jokes you'd like to share?"

Virgil got a call from Becky as they were cruising the hospital's parking lot, looking for a spot. Virgil had learned his lesson about parking where he shouldn't at a hospital, cop or not. He found a spot, asked her to hold on as he maneuvered the truck into the space. Once he was in his spot he said, "Sorry, I can't park and talk at the same time. It's like looking for an address with the radio on."

"You're starting to sound like an old man."

Virgil ignored her jab. "What's up?"

"Remember way back when you hired me away from Ron after they canned you from the MCU?"

"Yeah. What about it?"

"Well, we were talking about salary and I mentioned

that I come from a little money. Got a trust fund and all that."

"Yeah, Becks, I remember. If you need financial advice, I can hook you up with Said's guys. They helped Sandy and me out after Shelby County."

"No, no, it's not that. I take care of my own money. That means I keep a constant eye on the market news."

"If you're about to give me a hot stock tip, it'll have to wait. Murt and I are getting ready to go talk to Bob Long."

"Then my timing couldn't be better, because you just mentioned the two guys I'm calling about...Said and Long."

"Why? What's going on with them now?"

"Just this little nugget. It's all over the financial news that your friend and partner, Rick Said, is making a run on Long's company. He's buying stock from anyone who'll sell, and he's doing it at a premium. They're saying by day's end, or tomorrow at the latest if things keep going the way they are he might have control of the company."

And Virgil thought, *Oh no.*

BOB LONG, AND HIS WIFE JULIE, WERE IN THEIR SON'S hospital room. The anesthesiologist was getting ready to administer the drugs to Pete to wake him up. They watched as the doctor screwed the end of the syringe into the IV port and slowly pressed the plunger. "This should only take a few minutes. He'll come around slowly, like he's waking from surgery. He may be a little confused, and his speech might be somewhat slurred. It's common, and nothing to be concerned about."

A few minutes later Pete finally came around, and the doctor was right...he was confused and his speech was sluggish and slurred. His parents spent a few minutes reassuring him that everything was okay, telling him to relax, and letting him know they were there for him, no matter what. "We're not going to leave your side, Son. Everything is going to work out. You'll see."

When Bob Long's phone buzzed at him, he looked at the screen, then his wife, and said, "I'll only be a moment." He stepped out in the hall, looked at Jensen and his other two men and said, "Stay put."

"Sir—"

"I'll be right down the hall. Please don't make me repeat myself."

"Yes sir."

He put the phone up to his ear and said, "Now isn't exactly the best time, Tim." He was speaking to Tim Cook, his chief financial officer.

"Sorry, Bob, but you're going to want to make time for this."

"What is it?"

"They started out slow, so we didn't notice at first. Our analysts thought maybe someone leaked the story to the press about the mobile voting. But I had dozens of our people scour the Internet and they came up empty.

No story, nothing. Then bigger and bigger chunks started getting bought up and now it's all over the financial news networks—"

"You're calling to tell me that our stock price is up and we're having a good day?"

Though Bob Long couldn't see it, Cook had his hand on his forehead, pulling his hair back so hard he was ready to rip it out. "Yes, the stock is up. Way up. But that's not why I'm calling. I warned you about dumping those extra shares into the market."

"We needed the capital for the change over. You know that."

"I do know that. I also know this: There's a hedge fund guy in New York who's involved and they took some very large chunks. In fact, they still are. They've managed to get enough already that it's too late to implement a flip. And the hedge fund guy? He's been hooked up with Rick Said for years. We're not sure what to do, here, Bob."

Bob Long squeezed his phone so hard he heard it crack. "You're telling me that Rick Said is making a run on Ar-Tell?"

"That's exactly what I'm telling you. As a matter of fact, he's approaching the finish line as we speak."

VIRGIL AND MURTON WERE IN THE LOBBY WAITING FOR the elevator to arrive. Virgil had his phone to his ear.

"Who are you calling?"

"Who do you think?" When the call was answered Virgil said, "I need to speak with Rick Said, right now, if you please."

"I'm sorry, sir," Said's assistant responded. "Mr. Said is on a conference call with his finance team and cannot be disturbed."

"Break into the call and tell him it's detective Virgil Jones. He'll take my call."

"Detective, please, you'll have to forgive me, but he left explicit instructions that he was not to be disturbed."

Virgil knew he wasn't going to get to Said unless he did something drastic. He hated himself for doing so, but he played the only card left in the deck. "Tell him it's about his niece, Patty Doyle."

There was a pause before the assistant said, "One moment, please."

When Said came on the line Virgil heard a side of him he hadn't heard since the day they met. "I don't know what kind of stunt you're trying to pull Jonesy, but I spoke with Patty not twenty minutes ago and I know she's well and fine. Using her to get to me is beneath you."

"That may be true, Rick, and whether it is or isn't, I'm sorry. But I need to know what's going on with Bob Long, and I need to know right now. Why didn't you tell me it was his company that holds the leases on the AI boxes, and further, why didn't you tell me you're making a run on his company?"

"Just because we're partners in a single venture doesn't

mean I inform you of my every move. What's your interest in Bob Long?"

The elevator dinged and Virgil and Murton stepped inside. "I just stepped into an elevator," Virgil said. "I don't want to lose you."

"I have to go anyway," Said said, "But answer my question. What's your interest in Long?"

"He's a person of intense interest in two homicides. We're almost certain he ordered one of them. He may also be responsible for blackmailing the state senator who is trying to get the mobile voting bill pushed through."

"Holy shit. That's good information."

"And you can't use any of it, Rick."

"And you shouldn't have used Patty to get to me, especially when I'm out here trying to save your financial ass. I'll call you back." The line went dead.

Murton looked at Virgil. "You may have lost a friend."

"It wouldn't be the first time, would it?" Then, "Based on the way things are going, it probably won't be the last." Murton stared at the elevator buttons without replying. When the door opened, they stepped off, turned the corner and found themselves face to face with Bob Long and his security men.

VIRGIL LOOKED AT LONG—HE RECOGNIZED HIM FROM the news articles and stories about his son, Pete—and said, "Excuse me. Bob Long?"

Long looked at Virgil and Murton, and said, "Yes, who are you?"

"I'm Detective Virgil Jones, and this is Detective Murton Wheeler. We're with the state's Major Crimes Unit and we need to have a word with you, sir."

"I'm sorry Detectives, but I don't have time right now. You'll have to excuse me. Call my offices and make an appointment. Maybe I can make some time for you. On second thought, probably not. If that doesn't work for you, I suggest you contact my lawyer." He moved to bypass Virgil and Murton, but they sidestepped with him and didn't let the men pass.

"Pretty quick to mention the lawyers, there, Big Bob," Murton said. "Feeling guilty about something? Garrett Wright, maybe?"

Jensen got right on Murton. "That's Mr. Long to you, Detective. Unless you've got a warrant, it's time to stand down. Mr. Long has important business to attend to and we're leaving whether you like it or not. I strongly suggest you do not try to stop us."

Murton leaned forward a few inches...enough to make his presence felt. "And if we do?"

"Then you won't simply be visiting this hospital, you may find yourself in the unfortunate position of being a patient."

"Are you threatening a state police officer?"

Jensen shook his head. "Not at all. I'm merely offering one of many different scenarios that might play out."

Then he leaned in close and whispered in Murton's ear. "If you don't get the fuck out of our way, that is."

"Jensen, step back," Long said. "Now."

Murton waved his hand in the air in front of his own face. "Whew. Someone needs a breath mint. Maybe you should stop in at the gift shop on your way out."

"Murt," Virgil said. He had his .45 in his hand, somewhat discretely behind his back. "Let them pass. From what I hear, Bob has important issues to attend to...like trying to save his company."

"What do you know about—" Then Long caught himself. "You said your name was Jones?"

Virgil gave him a grin. "That's right. Virgil Jones. My friends call me Jonesy. You can call me Detective."

"You're one of Said's partner's, aren't you?"

Virgil let his grin grow into a full blown smile, though his eyes remained cold. "That's right, Bob. Too bad about your company. If you'd have stuck with what you had, we probably wouldn't be talking to each other right now."

Long lunged at Virgil who suddenly had his .45 from behind his back, pointed squarely at Long's face. Jensen grabbed Long's arm and yanked him back.

"I'm going to take you and Said for every nickel you've got if it's the last thing I ever do. You've got my word on that."

A crowd of onlookers was starting to gather, and Virgil could see two security guards heading their way. He reached into his shirt and pulled his badge out, then slipped his gun back in its holster. "The word of a murderer and blackmailer doesn't carry much weight with me, Bob."

When the security guards got there, one of them looked at Virgil, his badge hanging from his neck. "Is there a problem here, officer?"

"It's Detective. And no, everything is under control. These gentlemen were about to leave."

"That's right," Jensen said. "We're leaving." Then he turned and looked at Murton. "I'll see you down the track."

Murton winked at him. "Count on it, Sunshine."

CHAPTER TWENTY-THREE

When Virgil and Murton walked into Pete Long's room, they came face to face with his mother, Julie. She looked at the badges hanging from their necks, glanced quickly back at her son, then said, "What's this all about, Detectives. And what was all that commotion out in the hallway?"

"The commotion in the hallway was a brief exchange between myself and one of your husband's thugs," Murton said.

"He doesn't have any thugs, as you call them. They are his personal security detail. Bob's had some threats over the years and we thought it wise that he remain protected."

"How is your son doing, ma'am?" Virgil said. "We'd like to speak with him if possible."

Julie Long ignored Virgil's question, and addressed his statement instead. "Why?"

"We'd also like a word with you," Murton said.

"My son has only been awake for a few minutes now. He's having trouble with his speech. The doctors said that's to be expected. He's in no position to answer any questions."

Murton tried again. "We'd like to speak with him regarding his injuries on the ball court."

Julie's eyes narrowed a fraction, her lips parting, but she caught herself before she spoke. Murton knew what she was thinking. "That's right," he said. "You're thinking there's no real way for you to talk about it without casting suspicion on your husband."

"I'm sure I don't know what you're talking about," she said.

"Then you haven't heard what's happened to Senator Wright's son, Garrett?"

"Of course I have. It's been all over the news. What does that have to do with Bob?"

Virgil laughed out loud. "Surely you know by now who injured your son, ma'am."

"I don't know what you're talking about," she lied.

"Yes you do," Murton said, "It's written all over your face. Garrett Wright took your son, Pete, down hard on the court and inflicted the type of injury from which there is no recovery. I think you know exactly what happened to young Garrett Wright."

"And you're suggesting my family was a part of that?"

When Pete spoke his voice was dry and course. It

sounded like sandpaper being brushed against a piece of steel. "My fault."

Virgil stepped around Julie Long and moved right next to the bed. "What was that? Say that again?"

"Move away from my son, Detective. It's not a request."

"My fault," Pete croaked out again.

"He's just come out from under anesthesia," Julie said. "He doesn't even know what he's saying." She started to move toward Virgil, but Murton stopped her. "Take your hands off me this instant."

"Let's step out in the hall, Mrs. Long," Murton said.

"I will not. That's my child and you have no right to speak with him without my permission."

"He's of legal age," Murton said. "Now walk out in the hall with me like the lady I know you are, or I'll put you in restraints and walk you out myself. It's your choice."

She let Murton pull her away, looking over her shoulder the entire time. "Don't you say anything, Pete. Do you hear me, don't say a word."

VIRGIL PULLED A CHAIR OVER NEXT TO PETE'S HOSPITAL bed and sat down. "What are you trying to tell me, young man?"

Pete looked at Virgil and said, "Throat. Water. Hurts to talk."

Virgil got a glass of water and held it for Pete as he

sipped from the straw. When he was finished, Virgil set the glass down on the bedside table and waited.

"Uncle," Pete said.

"What? Start over, please. A moment ago you said it was your fault. What did you mean by that?"

"My uncle came in...showed...pictures to me. I picked him out. Uncle Ave said...he'd...take care...of everything."

"Jacob Avery is your uncle?" Virgil asked.

Pete shook his head slowly. "Not real uncle. Only... called him that. The guy in...the pictures. Uncle Ave showed me and said...everything was going...to be...okay. Have you caught him yet?"

Virgil knew Pete wasn't asking about Avery. He was asking about Garrett Wright. But he didn't have the heart to tell the young man the entire truth. "Yeah, they got him. He won't be bothering you anymore. Uncle Ave works for your father?"

Pete nodded. "He's a good man."

Virgil wasn't exactly sure how to respond to that statement.

AS THEY WERE WALKING OUT TO THE PARKING LOT, Virgil told Murton everything Pete had said. "Did you get anything out of his mom?"

"A lot of threats of lawsuits, proclamations of friends in high places, you know, that sort of thing. So, Avery—who works for Long—gets some photos, shows them to

Pete, who picks out his attacker, and then bang, Garrett Wright is dead. Shot from eight blocks away."

"That about says it."

When Virgil's phone rang again they were turning out of the hospital's parking lot. Virgil thought it was Said, calling back as promised, but it wasn't.

It was Cora.

When Virgil and Murton walked into Cora's office she glanced up for a moment, then reached into her desk drawer and pulled out a pack of cigarettes. "We've had a flurry of calls over the last thirty minutes. Care to guess what they were about?"

Murton looked around like maybe there might be a surprise attack about to happen. "You seem awfully calm. We sort of expected you to chew us out or something. You know, flaming nostrils, bulging veins in your forehead, the whole enchilada."

Cora lit a cigarette and cracked the window behind her desk. She took a few drags, then tipped the ash of her cigarette into a planter. She leaned back in her chair and said, "Oh, I was going to. Believe me. I had this big speech prepared and everything."

Virgil, who knew Cora better than anyone, could tell something was up. "So let's have it."

"I'm not going to say anything. I promised I wouldn't. I might listen though...mostly because I think it's something that I'll be able to hold in my mental managerial bank for quite some time." She pressed a button on her phone. Two seconds later the governor's door opened.

"Virgil, Murt. The governor and I would like a word with you both," Sandy said.

Murton looked at Virgil and said, "Uh oh."

Cora put her feet up on her desk, turned her head and blew a stream of smoke out the window, the smile still evident on her face.

THEY ALL SAT DOWN AT THE GOVERNOR'S ROUND conference table, a small four-top tucked into the back corner of his office. Virgil and Murton sat next to each other, with Sandy opposite Virgil and the governor opposite Murton. Once everyone was seated, the governor got right to it. "I had an interesting conversation with Bob Long. He says the two of you publicly harassed and humiliated him."

"Just doing our job, sir," Murton said.

The governor ignored him. "Bob Long is off the table. He's off your radar, he's not a suspect, he's not a person of interest, he's nothing and no one to the two of you. Can I be any more clear about that?"

Virgil turned slightly and looked at his wife...a *what the hell is going on?* sort of look.

"Don't look at her, look at me," Mac said.

Virgil snapped his head back and faced the governor.

"We'll get to whatever is going on here in a minute, but with all due respect, sir, to both you and this office, do not refer to my wife as *her*. You'll use either Sandy, or Lieutenant Governor, but I won't stand for anything less, from you or anyone else." Then, to drive his point home, "Can I be any more clear about *that*?"

"Virgil..." Sandy said.

The governor shook his head at Sandy. "No, you know what? He's absolutely right. I apologize to you both."

"Mac, what the hell is going on?" Virgil said.

"I was about to ask the two of you the same thing. I told you both that I wanted Garrett Wright's killer brought in and instead of doing that you're running around hassling the one man who is going to make mobile voting in this state—my state—a reality." He held up a finger. "No, no, let me finish. His company, together with Senator Wright, are the only ones out there right now who can push this thing through and I want it passed. Period. It will put our state on the cutting edge of voting reform all across the country. I believe other states will follow along with their local counterparts. It has the potential to reach the national level as well."

"That may be true, Mac," Virgil said. "But it won't be with Bob Long."

The governor leaned forward. "And why is that? Because Rick Said has all but bought his company out from under him?"

"And that's a bad thing?" Virgil said.

"Of course it's a bad thing...though I suppose not for

you. Said will abandon the blockchain and put all his resources into keeping his sonic drills operating at full capacity. He says he's ready to ramp up his operation and take it nation wide. Are you a part of that?"

Virgil shook his head. "No, I'm not. He made the offer some time ago, and I declined."

"Well at least you managed to get that part right."

Sandy put both of her hands on the table, palms down. "How about we all take a breath here for a second? Virgil, tell us what you know about Bob Long, and why you're interested in him when you and Murton were tasked with finding Garrett Wright's killer?"

Virgil suddenly discovered he didn't like being questioned by his own wife in an official capacity. Nevertheless, she was the lieutenant governor, and like it or not, he responded...though maybe not as tactfully as he could have. "You practically answered your own question."

"Meaning what exactly?"

"When Garrett Wright was killed, everyone immediately jumped to the conclusion that it was to send a message to his father, the message being to back off of the mobile voting bill."

"And you're saying that's not the case?" Sandy asked.

Virgil took a deep breath. "Yes and no. It's...complicated. Garrett Wright was not only a victim, he was a perpetrator as well."

"A perpetrator in what crime?" The governor asked, his voice tight.

"In the assault on Bob Long's son, Pete," Murton said.

"He is now, by all accounts, permanently paralyzed from the waist down because of an attack by Wright on a basketball court."

Sandy leaned forward. "Wait, that doesn't make any sense. You're saying that Bob Long killed Senator Wright's son, Garrett, because he was responsible for crippling Pete?"

"Again, yes and no," Virgil said. "First, Bob Long didn't actually pull the trigger. One of his men did. We think we know who, and I'll get to that in a minute. We believe that Garrett Wright's death was a result of two things that happened back to back: One, the injury he caused to Pete Long on the court, and two, as a way to apply pressure to the senator to keep the bill moving on the floor."

The governor sat back and ran his fingers through his hair. "That doesn't make any sense whatsoever. Wright was the one pushing the bill. He and I have had many conversations about it over the last few weeks and he's all for it."

"He's for it alright," Murton said. "But not for the reasons you think."

"Explain that," the governor said. He snapped it at him.

Murton showed no emotion at the governor's outburst. "He was being blackmailed, Mac. He never wanted the bill to hit the floor. As a point of fact, he was totally against it."

"Why?" the governor said, much softer now.

"Because he didn't want to go to jail for solicitation of

a minor child," Virgil said. "Though we haven't yet seen it, we have it on good authority that there are photographs of the senator engaging in sexual activity with a minor, all of it set up in advance by Bob Long to get the senator to push the bill."

"Who's your source?" Sandy asked.

Virgil looked at his wife and said, "Wright's own daughter."

The governor folded his arms on the table and put his head down. When he raised himself back up, he looked at Virgil and Murton and said, "Why was he against it? Wright? The bill?"

"We interviewed his daughter, Melissa," Virgil said. "She told us how her brother intentionally injured Pete, and how she'd overheard her parents fighting about the encounter the senator had with the young woman. During that conversation she said her father felt that it would disenfranchise the voters."

"Oh, bullshit," Mac said.

"We're simply telling you what she told us," Murton said.

"No, no, that's not what I mean. I'm talking about the whole disenfranchise part. It's not true. Show me a registered voter who doesn't have a cell phone and I'll show you my ass." Then to Sandy: "Sorry."

Sandy smiled at him.

"The whole thing is done with an app," Mac said. "And a free one, at that. I've seen the demonstrations and our technical people have been over it with a fine-toothed comb. It's encrypted and totally secure."

Murton looked down and sort of shook his head. "Uh, yeah, about that..."

THE GOVERNOR REMOVED HIS FACE FROM HIS HANDS. "Please, Murt, I'm begging you, if this is some sort of joke..."

"It's not a joke, sir. We suspect the demonstrations you and your technical people saw were only part of what the app can do. But every single person who downloads the final version will be giving access of all their personal information, financial information, passwords...essentially everything on their phone to Ar-Tell without their knowledge."

"Bob Long isn't that smart," the governor said.

"That's just it, Mac," Virgil said. "Becky told us the way the code is buried in the system, she doesn't think Ar-Tell put it there."

"Who did?" The governor asked.

"We have no idea," Murton said.

Virgil shot Murton the side eye, but didn't say anything.

"This is a goddamned disaster," the governor said. "I'm willing to entertain suggestions on how to proceed."

"Avery is the key that unlocks everything," Virgil said. "If we can get to him, we can get to Long, assuming you've changed your mind about him being off the table and the radar and all that." He let a hint of sarcasm creep into his voice.

The governor pointed a finger at Virgil. "You know, I'm beginning to understand the love-hate relationship Cora has with you."

Virgil smiled. "It's all an act. She loves me."

The governor waved them out. "Go do your jobs."

Sandy looked at the governor. "If there's nothing else, Mac? I have to prepare my remarks for Garrett Wright's funeral."

The governor shook his head. "No, that's all for now." Then as the three of them were walking toward the door, "And for the love of God, someone please tell that woman it's illegal to smoke inside a state building."

WHEN THEY WALKED OUT OF THE GOVERNOR'S OFFICE, Cora looked up, put a fake smile on her face and said, "How'd that go, hotshots?"

Virgil and Murton looked at each other. "It went well," Murton said. "One of us is supposed to tell you that it's illegal to smoke inside a state building, but you didn't hear it from me."

"Me either," Virgil said. "He told me you loved me, though."

"He's mistaken," Cora replied. Then she looked at Sandy. "What about you? Anything clever to say?"

Sandy tilted her head. "Nope, but as a casual observation, I think your plant is on fire a little."

Cora looked at her planter and saw the smoke. "Shit." She dumped her coffee on the smoldering cigarette butt and it made a short little hiss like a snake. "I think I should quit."

Once they were out in the hallway, Murton said, "You think she meant quit smoking or quit her job?"

"I think she meant smoking," Virgil said. "She'd never leave Mac."

"You know," Murton said, "when we first walked in and she said mental managerial bank...I don't think she meant to use the word managerial. I think she was about to say master—"

Sandy punched him on the arm. "Murton!"

CHAPTER TWENTY-FOUR

By the close of business Said and his hedge fund managers had wrangled control of Bob Long's company right out from under him. Bob's wife, Julie, was livid.

"How could you let this happen?" She hissed it at him. They were at their home, Pete still in the hospital, but awake, alert and in no immediate danger. The Long's loved their son, but the hospital staff encouraged them to go home and get some much needed rest. The doctor told them it'd be good for Pete as well. "He doesn't need to see you both sitting here worrying over him. He needs to rest as much as possible."

They took the doctor's advice, but unfortunately, Bob wasn't getting any rest at all. Julie was on the offensive. "It all happened so fast," he said. His words were slurred from the scotch he'd been drinking since they'd arrived home. "I was distracted with everything going on with Pete."

"Oh, bullshit. The only time you ever cared about Pete was when he was on the court, making you look good."

"That's not true and it's a cruel thing to say."

"It is true," Julie said. "And the truth hurts, doesn't it? Do you know how many times people laughed behind your back when you'd stand up and shout, 'That's my boy, that's my boy.' Everything isn't about you, Bob, no matter how hard you try to make yourself feel like it is."

Bob had been drinking so much he was starting to repeat himself. "That's not true. Nobody laughs at me. I'll figure a way out of all this."

"Out of what? We're broke now and it's all your fault."

"Is that what we're talking about? Money?"

"Of course that's what we're talking about, you idiot. It's all over the news. The financial anchors are calling you the laughingstock of the stock market."

"They are not," Bob said, though when he glanced at the television in the corner he did see two analysts laughing about something. He couldn't hear what was being said because the sound was muted.

"Oh yeah," Julie said. "I'll bet Rick Said is laughing his ass off right now. What were you thinking dumping all those shares into the market?"

"I wasn't thinking...I was raising capital for the blockchain to implement the mobile voting platform. You know this. Everything was going exactly as planned until

—" Long's phone buzzed at him and he pulled it out, answered without looking at the screen and shouted, "What?"

Then the color went out of his face and he dropped his glass on the floor where it shattered to pieces, the scotch splashing against the furniture and rolling down in droplets just like the tears that suddenly began to spill from his eyes.

ROBERT HAD THE NIGHT OFF FROM THE BAR, SO VIRGIL and Sandy invited him over to have dinner with everyone.

"I know it impolite to ask, me, but what are you having?"

"Thought we'd grill up some chicken, why?"

"You not gonna let Virgil grill the chicken are you?" He put a little emphasis on the word grill.

"I was sort of hoping you could give him some pointers," Sandy said.

"Oh boy. Okay. I be there as quick as I can, me. Tell Huma to try and keep him distracted. Don't even let him light the grill, no. Hide the matches, or someting. Do whatever you have to do, you."

Sandy laughed and told him not to worry. They'd wait for him. She went out on the deck and sat down. Murton and Becky were there as well, and even though Virgil was doing his level best not to talk about work, this time it was Sandy who raised the issue.

She wrapped her arm inside of Virgil's, looked at Murton and said, "Is it my imagination, or did this one here look a little uncomfortable when I was acting in my official capacity earlier in the governor's office?"

"I'm staying out of it," Murton said. "But yes."

Virgil shook his head. "Not true at all. I was fine," he lied. "Besides, you were the one who said, 'uh oh,' not me."

"I was speaking on your behalf," Murton said. "It's what partners do for each other when they know the other is in distress."

"I wasn't in distress."

"Then how about explaining the looks on your faces?" Sandy said.

Virgil shrugged. "It was a 'what the heck is going on here' look."

"That's not the look I was referring to," Sandy said. "Mac missed it, but I didn't. I'm talking about the look you and Murton gave each other when we were discussing the hidden code inside the mobile voting app."

Becky punched Murton in the arm. "Oh my God. You guys didn't tell them?"

"Tell us what?" Sandy said, unraveling herself from Virgil's arm. "What's going on?"

"How about we light the grill?" Virgil said. "I'm getting hungry."

"Nobody's lighting anything until I get some answers," Sandy said.

Virgil stood and looked at Sandy. "Maybe we should talk about this in private."

"Why? Clearly Murton and Becky already know whatever it is you're not telling me."

Virgil sat back down. "Okay, fair enough, but you have to remember Becky works for me and Murt. And Murt and I work for the state."

"That's a real news flash, Virg," Sandy said. "Now quit stalling and spill it."

"We didn't tell you because if we did, then you'd feel obligated to tell Mac."

"And Mac can't know whatever it is you're not saying?"

"That's right," Virgil said. "It's a plausible deniability thing. One that extends to you as well."

This time Sandy stood up. "Excuse me for a moment."

"Where are you going?" Virgil said.

"To think."

"You want me to light the grill?"

"No. Do not light the grill. Don't even look at the grill." She walked away, down off the deck, and toward the pond.

Murton looked at Virgil and said, "Are you going to tell her?"

Virgil waited a few seconds before he answered. During the pause, Becky jumped in and said, "I think you have to, Jonesy. She's your wife."

"She's also the lieutenant governor. If I tell her about the code, she'd be obligated to tell Mac."

"I think you're both missing the point," Murton said.

"She already knows there's a piece out of place. If Mac found out she knew something, even if she didn't know the entire truth, it wouldn't go over well...probably for any of us."

When Sandy came back up on the deck, she sat down and took Virgil's hand in her own. "I knew this day or this type of thing would happen eventually...that there would be some sort of conflict between us as a couple, and us as two people who work for the state under the leadership of the same man."

"Me too," Virgil said.

Sandy squeezed his hand. "Good. Then hear me when I say this: You are my husband. You guys are my family. And family always comes first. Always. That means whatever you know, I know. What happens after that is something we'll figure out together."

They all spent a few seconds looking at each other, then Virgil pointed at Becky with his chin and said, "Becks...go ahead."

Becky spent the next few minutes telling Sandy what she'd learned after reviewing the code. When Sandy finally knew the whole story, she shook her head and said, "I wish I didn't hear any of that."

Just then Delroy and Robert came around the corner. "Heard any of what?" Robert said. Then without waiting for an answer, he looked at Sandy and said, "I see you didn't let him light da grill, you. Good work, mon."

When Sandy didn't answer, Delroy took stock of the situation and said, "What going on, here? Everyone look like maybe they seen a ghost or someting. Where's my lovely Huma Moon, by da way?"

"She's inside with the boys," Sandy said. "I'm sure she's eager to see you."

Delroy laughed his big Jamaican laugh and said, "Yeah, mon. Who wouldn't be?"

ROBERT WAS DEMONSTRATING THE PROPER WAY TO KEEP the grill at the right temperature so the chicken wouldn't burn to a crisp as it usually did whenever Virgil tried to cook it. "Da secret, mon, is to cook it slow. It not a hamburger or a steak, no. And you got to keep the lid closed. If you do, it help seal da juices inside, mon."

Virgil's phone buzzed and he pulled it out. "Jones."

"Jonesy, it's Rick. I'm wondering if we might have a word?"

Virgil thought Said sounded happy enough, regardless of their previous conversation. "Sure, Rick, but listen... that business about Patty? I'm sorry. You were absolutely right. I was out of line."

There was a fractional pause before Said answered, but when he did, his voice was calm and even. "All is forgiven. But don't do it again. I've got this great system in place. It's called voicemail. If you leave me one and tell me it's urgent, I'll see it and get back with you as soon as is humanly possible."

"Got it," Virgil said.

"The caveat to that though is this: If it *is* about Patty, I want to know no matter what."

"Got it," Virgil said again. "So what's up?"

"Everything. I met with the board of Ar-Tell. My company now has a controlling interest and I'll be acting as the CEO until I can find someone to permanently fill the position. I'll remain as chairman of the board."

"Congratulations," Virgil said. "Hold on a moment, will you?" He turned to Robert and said, "Can you take over here? I've got to talk to someone for a minute?"

"Ya, mon. Let the professionals do their ting."

Virgil stepped off the deck and wandered down into the backyard. "Sorry," he said back into the phone. "Where were we?"

"You had just congratulated me. So, thank you. It wasn't easy, it cost me a fortune, but my finance people tell me if we play our cards right, we'll be fine. Anyway, I'm not worried, mostly because I just got off the phone with the governor. He wants me to keep the mobile voting platform in place. I've already reviewed the platform and the people, and I think with a little strategic restructuring, I can have Ar-Tell do both. They can keep producing the AI boxes we need for the drilling rigs, and move forward with the blockchain mobile voting system."

"That's great," Virgil said without inflection.

"Yeah, Mac was absolutely thrilled. You, on the other hand, sound like I may have recited my grocery list or something."

"No, no, sorry, I've got a lot on my plate right now."

"Who doesn't?"

"Listen, Rick, how soon will Ar-Tell—"

Said interrupted him. "See, I always knew you were a businessman at heart. Don't worry, partner, the drilling operation will continue uninterrupted. I've already made sure of that."

"That's great news, Rick, but it wasn't what I was going to ask. How soon will Ar-Tell be pushing this mobile voting app out to the people?"

"It's already out there. Granted, it's in the beta stage so we can get the bugs worked out, but it's essentially ready to go. Have to ramp up the AI boxes first because we'll need that revenue for the mobile voting, but it should all work out. Eventually there'll be a big campaign to inform the general public and all that. Mac and Sandy and I are meeting tomorrow to discuss the particulars."

"Huh."

"What?"

"Nothing...she didn't say anything to me, is all."

"That's because she might not know yet. I just got off the phone with Mac. He said he was going to call her."

Virgil spun around and looked at the house. He saw Sandy standing at the edge of the deck, her phone to her ear. "Yeah, I think she's speaking with him now as a matter of fact."

"Yeah, that sounds right. Boy that's a shame about the Long's huh?"

"Rubbing salt into the wound you created, Rick?"

Said waited a moment before he spoke. "I won't hold

that last statement against you, Jonesy, because you clearly don't know what I meant."

"What did you mean?"

"I was speaking of Pete Long, and his father, Bob. They're both dead."

This time it was Virgil who paused. "Hey, Jonesy, you with me?"

"What happened?" Virgil said.

"I don't have all the particulars," Said said. "But apparently Pete had a blood clot that developed during or after his surgery. He had a massive stroke and died at the hospital."

"Jesus. What happened to Long? Bob, I mean?"

"I guess both Long, and his wife, Julie, were at home when they got the news. Looks like Bob had been drinking pretty heavily. Anyway, the medical people said the combination of alcohol and stress caused him to have a massive heart attack. Julie was driving and when she looked over and saw him in distress she lost control of the car and drove right down into the ravine. They rolled a few times and totaled their Benz. They had their security detail following them...they're the ones who called it in. Anyway, he was pronounced DOA at the hospital."

"And Julie?"

"She came out of it okay. She was buckled in, but Bob wasn't, so...she'll be all right. A few minor cuts and abrasions, some pulled muscles, I guess, but she'll make it. Her whole family is gone now though. Listen, I've got to run. Lots to do. Let's try to get together next week and talk about Shelby County. Go over the numbers and all that."

Virgil said they would, then finished the call and walked back up to the house. Sandy was wrapping up her call with the governor.

"He tell you about the Long's?" Virgil said.

Sandy nodded. "I've got a meeting tomorrow with Said and the governor. They want this app out as soon as possible. What am I going to tell them, Virgil?"

Virgil put his arm around his wife. "I don't know yet. Let's see how it all plays out."

Robert turned from the grill and said. "Time to eat. Da chicken, mon...it look perfect. What a surprise, no?"

CHAPTER TWENTY-FIVE

The timing worked in Avery's favor and he dumped the building superintendent's body in the woods near the back of Bob Long's property, finally glad to be rid of the damned thing. When he pulled back out on the road he turned toward the Long's house. A little house cleaning was in order, and Avery knew exactly what he was going to do. And those other three nut jobs on his security staff? They didn't bother him. He could take them out either from a distance, or up close and personal. He was as good with a side arm as he was with his long guns. And he was quick. They sat around and played cards all day, while Avery stayed sharp at the range. Former Army Rangers? Yes. In shape, sharp, and ready for anything? Hardly. All three were a joke, and they'd never know what hit them.

He turned into the Long's drive—the driveway was long...something that good ol' Bob loved to joke about—

and made his way up to the house. There were no cars anywhere, the garage was empty, and the front door hung open like the mouth of an old man who had a bad tooth.

He'd come fully prepared to make a mess. He had flash-bangs on his belt, zip-ties in his pocket, two 1911 style handguns attached to holsters strapped to his thighs, and a bulletproof vest.

None of it was necessary though. When he walked inside, he discovered no one was home. He found a broken glass on the tiled floor, and a small puddle of bourbon or scotch with little shards of glass floating on the surface of the oily liquid.

He thought, *Huh. Gonna be easier than I thought.*

He hurried back out to the car, grabbed his rifle case, and ran through the house and up the stairs. The gun safe was in the back of the massive master closet. As former head of security, Avery knew the combination. Unless they'd already changed it, that is.

They hadn't.

He pulled the heavy door open, then popped his case. He hated to part with the rifle, but he'd known all along that it might come to this. He removed one of the rifles from the safe, the one identical to his own and set it aside, then put his in its place. The one from the safe went into the carrying case and once all that was done, Avery closed everything back up, ran down the stairs, and into Long's office. He took the painting off the wall...a fake of some kind meant to impress anyone who knew nothing about art, and punched in the key code for the wall safe.

The pictures were right there, in a manila envelope sitting on top of a few stacks of cash. Avery thought about taking the money, but he didn't need it, so he left it alone. He grabbed the envelope, closed the wall safe, put the painting back, hopped into his car, and drove away.

After dinner, Virgil pulled Robert aside and asked if he could speak with him in private.

"Yeah, mon. Everyting irie?"

"That's what I was hoping you could tell me." Robert had a puzzled expression on his face, one Virgil didn't often see. "You up for a little stroll?"

"Yeah, mon. Always."

They walked down near the pond, next to Mason's cross and stood quietly for a few moments, Virgil gathering his thoughts.

When he turned to his friend, he saw him looking at the cross. Virgil looked as well, but didn't see anything. "You and Delroy have known each other a long time, haven't you?"

Robert nodded. "Oh yeah. We go all da way back, mon."

"Was there ever a time in your lives that you guys weren't friends?"

"What you mean, you?"

"I mean, say, as young men, or adults even, before you came to thc states...did you guys always work together or was there a time when maybe you didn't see each other for a while?"

Robert put the puzzle back on his face. "No, mon, no. Me and Delroy, we like two peas from da same pod. I thought you knew dat, you."

"I did...I do. I was wondering about something though. Maybe it's none of my business..."

"Dat mean maybe it is, den, no?"

Virgil loved the simple Jamaican logic. "I suppose that's one way of looking at it."

"You know how to dance, you?"

The shift in the conversation caught Virgil off guard. "Excuse me?"

"I asked if you know how to dance, you."

"Why would you ask me that?"

"Because you said you wanted to talk to me about someting and whatever it is, you haven't said it yet, mon."

"Did Delroy ever have a child? Does he have a child?"

Robert turned back toward the water, tipped his head to the side and nodded at the same time. When he spoke, his voice was soft and quiet. "How'd you know about that, you?"

"I managed to put a few pieces together during a previous conversation."

"With Delroy?"

"Not so much," Virgil said.

Robert was still staring at the water. He waited a long

time before he spoke. "I know you remember dat night when we were all here for you, mon. Da moon was out, da torches were lit, dat woman of yours look as lovely as I've ever seen."

"You're speaking of when I was on the meds, aren't you?"

"Yeah, mon. Meds maybe not the right word though. More like poison, no?"

"I guess so. They helped me though, Robert. They got me through something that I wouldn't have been able to handle without."

"And they also took hold of you too."

"Yes, they did, but that's all in the past now. Why are you bringing up that night?"

"Because of this, mon: Do you remember what I did, me, da way I got in the water."

"Of course."

"But at the time you didn't know. You had to ask Delroy. He told you, *He pray for you.*"

"I don't understand what you're trying to tell me, Robert."

"I'm not trying to tell you, Virgil. I am telling you. It my way, is all, mon. I pray for Delroy every single day. Putting dat shirt under da willow tree was his idea."

"I know. It was a beautiful gift."

"It more dan dat, mon, and you know it. It not the first time it ever happen either, no."

"You're saying Delroy lost a child and buried their clothing under a tree?"

Robert again took a long time before he answered, and Virgil let him. If he knew anything about Jamaicans, it was that they couldn't be rushed.

"These questions you have, I don't need to know why you ask them, me. To be true, I don't even tink I should be da one to answer."

"I don't think Delroy wants to talk about it."

"Den maybe you ask someone else, you."

"Who?"

Robert turned and looked over Virgil's shoulder. "Maybe da man standing right behind you. If you get the chance, please tell him how much I miss him. I tink I go back up to the house and say goodnight to everyone now."

Robert walked away and when Virgil turned, he saw his father standing next to the cross.

THE FIRST TIME HE EVER SAW HIS DEAD FATHER UNDER the willow tree, Virgil was high as a kite on prescription pain medicine and after the encounter he spent a long time questioning himself about the validity of the event. In the beginning, when he first appeared, it was Mason who spoke first, not Virgil. But over the course of the years, when Mason appeared to him, sometimes it was Virgil who would speak first. But not this time.

"He's a fine man, that Robert."

"He wanted me to tell you how much he misses you."

"I see you're starting to put it all together," Mason said. He was eating an apple.

"Am I?" Then, "I don't think I've ever seen you eat before. Is that an apple?"

"It is. It's good too. I heard what you and Robert said to each other. It seems as though you'd have, at a minimum, a rudimentary understanding of the situation."

"Delroy lost a child at some point in his life."

Mason nodded, the look on his face blank. "That's right. It was a long time ago."

"Did you know about this...before, you know..."

"When my body was still alive? It's okay to say the words, Son."

"It might be okay, but it isn't exactly easy. But yes, that's what I was referring to."

"No, I didn't. He never told me. Neither did Robert if you were going to ask that too."

"What can you tell me about it?"

Mason seemed to consider the request, the way a politician might when asked a difficult question before a room full of reporters. "I suppose I can tell you everything. The real question is should I tell you anything, and if so, what parts, and why?"

"Why would you hold any of it back?" Virgil asked.

"Because there are things yet to happen, Virg. Things that have to play out, and it's not my place to interfere."

The conversations Virgil had with his father often felt circular in nature, but this time he felt like he finally had his father on the ropes and boxed into a corner...which was not an easy thing to do, or even admit to himself. Nevertheless, he pushed forward. "But you yourself told me—on more than one occasion, I might add—that everything happens at once...is happening at once."

Mason took another bite of his apple, tucked the fruit into the corner of his cheek and said, "That I did."

"And even though that still doesn't make sense to me, I'd like to know what you know about Delroy's child."

"Why?" Mason asked. "What would you do with the information?"

The question caught Virgil off guard. His father had done a little duck and cover and was now out of the corner, no longer on the ropes, but back in the middle of the ring. "I guess I'm not sure. Try to be a better friend to him. Be more supportive. Things like that."

"And you need to know about what happened to his child in order to do that? What does that say about the nature of your friendship as it stands right now?"

Virgil was getting frustrated. "I don't think it says anything. Delroy is one of the finest humans I've ever known."

"Me too," Mason said.

"Last time we spoke you said something to the effect of every major case I've ever worked has put either my family or friends in direct grave danger. Do I have that right?"

"You do. That's what I said."

"Are you trying to tell me that Delroy is in some sort of danger?"

"No, Son, he isn't. But he needs you."

"I don't understand."

"You will, when the time comes."

Virgil laughed out loud. "This from the guy who says time isn't real and everything happens all at once?"

Mason let out a little chuckle, the way a parent might when a child asks where babies come from. "I told you that time isn't real, and that's true because it's the only way I could say it that makes sense from your perspective."

"I hate to be the one to point it out to you, but it still doesn't make any sense."

"That's because it's so complex. Time—if that's what we're calling it, and I guess we are—isn't only linear. There's so much more than *right now*...or before and after for that matter. Time has length, and width, and depth and so many different dimensions that the best physicists in the world won't discover or understand for eons."

"But you do?" Virgil said.

Mason nodded. "In some ways, yes. But I find I have a better understanding of events past, over those about to take place."

"Even though, according to you, everything is happening at once."

"It's difficult to explain in ways you'd understand, Son."

"How about you try?"

"I thought you wanted to know about Delroy?" Mason said.

Virgil flapped his arms in the air and let them fall to his sides. "Of course I do. But you keep going off on this weird tangent about the mysterious and complex nature of all things magical and mystical about the universe."

Mason tipped a finger at him. "And that right there is why you can't understand. I'm not going off on a tangent, as you say. I'm trying to help you grasp the bigger picture."

"Maybe I don't want the bigger picture right now. Maybe all I want is this one little nugget of information. Maybe that's all I need to help a friend."

"That's a lot of maybes. And maybe you're wrong, Virg. Let me ask you this: How's Wyatt? Your little miracle boy, as you and Sandy call him."

A little heat went out of Virgil's voice. "He's the best, Dad. The absolute best."

"That he is," Mason said. "Do you remember the first time you saw him? In the park, when you were chasing him up that hill?"

Virgil nodded. "Yes, of course. I didn't think it was real at the time."

"But now you do?"

"Yeah, I do."

"Have you ever asked yourself why any of that happened?"

This time it was Virgil who waited a few minutes before he answered. Finally, he said, "I have."

"And?"

"It was a warning. He told me that if I didn't get off the pills I was going to die."

"And on whose behalf do you think he was speaking?"

"I don't understand the question."

"I think you do. Was he worried about his father to be? Yes. But he was also worried about whether or not he'd get a chance to be with his family. He was looking out for himself, Virg, even before he was born. We all are. We all do. It never stops."

"And this has to do with Delroy how, exactly?"

Mason shook his head. When he spoke, his voice took on a robotic tone, as if the words were coming through him instead of from him. "When Delroy was still living in Jamaica, he and his girlfriend at the time lost a child, a baby girl. She died at birth. He carried her into the hills and he and Robert buried her themselves. They planted a tree over her grave."

Virgil didn't know why he asked the next question, but he did anyway. "What kind of tree?"

"A pond apple tree, Virg." He held the apple up for a second. "Where do you think I got this?" He took a final bite of his apple and tossed the core into Virgil's fire pit. What he said next so surprised Virgil he had to sit down.

"Jacob Avery isn't the person you think he is, Son."

"Then who is he?"

"He's a man, just like you, with a job to do. Though I will admit he's taking his sweet time to do it."

"What's his job?"

"It'll come to you. Stay tuned, Virg."

CHAPTER TWENTY-SIX

The next morning Virgil and Sandy drove into the city together. He'd drop her at the statehouse before going to the bar—Emily Baker was still out on sick leave—and it was a chance for them to discuss how she was going to handle the meeting with the governor and Said.

"I'm not exactly sure," Sandy said. "In fact, you can remove the word exactly from my last statement. The truth is, I'm not sure at all."

"Maybe if the whole thing could be delayed somehow," Virgil said. "Isn't there some sort of procedural trickery you could use to delay the vote?"

"*Trickery?*"

"You know what I mean. At least until we figure out what's going on."

"It's not that simple, Virgil. I think the vote is going to

go forward, and based on what I'm hearing, it's going to be close. Very close."

They talked it back and forth all the way to the statehouse, and by the time they arrived, a solution to Sandy's dilemma still had not presented itself. Virgil did the only thing he could do. He kissed her goodbye and wished her luck.

BECKY HAD STAYED UP ALL NIGHT—AT VIRGIL'S request. The request wasn't actually that she not go to sleep—the request was for her to find a phone number by any means possible. She finally had it, though it wasn't because she'd actually found what she was looking for...it happened because the people the number belonged to noticed that she was looking.

Virgil and Murton were sitting on the sofa in Becky's office above the bar. Murton had stayed with Becky because he didn't want her to be alone all night, and he sat with his arms crossed, his chin resting against his chest. Virgil had arrived an hour or so ago. He kept glancing at the clock on the wall, then at Becky, then the telephone. He kept repeating the same process until Becky told him to knock it off.

"You're making me dizzy," she told him.

"And you're preventing me from getting any sleep," Murton added without lifting his head.

"They said they were going to call at seven. That was fifteen minutes ago. Are you sure that's what they said?"

Becky gave him a look. "Yes, I'm sure. They sent it via text, so I've got it in writing. I showed it to you twice already."

"Yeah, yeah," Virgil waved her off.

"Don't yeah, yeah me, mister. I'm the one who's been up all night trying to find what you wanted. I would have much rather been at home, in my own bed and—"

The ringing of the phone cut her off. She hit the speaker button and said, "Hello?"

"Becky?"

"Yes. To whom am I speaking?"

"You should know...you've been looking for a way to contact us all night. Don't be frustrated it took you so long. We're good, and we're careful."

Virgil and Murton were still on the sofa, but they were both now leaning forward, listening.

"I'm not frustrated," Becky said. "I'm tired."

"Yes...fatigue. The enemy of coders all across the globe. I can tell that you've got me on speaker. Can I assume you're not alone?"

"I'm not," Becky said.

"Nor am I. Do you have the ability to secure the line at your end? We are secure here."

"We are too," Becky said. "I've got Virgil and Murton here with me."

"Wonderful. Well, I imagine I'm not the one you want to speak with, so I'll back away now, but before I do, I want you to know how impressed we were not long ago when you found an open socket layer, then bounced that packet through Ukraine. Not many people could have done that so quickly, and as skillfully as you."

"Thank you," Becky said.

"You're welcome. Let me put her on now. I'm starting to get the evil eye over here."

"I'M GUESSING YOU'VE GOT MORE THAN A FEW questions."

"Hello, Nichole," Virgil said. "And you're right. We do."

"Fire away, then. But before you do, I hope you haven't prejudged us."

Virgil thought for a moment before he responded. "I wouldn't say that...that we've prejudged you. But we're all having a hard time understanding how and why you and your brother are involved in all of this."

"The how part is simple, and I'll get to that in a moment. The why is a bit more complex. But before we get into any of it, I need to know something from you."

"What's that?"

"Actually, Becky will probably have to answer. How did you trace it back to us? The hidden code?"

"We didn't actually trace it back," Becky said. "But you should tell your brother that while his coding is excellent, like a poker player, he has his tells. The code...it's practically signed."

In the background, over the speaker, they heard an oriental voice say, "See? What Wu say? Nobody ever listen to me."

"Not now, Wu," Nichole said. Then back into the phone, "How we got involved, Virgil, was simple. One of the engineers at Ar-Tell—their Chief Technology Officer, if I'm not mistaken—put out a request for our help on the dark net. Well, not our help specifically...it was more like a general request, and we responded."

"A request for what?"

"The coding for the AI boxes that run your sonic drill rigs. How's everything going out there at the site, by the way? Patty doing well?"

"Yes, Patty is fine and the cultural center is all but complete, thanks to your foundation's contribution."

"Excellent," Nichole said. "Then let me ask you this: Why do you sound so confused about my answer?"

"Probably because we had no idea that your brother and Wu wrote the code for Ar-Tell. To be honest, I didn't even know about the boxes until a few days ago."

"The Ar-Tell people worked on it for almost sixteen months and got absolutely nowhere," Nicky said in the background. "They were ready to give up."

"That's right," Wu said. "Me and Nicky had the proper coding in place, then up and running in less than eight weeks. It was a slice of pie."

"It's piece of cake, Wu," Nicky said.

Wu laughed. "He fall for that one every time."

"Did Rick Said know about any of this?" Virgil said.

"Not to our knowledge," Nichole said. "Those lease payments he makes to Ar-Tell every month for our code on the boxes? A full seventy-five percent of it comes back to us, although given what's happened over the last few days, I imagine that will have to be renegotiated."

"You're speaking of Said taking over Ar-Tell?"

"Yes, among other things."

"What other things?" Virgil said.

"Things that have yet to happen," Nichole said.

Virgil thought the conversation was starting to sound like the ones he often had with his father. "Like what?"

"Let me put it this way, and Becky please, no disrespect, but you didn't catch everything when you examined the code. Nicky wrote it with one goal in mind the entire time. He wanted you to find it, and he wanted you to know that it came from us."

"Why?" Becky asked.

This time it was Nicky who answered. "Because when Ar-Tell wanted to implement the blockchain for mobile voting, they needed help with that too. Who do you think they turned to?"

"You and Wu put the blockchain together?"

"We write app as well," Wu said.

"None of that answers Becky's question," Murton said.

"Hello Murton. You still owe Wu."

"I know, I know," Murton said. "I'm still trying to figure out how to pay you back for saving my life."

"Maybe someday you return the favor, though Wu hope it never come to that."

"Me too," Murton said. "So, Becky's question? Why did you want us to know that it all leads back to you guys?"

"We only found out at the last minute that Bob Long and his company were getting ready to screw us," Nichole said. "We had no idea that he was going to abandon the AI boxes. That income, as you can imagine, is significant. We count on it to keep both our humanitarian efforts here on the island in place, as well as the future funding for the cultural center. We knew Said was getting ready to ramp up the sonic drilling and put it out there for the world. It would have been a windfall for us."

"It's not like you need the money, Nichole," Virgil said.

"No, but you know how it is, Virgil. Nicky and Wu need something to do. Plus, as any good financial advisor will tell you, you never dip into the principal. Anyway, they had the blockchain built and ready to go. The only thing they were waiting for was the app itself. That's when we heard that Long was going to abandon the AI boxes. So Nicky and Wu dropped a little code in there that makes it look like the app is stealing everyone's personal and financial information and sending it to our servers. There's big, big money in identity theft these days."

Becky caught it. "What do you mean makes it look like?"

"Do you have your computer up?" Nicky asked.

"What do you think?" Becky said.

"Go into the app's directory and find the file called PB-TTI-M. Let me know when you've found it."

Everyone sat quietly on both ends of the phone while Becky did her search. After a minute or so, she had it. "Okay, I've got it."

"Alright, stand by while I create a temporary key. The files are encrypted."

A minute or so later the key came through. "Got it," Becky said.

"Good. Open the file and look at line, uh..."

Nicky snapped his fingers a couple of times and Wu said, "Fourteen hundred and thirty seven."

Becky scrolled down to the proper line and looked at the screen. She studied it for a moment then said, "Huh."

"What does that mean?" Virgil said.

"Just a second," Becky said. "I need to ping this and verify it."

"What does that mean?" Virgil said again.

"Please stop asking me that. It'd take longer to explain than to do it."

Virgil sat back and crossed his arms. He let out a little huff.

"Don't get your testicles in a twist, Virgil," Nicky said. "I'll answer your questions while Becky is verifying what we've told her."

"My testicles are not twisted," Virgil said. He actually had a little whine in his voice.

"Then quit huffing like a teenage girl. Becky is sending

out a signal to a server...it's called a ping. The ping will verify where the server is located, which is where the information would end up if anyone were to use the app. It will also send a sample data set of the type of information collected."

"Okay," Virgil said. "Although I don't know why Becky couldn't have told me that."

Becky ignored him as she studied the screen. When she finally figured it out, she said, "Man, you guys are amazing. Do you think it will work?"

"Will what work?" Murton asked.

"It work," Wu said. "We've been testing out here on the island for over a month. So far so well."

"It's so far, so good, Wu," Nicky said.

"Every. Single. Time." Wu said.

Even Murton was starting to get annoyed. "Will someone please tell us what's going on?"

"THEY'RE NOT STEALING ANYONE'S PERSONAL OR financial information," Becky said. "They only wanted it to look like they were."

"Why?"

"We've already answered that," Nichole said. "Bob Long tried to screw us over on the AI box leases. So we played along, built his system, and dropped our code in there so it would look like that's what he was doing."

"But here's what I don't understand," Virgil said. "Bob

Long is dead, Rick Said has control of Ar-Tell, and he intends to go forward with the blockchain mobile voting. If he does, he'll be accused of stealing private information from individuals all over the state."

"No he won't," Becky said. "The only information the app collects is the type of phone, its processing power, and location. No different from most any other app on your phone right now."

"Then why bother?" Murton said. "Sounds like a whole lot of work for nothing."

"Because this isn't only about mobile voting in the state of Indiana," Nichole said. "That can still happen, and I hope it does, but this is bigger than that. Much bigger."

"Bigger how?"

Becky turned in her chair and faced Virgil and Murton. "They're rebuilding the Internet."

"I told you she was good," Nicky said.

"Wu not argue."

Virgil shook his head. "What? How is that even possible? It sounds like something you'd read in a novel or something."

"It's completely possible, Virgil," Nichole said. "Our web, unlike the current one, will be decentralized, using connected devices to create a new and alternative framework for the Internet that bypasses major tech companies by using the computing resources found in everyday life... like smartphones."

"She's right," Nicky said. "There's more power in one

single smartphone than all the computers they used to put a man on the moon...if you believe they did, that is. I'm a believer, but I'm just saying. Anyway, hook millions of those together and you'll provide an alternative foundation meant to take back control from powerful Internet giants like Google, Facebook, and Twitter, while also creating a more secure and private system.

"Look at it this way: The Internet's data is currently managed largely on centralized, private servers owned by various large companies, what everyone now calls The Cloud. Google, Amazon, Microsoft and a handful of other companies operate these systems, providing the backbone both for their own services and for those of others. All we're doing is providing an alternative method of accessing the Internet without relying on a tech giant... or giants to let us."

"Sort of sounds like that show on HBO," Murton said. "What's it called?"

"Silicon Valley," Wu said. "Where you think we get idea?"

"One last question," Virgil said. "No one knew Said was going to make a run on Ar-Tell until it was actually happening. What would you have done if he hadn't been successful, or if Bob Long hadn't died and still controlled the company?"

"Simple," Nichole said. "Nicky...?"

"Becky, open the file PB-TAT-M. The key I sent will unlock that one as well."

Becky laughed. "I already did." She looked at Virgil

and Murton. "It would have stripped the other file, everyone's phone would have sent their personal private data to a secure server owned by Bob Long's company, and he would have had some serious charges levied against him."

They all thought about that for a few seconds, then Murton said, "Where do you guys come up with these file names? What do they mean?"

Nicky put on his best Jamaican accent and said, "PB-TTI-M means ping back to the island, mon. PB-TAT-M means ping back to Ar-Tell, mon."

Virgil chuckled...not at the file names, but Nicky's accent. "Listen guys, can you give us your number, a way to reach you if we need to?"

When Nichole spoke, she was serious. "Yes, but it is not to be shared. We value our privacy. I hope we're clear on that."

CHAPTER TWENTY-SEVEN

After the phone call had ended, Virgil looked at Becky and said, "Can they do it? Could it work?"

Becky thought carefully before she answered. "Can it work? Yes. Can they do it? Maybe."

"Why do you say maybe?"

"Because they need a way to get a ton of people to download the app. If they do, then yes, they could pull it off."

"So it comes down to Mac and Senator Wright getting the bill through. If that happens, that app will be all over."

"It looks that way. If the bill passes, and the process works in our state, you know other states are going to want to jump on the bandwagon. If that happens, a decentralized Internet could be up and running in no time at all. I'll tell you this: I hope they pull it off."

"Why?"

"You know why, Jonesy. These giant tech companies are controlling almost every aspect of our lives. It's like they're out to take over the world or something."

"That seems a little extreme to me, Becks."

"You call it extreme, I call it forward thinking. If you don't believe me, take a look at some of the things guys like Elon Musk, or Mark Zuckerberg are proposing. Zuckerberg wants his own currency for Christ's sake. Nobody knows when to say enough is enough, already."

Murton looked at Becky and said, "Better slow your motor, there, sweetheart. You're starting to sound like Jonesy."

Becky punched Murton in the shoulder. "Shut up."

AFTER EVERYONE HAD HUNG UP, NICHOLE LOOKED AT her brother and said, "Do you think they suspected anything?"

"I don't see how they could. The connection was set up before we ever made the call. The delay was virtually minimal, and you know Wu...no one listens to him anyway."

Wu's voice came over the speaker. "Wu still here you know."

Nicky laughed. "I know. I'm just messing with you, Wu. How's Indy? You and Linda having a good time?"

"No, we are not. It is noisy and everyone is in a hurry all the time. When do we get to come back?"

"When all this is over, Wu," Nichole said. "Shouldn't be too much longer." Then to her brother, "That was great, the way you guys improvised which line of code to look at...the way you snapped your fingers. And Wu, you played right along. It was perfect."

"Thanks," Nicky said. "All in a day's work. Speaking of work, I'm heading down to the beach now." Then into the speakerphone, "What are you going to do, Wu?"

"Wu need to be at Ar-Tell in one hour. This Mr. Said? He is a nice enough man, but he a slavedriver."

"Remember, Wu," Nichole said. "All you have to do is make sure that the code stays put. You're in charge of the team working on the app, so it shouldn't be a problem."

"I hope they hurry up with the whole thing. Linda is desperate to get back. Wu too."

"And Linda knows what she has to do?"

"Yes, yes. How many times you ask Wu that?"

"Don't get snippy, Wu. I'm the one trying to make sure everyone is safe."

"Sorry. Wu not snippy. Wu exhausted. We are ready. Ready to come home too."

ROBERT WAS IN THE KITCHEN, GETTING READY FOR THE day's customers. He'd seen Virgil, Murton, and Becky's vehicles outside, so he knew they were upstairs. He scrambled some eggs, dropped in some peppers, onions, sausage, and Jerk sauce, then placed the three plates with silverware and napkins on a tray, along with a pot of Jamaican Blue Mountain coffee, and carried it all upstairs.

Murton heard him coming up the steps and opened the door. The aroma of the food and coffee made his face light up. "Robert, my man, I don't think I tell you often enough how much I love you."

"Yeah, mon. I tink you right, you. But let's keep it between ourselves, no?" He handed everyone a plate, then said, "Back to work, me." He glanced at Virgil before going down the stairs. "You get the information you wanted, mon?"

"Yeah, I did, Robert. Thank you."

"No need to tank me, you. I hope everyting work out, mon."

"I'm sure it will." Virgil said.

Robert didn't reply. He looked at Virgil for a moment then went back down to the kitchen.

"What was that all about?" Becky said.

Virgil opened his mouth to answer and left it hanging there. He wasn't exactly sure how to respond. He wanted to protect Delroy's privacy, but he didn't want to deceive Murton and Becky either.

"Either say something, or close your mouth," Murton said. "You've got some egg on your teeth, there."

Virgil closed his mouth and licked his teeth. He was still trying to figure out what to tell Becky and Murton regarding Delroy's past when his phone vibrated at him.

"Saved by the vibrator," Becky said.

Murton turned his head, tucked his chin and looked at her. "Really?"

Virgil looked at the screen and saw the number was blocked. "Guys, please." He thought he knew who was calling so he put the phone on speaker, pressed the answer button and said, "This is Jonesy."

"The other night when I stopped into your bar it was to say hello," Avery said. "This time I'm calling to say goodbye. Don't bother to try and trace this call, either. It's a burner, and I'm on the move. It'll be crushed when we're finished speaking."

"Where you headed, Ave?" Virgil said.

"Oh, you know, whichever way the wind blows, that sort of thing."

"So you've finished your work here and it's time to move on? It's that simple?"

"There's nothing simple about it, Jonesy."

"Meaning?"

Avery was silent for a few moments. Virgil looked at Murton and shrugged. Murton rolled his wrist. The message was clear. Keep him talking.

"We were friends once, Jonesy. I saved your life when we were in the box."

"I gotta tell you something, Ave, and I hope you believe me. I'll be forever grateful for that. Murt and I both. We wouldn't be here right now if it wasn't for you."

"I paid the price though, didn't I?"

"You came out of it alive," Murton said.

"Hey Murt. Should have guessed you'd be there."

"Always. And we all paid a price, Ave. Believe it or not, some of us still are."

Avery laughed. "Who do you think you're talking to? I pay the price every time I look in the mirror."

Virgil leaned toward the phone. "Ave, we fought in the same war."

"Yeah, and this isn't it."

"No, I guess not," Virgil said. "But you did save our lives. There's no need for us to be fighting against each other now."

"You don't get it, do you Jonesy?"

"Get what?"

"That we're not fighting against each other. I've been trying to help you all along. No matter what happened between our fathers, I've always considered you guys my friends."

"If you turn yourself in I'll make sure you're treated fairly. Name a place and I'll meet you there. You can tell me how you've tried to help. I'll testify on your behalf."

Avery laughed again. "That's not going to happen, buddy. Your old man tried to be kind and helpful to mine and he still ended up in the chair. I don't think I'm going to let the circle close on this one, my friend. Maybe I'll see you again, sometime."

"Ave, wait. Tell me one thing."

"What?"

"Why did you do it? Why did you kill Garrett Wright?"

"You see...that right there is why you'll never get me to come in voluntarily."

"What are you talking about?"

"I didn't kill Garrett Wright."

This time it was Virgil who laughed. "We lying to each other now?"

"I always knew you'd turn out to be a heartbreaker, Jonesy. I never thought it'd be mine you broke though. I'm not lying. Have I killed? Yes. But I didn't kill Garrett Wright. I swear to you I didn't."

"Then who did?"

"Get a warrant for Bob Long's house. You'll find most of what you're looking for there."

"I guess you haven't been watching the news. Bob Long is dead. So is his son, Pete, by the way."

"I have been watching," Avery said. "I know all about it. Get your warrant anyway."

"You're saying one of Long's other security men killed Wright with a single shot from eight blocks away? That was a hell of a shot, Ave."

"It sure was. But not impossible if you know how to shoot. I won't say it again because I'm going to hang up now. Get the warrant. There's a gun safe in the back of the master bedroom closet and another safe in Long's office behind a painting on the wall. I'll text you the combinations. And Jonesy?"

"Yeah?"

"Don't try to find me."

"That's my job, Ave."

"Not if you're looking for Garrett Wright's killer. And job or not, here's two things to consider: One, you won't be able to find me, and two, on the off chance you did, friends or not, it wouldn't end well. A guy can only extend the hand of friendship so far, no matter the past."

For some reason, Avery's comment reminded Virgil of the conversations he'd had with Robert and his father regarding Delroy.

AFTER AVERY ENDED THE CALL WITH VIRGIL, HE SENT the combinations via text, then removed the battery from the burner and tossed it out the window. Then he pulled the SIM card, and after a mile or so, threw that out as well. Then he snapped the phone in half, ripped out the circuitry and let the pieces drop from his gloved hand as he rolled down the road.

When he arrived at the house, he left his car running. He'd only be a moment. He walked up the front sidewalk and onto the porch, then rang the doorbell. When the door opened, he reached into his pocket and pulled out the medallion. It was close in size to a half-dollar coin, and featured Indiana's state seal. He handed it over and said, "Are you sure you're up for this?"

"Of course. We appreciate your cooperation."

Avery nodded without saying anything else. He turned, got back into his car and drove away.

Murton was shaking his head. "He's playing us. Or trying to, anyway."

Virgil didn't agree. "I don't know, Murt. He sounded sincere."

"You heard what you wanted to hear, Jonesy. The man is a killer. The war twisted him out of shape and no amount of conversation here is going to change that."

"Maybe not," Virgil said. "But let me ask you this: What do we have to lose? If he's lying about not being Garrett Wright's killer, he remains the primary suspect. But if he's telling the truth—and I sort of think he is—Wright's killer is still out there. What if it was one of Long's other security people who took the shot?"

"What about what Ross told us?" Murton said.

"What about it? He said he could make the shot. He also said any well-trained shooter could too. Let me ask you something: Why are you resistant to getting a warrant on the Long's residence?"

It took Murton a moment to answer, and when he did, the words he spoke didn't surprise Virgil. "Because I want him to be telling the truth, even though I suspect he is not. The man saved our lives, Jonesy. It's a pretty hard thing to reconcile."

CHAPTER TWENTY-EIGHT

They'd been at it most of the morning and ended up going in circles. The governor was pressing Said hard, and Said was pressing right back. It was his company, after all. Sandy felt like she was sort of caught in the middle, her loyalties to the governor and the state on one side, and her loyalties to Said, who provided a substantial income for her family from the drill operations, on the other.

"I fail to understand why the blockchain can't be the priority," the governor said.

Said took off his glasses and rubbed his face. "Mac, we've been over this twenty times already. We simply can't do both at once. My company has been preparing for over a year to expand the sonic drilling technology...not only across the country, but around the world. We have committed massive amounts of capital toward that singular objective. Further, we have commitments in place that, should they dissolve, would cripple us financially. Can we do both...ramp up production on the AI boxes, and get the mobile voting platform up and running? The short answer is yes. Can we do both at the same time right now? No."

The governor was shaking his head. "But it's my understanding that the blockchain is built, the app is ready to go, and all you have to do is..." He sort of waved his hands in the air. "I don't know, press a few buttons and get the damned thing rolling."

Sandy leaned forward and said, "Mac, while I don't know all the particulars, I believe it might be a bit more complicated than pressing a few buttons, as you say."

"Yes, yes, I was simply trying to look past all the red tape that seems to be floating around the room."

"You know," Sandy added, "There is a chance that the bill won't pass."

"Oh, it'll pass," Mac said. "If there's one thing I know about this state, we're tired of always being last. We need to be first at something, and I believe this is it."

Sandy tipped a finger at him. "You might believe it, but the information I'm getting on an hourly basis is this: The vote is going to be close. So close, in fact, that we can't call it yet. I've got a white board in my office with all the names of each legislator listed, and where they stand. Every time I walk in there the tally is different."

"It'll pass," the governor said. Then he looked at Said. "And if it does, then what? We'll have legislation for one of the greatest advancements in free and fair elections in place and ready to go...one that could be adapted at the national level. And if it is, it will once and for all put the power of the people back in charge of their own country's destiny. Election interference from foreign agents will be a thing of the past. So tell me, Rick, what's more important? That, or drilling more holes in the earth?"

Said showed some teeth. "That's a gross mischaracterization of the issues on the table. We're doing more than simply punching holes in the ground, and you damned well know it. You said you wanted your state to be first in something for a change?" He pounded his index finger on the table. "Well this is it. We invented the sonic drilling technology, we used it...are using it down in Shelby County—with your blessing, I might add—and it could save the entire fucking planet. Now, which would you like? A short delay on a bill that may or may not pass, or both the drilling tech and the mobile voting, because the mobile voting won't happen without the revenue from the expansion of the sonic technology."

The governor, starting to show some teeth of his own, said, "It is not gross mischaracterization of the issues. Those are the facts. The bill is self-funded, which I know you know. So don't try to tell me that it can't be done, when I know perfectly well that it could."

Sandy finally decided she'd had enough of the back and forth. "Gentlemen, let's take a moment and remember we are all on the same side here. I'd like a word with both of you in private, one at a time." She hated to do it, because she didn't want to disrespect the governor, but she turned to him and said, “Sir, could Rick and I have the room for a few minutes?”

Mac stuck his tongue in his cheek, then said, “You’re putting me out of my own office?”

“Only for a few minutes. Please.”

The governor nodded tightly. “I’ll be out in the hall.”

Once he was out of the room, Sandy looked at Said. “You’re certain we can’t do both at the same time?”

Said nodded with a tinge of defeat. “I have a great deal of respect for that man, but he simply doesn’t understand the logistics of the matter. He keeps saying that the blockchain is built and the app is ready, and even those things aren’t entirely accurate. The blockchain is built... the infrastructure is there, and the app is in the beta stage, so it’s close, but none of that matters.”

“Why not?”

Said thought about how to frame his answer. “Look at it this way. It might not be the perfect analogy, but it’ll do for purposes of this conversation. Let’s say we’re talking about a pipeline, and let’s further say that we’ve invented a new type of material from which the pipes are made... one that will never decay, break, or leak, no matter what. Let’s call it our forever pipe. So you’ve got this forever pipe...or I should say the ability to make this pipe, and it can handle water, oil, natural gas, whatever. Doesn’t matter. But the problem in this scenario isn’t the pipe. The forever pipe is perfect. It’s the costs associated with the research and development that went into the pipe, and further, the costs of removing all the old pipes and replacing it with the new. You're talking massive amounts of capital to make that happen."

Sandy bit into her lower lip. "I get it. I understand the analogy. But we're not talking about pipes and infrastructure, Rick. We're talking about a digital thing. A thing, I might add that you yourself said was all but ready."

"Yes, but there's still a cost. Look, I'm going to share something with you and I would appreciate it if you kept it to yourself. This hostile takeover of Ar-Tell...it cost me. A lot. I'm working with a house of cards here and it wouldn't take much of a breeze to blow the whole thing away. The fact of the matter is this: We can't afford it. Not until the expansion of the sonic drill units is underway, and those units start producing."

Sandy nodded. "I understand, and look, I'm no financial whiz or anything like that, but what about the banks, or even private equity?"

Said smiled at her the way a parent does at a child who just drew their first picture. "Not possible. They'd take one look at the financials and laugh me out of the building."

"How much are we talking about?"

"Rough numbers? To do both at the same time? About fifty."

Sandy squinted at him. "When you say fifty, you're not talking about thousands, are you?"

"No, I'm afraid not. We'd need fifty million, and we'd need it all at once. No one is going to put up that sort of money. We've got a balance sheet that's so off-kilter it makes the Leaning Tower of Pisa look like a marvel of modern engineering."

They sat quietly for a few minutes until finally Sandy said, "Okay, let me speak with him...Mac. If it can't be done, I guess it can't be done."

SAID GATHERED HIS BELONGINGS AND LEFT THE OFFICE, taking the side door so he wouldn't have to speak with the governor. Sandy opened the outer door and found Mac leafing through a golf magazine.

"I can have my office back now?"

"Of course. And thank you. Let's go back in and talk."

They went back into the office, sat down, then the governor looked at Sandy, raised his chin a fraction, and said, "Tell me."

"It's not going to happen, Mac. He doesn't have the capital to do both at once."

"How much are we talking?"

"He said fifty." Sandy noticed the governor didn't inquire whether it was thousands or millions. He knew.

"Private equity?"

Sandy shook her head. "Says nobody will touch him after the buyout of Ar-Tell. He's way over extended."

"What time is the vote scheduled to take place?"

"What does it matter?" Sandy asked.

"It matters because if there's anything I've learned about politics and big business it's this: You take things one step at a time, you put one foot in front of the other, and you never quit doing that until you're completely out of options."

"I think that's where we are now, sir, if you'll pardon me for saying so."

"It looks that way, doesn't it? Anyway, the vote? What time?"

"Three, this afternoon."

"This meeting never took place. Make sure the bill stays on the floor. I want that vote to go through, no matter what. Are we clear on this?"

"Absolutely, sir," Sandy said, her voice tight. She stood from her chair. "If you'll excuse me, I've got the graveside eulogy for Garrett Wright."

"Sandy..."

"It's okay, Mac. I understand. We tried. I hate to see you disappointed, is all."

The governor smiled. "Disappointed? Who says I'm disappointed. I live for this sort of thing."

Once Sandy was out of the office, the governor picked up the phone and called Becky. "How's my favorite researcher?"

"Since I'm your only researcher, that's not much of a compliment. How are you, Sir?"

"I'm fine, Becky, fine. But I have my back against the wall on an important issue, and I need your help."

"You realize don't you, that you're asking for help from the one person you and Cheese were ready to throw to the wolves not so long ago?"

"Cora was only doing what she thought best, given the circumstances at the time. Besides, it all worked out. And please, stop calling her Cheese."

"How can I help, Mac?"

When the governor told her what he wanted, Becky thought, *Oh boy*.

VIRGIL, MURTON, ROSS, AND ROSENCRANTZ ALL DROVE their own vehicles out to the Long residence. It wasn't completely necessary, but a show of force was never a bad thing when serving a search warrant, and four cop cars turning into the drive made an impression, one that said, we're here and not to be messed with.

Because of the previous encounter with Long's security detail, they all wore their tactical vests, their side arms strapped to their thighs. Ross had his long gun, even though its value during a home search was practically nil.

They all exited their vehicles, and Virgil and Murton took the front. Ross and Rosencrantz went in opposite directions to cover the rear. Virgil gave them enough time to get to the back of the house, then he rang the doorbell and pounded on the door with the heel of his hand.

"Police. Search warrant," he shouted. He repeated the process three times, and when no one answered he stepped back, ready to kick the door in. Murton saw what he was about to do, and pulled on his arm to stop him.

"What are you doing?" Virgil said.

Murton gave him a dry look. "I was about to ask you the same thing. Take a good look at that door. The only thing you'd break is your leg. Like we need that again. Wait here."

Murton walked back to his car and popped the truck. When he returned he had a twenty-pound sledgehammer in his hand. "Step back."

Virgil got out of the way, and Murton put both hands on the giant hammer, and swung at the door, right above the knob. He put his whole body into it, like a baseball batter who'd been given the signal by the third base coach to swing for the fence. The door cracked, but otherwise held fast. It took two more swings before it finally let go. Murton held the hammer over his right shoulder with both hands and said, "See?" Then he pushed the door open.

Jensen and his men were right there waiting for them.

Ross and Rosencrantz met up at the back of the house on an elaborate, multi-level, red-bricked patio. They couldn't see all the way through the house to the front, but they could hear Virgil beating on the door.

Then the beating stopped. Rosencrantz tried the back door, but it was locked.

He put his face up to the glass and peered inside, but all he could see was a well-furnished kitchen, half of a dining room, and a hallway that looked like it led to the garage. He looked through a couple other windows for a few moments but the layout of the house made it impossible to see much of anything. When he heard the sound of the sledgehammer hit the door, he pulled his head back and said, "Must be a hell of a solid door. Take a look through one of those other windows on your side and see if there's anything to see." He heard the sledge hit the door again, and then one more time. "Or, maybe we should bust out this glass and go let them in." When he didn't get a reply, he said, "What do you think?"

When Ross didn't answer, Rosencrantz started to turn around. "Hey, I'm talking to you—" That's when Rosencrantz heard the gunfire, two quick shots in a row. The shots were so close together they were almost simultaneous.

Rosencrantz instinctively turned and ducked at the sound of the shots, and when he did, he discovered that Ross was nowhere in sight.

CHAPTER TWENTY-NINE

Ross heard Virgil banging on the front door, but he also happened to catch a bit of movement out of the corner of his eye. He was looking through a different window on another level of the patio, one Rosencrantz had pointed to when they rounded the corner. The movement came from a short hallway that looked to lead right up to the front door. Had he seen a gun in the man's hand? He wasn't sure. But Ross, never one to run from danger, assumed the worst, and took off toward the side of the house by the garage.

When he twisted the knob, the door opened right up. The garage had a seven series BMW parked in one stall. The other two were empty. He ran toward the interior door, and as quietly as possible, twisted the knob, then stepped inside. He took a half second to get his bearings, then turned toward the front of the house, moving along the hallway, his back to the wall, his head on a swivel watching both the front and the rear.

The hallway opened up into a massive foyer with a wide stairway to the upper level. The stairway was open on both sides. When he saw the men, their guns drawn and pointed at the door, he pulled back, and waited. Either Virgil or Murton had already hit the door once, but it was holding.

The three men were spread out, standing in the open at the bottom of the stairs with their handguns pointed at the door. When the door was hit again, this time it almost gave way. Ross brought his long gun up and pressed his shoulder against the side of the wall. He was only twenty feet away.

The door was hit a third time and the latches finally ripped free. Ross wasn't looking at the guns the men held. He was looking at their faces. They were standing not quite in line with each other. One of the men was slightly forward of the other two. His face was calm, relaxed even. The other two were jittery. He saw it in their profiles, the movements of their heads, the slight crinkling of their eyes. When the door swung open, Ross fired two shots close together and two of the men went down.

He didn't get a chance at a third. There wasn't enough time.

Virgil heard the shots and spun back out of the doorway. But Murton had already stepped inside.

The back-to-back shots startled Jensen, and he took his eyes off the door for a fraction of a second as his men fell to the floor. He fired at the front door without looking, his shot missing Murton by more than a foot. By the time he got his attention where it should have been, it was too late.

Murton had been ready all along.

Murton saw the two men go down, and saw Jensen turn slightly at the sound of the gunfire. Jensen brought his weapon up and fired at the front door, but his aim was poor and Murton didn't even flinch, his momentum carrying him forward, his hands still on the massive sledgehammer resting on his shoulder. He took one more step, then flung the hammer at Jensen, and it caught him in the center of his chest. He dropped his gun and fell flat on his back.

Virgil spun into the room and heard glass breaking in the back of the house. He ran that way.

"Ross on your left," Ross called out to Virgil and Murton to let them know he wasn't a threat. Virgil discovered Rosencrantz in the main hallway, told him to stay put, and ran back to the front.

"Murt?"

"Three down" Murton said. "All dead."

"Alright," Virgil said. "Let's clear it."

Rosencrantz and Ross covered the lower level, and Virgil and Murton took the upstairs. Five minutes later they were all back in the foyer. With the exception of themselves and the three dead security guards, the house was empty.

Virgil was amped up. He glanced at Ross, then turned his attention to Rosencrantz. "He disappear on you?" He was speaking of Ross.

Rosencrantz shook his head. "I made a command decision to have him look around." It wasn't a full and complete lie.

Virgil looked at him like he wasn't sure if he was telling the truth or not. He let it go and looked at the two men Ross shot. Both of them had bullet holes in the sides of their heads. Then he looked at Jensen and the giant sledgehammer on the floor next to him.

"I can't wait to read your after-action report on this one," Virgil said. Then he added, sort of dryly, "Thor."

Murton shrugged. "I acted in a manner consistent with the duties of my position during a time when I felt my life and the lives of my fellow officers were in extreme danger. I think the sledgehammer must have cracked his sternum and stopped his heart."

"Uh huh. And what if you'd have missed? He got a shot off."

"I wouldn't have," Ross said.

"He's right," Rosencrantz said. "He never misses."

Virgil pulled out his phone and made a call. "You guys out there?"

"Yep," Lawless said. "Just waiting on your call. We heard the gunfire. Everyone okay?"

"Yeah, we're all fine. But we've got three dead guys. Get the county coroner started this way, then come up here so we can open those safes, will you?"

"Turning in now," Lawless said.

Ross visibly swallowed. "Is Mimi with him?"

"Yeah, why," Virgil said.

"No reason," Rosencrantz said, maybe a little too quickly. "You know, this is a pretty big place. There's a few outbuildings as well. Maybe Ross and I should go take a look around outside or something."

"Good idea," Virgil said. "Keep an eye out for Mrs. Long. I don't know where she is, but if she shows up we'll want to keep her out of the house."

"You got it, Jonesy," Ross said.

They turned to walk out the door and Virgil said, "Hey kid?"

Ross turned and looked at him. "Yeah?"

"Nice shooting."

"It was twenty feet. I think I yawned between shots."

Lawless took care of photographing the dead security men, and making a report of how they died, where, and when...all the particulars they'd need later on. Virgil, Murton, and Mimi went upstairs and found the gun safe exactly where Avery had told Virgil it would be... at the back of the master bedroom closet. Mimi dusted the keypad and dial, got whatever prints she could, then after making sure Virgil and Murton both had gloves on, told them they could open it up.

Virgil entered the combination and the lock clicked open. When he pulled the door he found a row of rifles and shotguns with one empty slot. "See your flash, Meems?" Virgil said.

"Better not call her that," Murton said.

"Why not?" Mimi said. "I sort of like it."

Virgil ignored them both and shone the light at the bottom of the gun case. A fine layer of dust was visible on the bottom of the felt, and he could see the outline where a rifle had rested previously. He turned to Mimi and said, "Get a photo of that, will you?"

Mimi took her camera from its case and clicked off a few shots. As she did, Virgil took out his phone and called Ross. "Where are you?"

"Outside. We cleared all the outbuildings. Nothing to report."

"Okay, Tell Rosie to keep looking, but I'd like you to come back up to the house. We're upstairs in the master bedroom closet. Need you to look at something for me."

"On my way."

Five minutes later Ross stepped into the closet, and Virgil pointed into the safe. "Take a look at that impression in the felt. See the dust, too?"

"Yeah. What of it?" He had his rifle slung over his shoulder.

"Can you tell what kind of rifle that is?"

"There is no rifle there, Jonesy."

Virgil gave him a smirk. "You're a riot. Can you tell or not?"

Ross bent over and looked closely at the impression. Then he stood upright, looked at Virgil and said, "Court of law, or two guys standing in a closet shooting the shit?"

"Two guys," Virgil said.

"Then yeah, I can tell you. It's this kind." He unslung his M24, grabbed it by its stock and was about to set it in the safe when he glanced at Mimi and said, "Is this okay?"

Mimi bit into her lower lip, then smiled at him. "Of course. Go ahead and put it all the way in."

Ross almost dropped his rifle.

Murton had to turn away, and Virgil looked down at the floor as he rubbed his forehead. Ross got his wits about him and gently set his rifle in the empty slot. The felt impressions and the dust pattern matched exactly.

Virgil looked at Mimi and said, "Get a picture of that as well."

Mimi ripped off a couple more shots, and when she was finished Virgil told Ross he could take his rifle and go back outside to help Rosencrantz. When he was out of the room, Virgil looked at Mimi and said, "It's not necessary to torture him, Meems."

Mimi smiled. "A girl has to get her fun where she can find it."

Virgil didn't know how to respond to that, so he kept his mouth shut on the issue. "How about we go check out the other safe, then you can come back here and print these guns?"

"You're the boss," Mimi said.

Rosencrantz discovered that he needed to pee. He went into the woods and when he was deep enough in that no one could see him, he unzipped and sprayed a little DNA. That mission accomplished, he thought he'd walk the woods line out to the road to make sure there was nothing of evidentiary value.

He was at the far edge of the property when he noticed an odor of a dead animal. He was going to turn back, but thought, *What the hell, I'm out here.*

The closer he got to the road the stronger the smell became. He was all but certain someone had clipped a deer or something and it had crawled off into the woods to die.

The trees were thick and even though the wind was calm, the smell seemed to be coming from every direction at once...it was that strong. He was almost all the way out to the road when he saw the body. It was about thirty feet away, the smell now so bad he had to cover his mouth and nose with his shirt. He marked the location by hanging his handcuffs on a tree branch, then backed away. When he was out of the woods, he took out his phone and made a call.

Bob Long's office contained only one piece of artwork, the rest of the walls covered with pictures of Pete playing ball. Virgil had Mimi dust the painting's frame, then with that done, they took it from the wall, and she repeated the process with the safe. Once she had everything she needed, she stepped back and said, "All yours."

Virgil again punched in the code that Avery had given him, and the safe popped open. Inside they found a manila envelope sitting on top of a few stacks of cash.

Mimi sighed. "Sometimes I hate this job."

Murton looked at her and said, "Why?"

She pointed into the safe with her chin. "Right there. Perfectly good cash that will go into some government evidence locker, never to be seen again. It's almost a tragedy." She removed the envelope by its edges, then set it on the desk and began to recover any prints she could. When she was finished, she opened the envelope and let the contents slide out on top of Bob Long's desk. The photo's showed Senator Wright in a motel room with a young woman.

"Get individual photos of each of these pictures before you print them," Virgil said.

Mimi looked at him and said, "I know how to do my job, Jonesy."

"Yeah, yeah, okay. Sorry."

Virgil's phone buzzed.

SANDY WALKED OUT OF HER OFFICE AND MADE HER WAY down the back stairwell that led to the parking garage of the statehouse. When she approached the vehicle, a black Lincoln Town Car, she glanced at the woman standing next to the car and saw the coiled wire that poked out of her collar and ran up to an earbud. She also saw the medallion, indicating she was her detail driver for this trip. She'd not seen the woman before, but the state had plenty of drivers, so it didn't strike her as unusual.

The woman adjusted her posture, stood up a little straighter, opened the rear door, and when Sandy was close enough, she said, "Good afternoon, ma'am."

Sandy smiled at her, said hello, then said, "Please, call me Sandy. Do you know where we're going?"

The woman lowered her chin a notch and nodded. "Yes, of course. Crown Hill Cemetery, for the burial of Garrett Wright."

"That's correct," Sandy said as she climbed into the car. "Let's not dally. I can't be late."

"Yes, of course," Linda said as she closed the door. As she walked around the rear of the vehicle, she reached up and tapped the earbud. "Wu, we're leaving now. Are you ready?"

"Wu ready. All done at Ar-Tell. But there has been a development. Listen closely."

CHAPTER THIRTY

They left Mimi to work the prints, but took Lawless with them into the woods. Rosencrantz had warned them about the smell, and he'd been correct. The body was ripe.

"How long has he been out here?" Virgil said.

Lawless was closer to the body than the rest of them, his mask protecting his sense of smell. When he answered, no one could understand what he said.

"We can't hear you properly," Virgil said. "Gotta ditch the mask."

Lawless slowly turned and gave Virgil a look, then stood and walked the twenty feet or so to where the other men were standing. He lowered his mask, and it hung below his chin, making him look like he had a giant bug strapped around his throat. "I said I can't tell you how long he's been out here, but I can tell you he's been dead for more than a few days. He didn't die out here either."

"How can you tell?" Rosencrantz said.

"Maybe I should be a detective," Lawless said. "I can tell because the heels on the bottoms of his shoes are caked with dirt and debris. You can see a trail where someone dragged him to where he is now. The trail leads out to the road."

"That's not exactly detective work," Rosencrantz said.

"Whatever, dude. You asked."

Rosencrantz turned and looked at Ross. "He whatevered, and duded me in the same sentence. Have the two of you been hanging out together or something?"

"Guys..." Virgil said.

Virgil was still gloved up, so Lawless gave him the man's wallet. When Virgil checked the driver's license, he didn't recognize the name. He quickly scanned the other items, and found fifty dollars in cash, a few miscellaneous receipts, and a business card that matched the man's name. The card identified him as the superintendent of the building where Garrett Wright's shooter had been. Virgil looked at Murton and said, "The missing building manager. Avery dumped his body here, on the Long's property. Why would he do that?"

Murton thought about it for a few moments, then shook his head. "I don't know. He was all but insistent that we get a warrant for this place. Maybe he was trying to point us at the body."

"To what end, though?"

"Don't know, Jonesy."

"Something's not right. He rents the room, then

doesn't want to be identified later, so he kills the building's manager. Then he drags him through the woods on his employer's property, and leaves him for us to find."

"Don't forget, the receptionist at Ar-Tell told us that Avery had been fired. Maybe this is a sloppy attempt at payback."

Virgil thought about it. "Maybe. But it seems a little too sloppy, if you ask me. Ave was always pretty squared away."

Virgil looked at Ross and Rosencrantz. "Circle around the body on both sides, then follow the tracks out to the road, or wherever they lead. See if there's any evidence he may have left behind. Chip, you better go with them."

The three men moved off deeper into the woods, with Rosencrantz on one side of the heel marks and Ross and Lawless on the other. They moved slowly, watching the ground all around them for anything that might be considered evidence. Rosencrantz was falling behind since he was working one side by himself. Lawless and Ross were well ahead, on the other side of the tracks.

"Say, Chip, you got anything going with Mimi?" Ross asked.

"No, of course not. She's not my type. Besides, she's my boss. It's against the regs. Why do you ask?"

"No reason," Ross said. "Forget I mentioned it. And for Christ's sake, don't say anything to Rosie."

Linda turned the Town Car off 38th Street and into the drive of Crown Hill Cemetery. Crown Hill, the third largest cemetery in the United States, encompassed over five hundred acres. Sandy had been to the cemetery many times before, though not so much in the last few years. Her father had been buried at Crown Hill long ago after he died rescuing a young boy from a fire.

The young boy had been Virgil. It's part of what brought them together later in life, as adults.

"What was that?" Linda said.

"I'm sorry, I must have been talking to myself. I said my father is buried here. His name was Andrew Small. He was a fireman. The station Chief, actually."

"I'm sorry for your loss."

Sandy was quiet for a few seconds. "Thank you. I am too. It was so long ago, but sometimes it feels like it was all last week. But even through all the grief, there's so much good that evolved as a result of his passing, things which I'm certain would never have occurred had he lived. That almost sounds selfish, doesn't it?"

"To tell you the truth, I don't think it does. I have friends who lost their father as young children to violence. It's such an awful thing."

"Careful," Wu said through the earbud.

"Yes, it certainly is." Sandy said.

Linda drove the Town Car through the massive Gothic arches, and pulled up next to the chapel's main entrance. She got out of the car and opened Sandy's door for her. "I'll be right here when you're ready, ma'am."

"Thank you," Sandy said. She started to walk away from the car, then turned back. "Your friends...did they find their way?"

This time it was Linda who paused before she answered. "I believe they have. Like you said, eventually goodness filled their lives. I don't think it would have worked out the way it did if their father had lived, and other kind people had not shown up in their lives."

"You've made your point," Wu said.

Linda reached up and adjusted her earbud. "This thing drives me crazy sometimes."

Sandy smiled and said, "I can imagine." Then she turned and walked inside.

VIRGIL AND MURTON WERE MAKING THEIR WAY BACK up to the house when the county coroner arrived. They flagged him down, and told him they had three in the house, and one in the woods.

The coroner let out a sigh, then jammed the transmission into park. "Please tell me they're fresh."

"The three in the house are," Murton said. "But the one in the woods has been there a while. He's pretty ripe."

The coroner shook his head. "You know, following you guys around is getting to be a full time job."

"We do what we can to protect the public," Murton said. "It is what it is."

"Wow, that's like, profound. Is Mimi out here?"

"Yeah, she's up at the house," Virgil said.

"Good. I think I'll start there." He dropped the van in gear and drove away.

Murton looked at Virgil. "He didn't even offer us a ride."

"You want to ride in the coroner's van?"

"Up front, sure. But not lying down in the back."

WHEN THEY WALKED BACK INTO THE HOUSE, THEY found the coroner chatting up Mimi in Bob Long's office. "Shouldn't you be doing something with those bodies?" Virgil said.

The coroner turned and looked at him. "Yeah, except I'm not sure—and neither is this lovely woman—if Lawless has everything he needs. So I'm on hold."

"How about you hold outside then. This is an active crime scene."

The coroner gave Virgil a dirty look and went back outside to wait.

"Thanks," Mimi said. "I thought I was going to have to break out the pepper spray."

"That bad?" Murton said.

Mimi considered the question. "No, I guess not. But when I'm working, I'm working. And listen, speaking of working, I pulled the prints from all those rifles upstairs. It's funny, you do this job long enough and you start to see patterns. They sort of jump out at you when you least expect them."

"What, exactly, are you talking about, Meems?"

"Just this: That room, where the shooter took the shot that killed Garrett Wright? We pulled a ton of prints out of there, as you'd expect with a rental. But when I took a quick look at the prints from the rifles, guess what? They match some of the ones we found in that room. Look, I've got them right here on my iPad."

She showed them the matching prints, and even though neither Virgil nor Murton were experts in forensics, they could tell the prints were a good match. "Not surprising," Murton said. "Avery was chief of security here for a long time."

Virgil was already shaking his head. "No, that's not right, Murt. Ave wore gloves. He wasn't lying. He wasn't the shooter."

"Guys," Mimi said.

"Hold on a second, Meems," Murton said. Then to Virgil: "Maybe he took them off for some reason."

"Guys?"

"Name me one good reason why he'd do that, especially after asking us to search this place?"

"GUYS?"

They both turned and looked at Mimi. "Yes?" Virgil said slowly.

"Avery wasn't your shooter. And neither are any of those dead guys out in the foyer."

"How can you tell?" Murton said.

"Because I'm good at my job."

"Well, that puts us right back at square one," Virgil said.

"Not necessarily," Mimi said.

"Meaning what?" Virgil said.

"Meaning I know who the shooter is...probably."

"Who? And how?" Murton said.

"Every single print on all of those rifles belongs to the same person, and they all match some of the prints we took from the apartment. They also match everything I've printed so far of Julie Long's personal belongings."

"*What?*" Virgil said.

"Yup. I think Julie Long shot and killed Garrett Wright."

MURTON LOOKED AT VIRGIL. "I'LL TELL YOU something, it all fits. Garrett Wright injured her son and paralyzed him for life."

"She'd have to be a hell of a shooter to make that shot, Murt."

"Which means she'd have to have a hell of an instructor."

"Avery," Virgil said.

"Who else? He worked here for years. The only problem is this: None of those weapons in the safe upstairs are a 30 cal, which is what Wright was killed with. That gun is probably at the bottom of the river."

"Unless she isn't finished yet," Virgil said. "If she's crazy enough to kill Wright for what he did to her son, can you imagine the thought processes running through her head now that she's lost both her son, and her husband. I think she's blaming all of it on Garret Wright."

Murton shrugged. "So what? Wright's already dead."

"But his parents aren't. And her husband was blackmailing Senator Wright into sponsoring that mobile voting bill. Then Said comes along and essentially steals their company right out from under them. I don't think that rifle is at the bottom of the river. I think she still has it, and intends to use it against the Wrights. Maybe Rick Said as well."

Murton saw the sudden change in Virgil's face. "Hey, what is it, Jonesy? You went about three different shades of pale, there."

"If you wanted to make a statement, the kind that let everyone know who was responsible for destroying your life, where would you do it?"

"In public," Murton said.

Virgil looked at his watch. "Garrett Wright's funeral is happening right now at Crown Hill."

Murton visibly swallowed. "Isn't Small there? Something about delivering the graveside eulogy?"

THEY RAN FROM THE HOUSE, VIRGIL ALREADY DIALING his phone, trying to reach Sandy. As they went through the front door Virgil noticed his truck was blocked in by the coroner's van. "Murt, keys."

"Still in the ignition."

They ran toward Murton's state issued Charger and Virgil climbed into the driver's side and cranked the engine. Murton didn't even have his door closed when Virgil hit the gas, the Charger's tires squealing to find purchase on the asphalt drive. Out of the corner of his eye, Virgil saw Murton struggling with the door. He gave the Charger's steering wheel a little juke to the right, and the physics of the maneuver caused the passenger door to close.

"Get on your phone. Keep trying Sandy until she answers."

Murton dialed Sandy, and after a few seconds he looked at Virgil. "Straight to voice mail. She'd have it turned off during the service."

"Send her a warning text. It'll be the first thing she sees when she turns it back on."

Murton typed in a text and hit the send button.

Virgil got to the end of the drive and turned out onto the road, the charger fishtailing through the maneuver. Murton hit the flashers and the siren.

"Try Said."

"I don't have his number."

Virgil took a hand off the wheel and tossed Murton his phone. He was coming up on a red light and Murton looked in both directions and said, "Clear."

Virgil blew through the intersection and focused on

driving while Murton tried Said. He was somewhat surprised when he got an answer.

"Rick, it's Murton."

"Hey, Murt. What's—"

"Rick, are you at Garrett Wright's funeral?"

"No. I was going to go, but then something big came up and I had to stay at the office. Listen, this is important: When you talk to Sandy, tell her—" He interrupted himself. "What the hell is going on? What's all that noise?"

Virgil was maneuvering in and out of traffic, leaning on the horn for the cars in front of him to get out of the way. They almost got blocked in by two delivery trucks that had no way to clear the lane. Virgil swung out wide to the left and found himself on a direct collision course with an oncoming car, and another vehicle as it began to pull out onto the street.

"On the left," Murton said, his voice calm. "Can't talk now, Rick." He ended the call.

"Got it," Virgil said. He took his left foot and stomped on the emergency brake, cranked the wheel hard to the right and put the Charger into a power slide, narrowly missing both vehicles. Then he stomped the pedal again, releasing the brake, and stood on the gas.

"Biker on the right," Murton said.

Virgil swung back out away from the cyclist, who shot them the finger as they went ripping past. Two blocks later they were on 38th Street. Murton killed the siren, but kept the flashers going. Three minutes later they turned into Crown Hill, passed under the Gothic arches, and pulled up right in front of the chapel.

When they ran up the steps and yanked the door open, they found the chapel empty.

Virgil thought, *What the hell?*

CHAPTER THIRTY-ONE

Virgil looked at Murton and said, "Let me have my phone."

Murton handed him the phone. "Who are you calling?"

Virgil didn't get a chance to answer because the connection was already made. "Cora, it's me. What do you know about Garrett Wright's funeral? It's at Crown Hill, right? Supposed to be happening right now?"

"Yes," Cora said. "You called to have me listen to you answer all your own questions?"

"Murt and I are at Crown Hill, and there's no one here."

"You at the chapel?"

"Yes. It's empty."

"That's because the service is being held graveside at the request of the family. What's going on? You sound like you're about to lose it."

Virgil hung up. He looked at Murton and said, "Outdoor service."

They ran back outside and looked in every direction, but didn't see a service being held anywhere nearby.

"This place is over five hundred acres, Jonesy. Hills, trees, tombstones, bushes, giant crypts...if Julie Long is our shooter, she could be anywhere."

"We've got to find the gravesite."

They got back in the car, and Virgil began driving through the massive grounds in search of Garrett Wright's funeral service, but with so much ground to cover, he had no idea which way to go.

"Forget about trying to find the grave site," Murton said. "We need some high ground." He pointed out the window to the right. "Over there. Head that way. See the hill?"

"I got it," Virgil said. He followed the path Murton had pointed out, and a few minutes later they were at the top of a hill. When they got out of the car they looked in every direction, but still didn't see anything. Murton ducked into the car and came out with a pair of binoculars. He jumped up on the roof of the Charger, and slowly scanned the entire property. Out of pure frustration, Virgil did the only thing he could. He tried to call Sandy again, but her phone was still off.

Julie Long was dressed all in black and she was down low in the grass, underneath a large flowering rhododendron bush. She was well hidden, and had her scope trained on the target area. She knew how to shoot, Avery had made sure of that. She'd spent hours and hours with him at the range for no other reason than pure enjoyment, and the challenge of long-range shooting. But when Garrett Wright had crippled her son, she didn't shoot for pleasure. She shot for revenge. Avery had tried to talk her out of it, but she insisted...persisted with such emotion that she be the one to take the shot that he reluctantly agreed under one condition: That he pick the spot and do whatever was necessary to cover her tracks. Julie agreed.

And it would have ended there. But her idiot husband lost their company to Said—someone else she wished were here today—then Pete and Bob both died. Now she was alone, broke, and if she was being honest with herself, broken in her mind. If she made it out of this alive, she'd go find Said and finish him off too. Maybe up close and personal. She closed her eyes for a few minutes to get her head in order. She had a job to do, one that left little room for error.

She had three targets in front of her, and the problem was who to take out first. Both the Wrights were going to die today. That was a given as far as Julie Long was concerned. But she wanted more than simple revenge, she wanted to make a statement, one that would rock the entire state...one that said the Long's were not to be fucked with. And that meant the lieutenant governor was going down as well.

She put her eye up to the scope and scanned the people seated under the tent. The Wright's were in the front row, of course, sitting right next to the lieutenant governor. She'd already dialed in her scope. She moved the rifle back and forth, pausing briefly on each person's face. Who first?

Eeny, meeny, miny moe. Who will be the first to go? She let out a giggle, and it made her sound like a little girl.

"I THINK I'VE GOT THEM," MURTON SAID. "CLEAR OVER on the far corner from where we are. I can see the top of the tent, but that's it." He jumped off the roof of the Charger and said, "Let's go."

Virgil got in the passenger seat this time because Murton had a better line on where they were headed. He looked over at Murton and said, "We've got two choices, Murt."

"Roger that. And neither of them are what any tactician worth his or her salt would call good. If we roll up and make a scene, Long...if it is Long, is going to start shooting. If we hang back and try to find her, she might start shooting before we can get to her."

"That about says it. I'm willing to entertain suggestions."

Murton thought about it as he followed the twisting

road through the cemetery. "I say we hang back...try to find her. She has to be reasonably close. There's too many obstacles for a direct line of sight. Plus, she'll be facing the service, shooting from the front."

Vigil gave him a tight nod. "Let's do it then. When we get close, stay back at least five hundred yards. We'll go in on foot from there."

IT'D BEEN A MISTAKE, RIGHT FROM THE BEGINNING, HE thought. A simple, tragic error in judgement that led him down the wrong path, like it'd been imprinted into his DNA before he was ever born. One pull of the wrong lever sent three men to their deaths, and Joe Avery to the electric chair. Yet the son, Jacob, joins the army and becomes a killer on behalf of the United States government. One man makes a mistake and dies at the hands of the government, while the other is paid to do so with purpose. How does that compute? But somewhere along the way something had clicked in his brain, and changed him in ways he thought not possible. He'd made friends in the service. Good friends. But after he'd been burned, he felt like it was more than skin and tissue he'd lost to the searing heat. He felt like he'd lost his friends, his direction, and often, his will to live. The killings...they somehow kept him alive. He knew it was wrong, but it was how he survived. It...fed him.

Those were the thoughts going through Avery's head

as he hid in the cemetery behind a massive tombstone, the suppressor of his rifle sticking out past the corner of the monument. He'd known this day would come, and finally, here it was. He put his eye to the scope and scanned the crowd of mourners.

VIRGIL AND MURTON CRESTED THE HILL ON FOOT, AND saw the burial site about five hundred yards away. Between them and the site were about a thousand different places a sniper could hide. They decided to spread out...not far—they'd keep each other in sight—but they needed to cover more angles. They had their vests on and their tac comms ready.

"Watch your ass," Virgil said. Then he stuck the earbuds in and said, "Mine too."

"Roger that," Murton said. "Let's go. And remember, she'll be down low, either behind a tombstone or in the foliage."

Virgil nodded and they spread apart, then began their advance. At the gravesite, the mourners were all in place, and the pallbearers were removing Garrett Wright's casket from the back of the hearse.

WU WAS BACK AT THE HOTEL. HE HAD EVERYTHING packed up and ready to go, except for his electronics.

Those would be last. He keyed his radio and spoke to his wife. "Where are you?"

"At the cemetery. They're getting started."

"Little behind schedule," Wu said.

"That works to our advantage."

"Only to a certain point. We want Miss Sandy back for the vote at the last minute so there is little time for debate."

Linda looked around to make sure no one was watching her. She didn't want it to look like she was talking to herself. "You're in the traffic control system?"

"Yes, the system is under my control."

"What about the cameras?"

"That may be a problem," Wu said. "There are coverage gaps along the route. You'll have to talk to me."

"That might be difficult, but I'll do my best. We need the timing to work out. Try to let me know in advance of the gaps."

"Wu will do."

"Good luck, love."

"Wu too."

JULIE LONG WAS GETTING TIRED OF WAITING. THE casket was in place, but the preacher kept rattling on about some Godly thing. She wasn't actually sure what he was saying because she was too far away to hear him. Plus, she thought, with preachers these days, who knew what was being said.

She'd already decided who was going to be the first to go. She'd wait until the lieutenant governor got up to speak, then she'd take her out first. It'd cause a hell of a commotion, but with the Wrights in the front row, the next two shots would be almost as easy. Long felt like the Wright's wouldn't abandon their son at his own funeral, and even if they tried to run, she was fairly certain she could pick them off. She was, after all, taught by the best.

AVERY MADE SURE HIS LINE OF SIGHT WAS CLEAR, WITH no other people in the way of his shot. When he saw Sandy stand and approach the podium, he adjusted his angle and put his finger on the trigger.

THE POWER OF THE SCOPE MADE THE TARGET'S HEAD appear to be the size of a basketball from about five feet away. The scope was dialed in, the wind was calm, and the shot would be so easy a three year old could do it. Then, suddenly over the comms, Ross heard Rosie's voice loud and clear.

"New shooter, new shooter. Target at your two o'clock. Readjust for distance. Range is one-seventy-five. Repeat, two o'clock, and one-seven-five."

Ross lifted his rifle, swung around to his two o'clock and twisted the dial on his scope for the new closer range all at the same time...a maneuver he'd practiced thousand of times over the years. His heartbeat didn't even increase with the new information or movements. "Target acquired."

"Background is clear. Sandy's at the podium, partner. Take the shot or we're going to lose her."

Ross exhaled and felt the familiar emptiness. And when he fired, for the first time in his career as a professional sniper, he missed.

AVERY HAD A COMPLETELY DIFFERENT ANGLE ON THE mourners, the crosshairs of his scope directly on Sandy's forehead. Virgil had done well for himself, Avery thought. His wife was a beautiful woman. He sighed with regret because he new he was near his own end now. He'd seen Virgil and Murton coming down the hill. It was now or never. He let his breathing slow, found the space between his own heartbeat, and then adjusted his aim.

When he fired it was a half-second before Ross. The shot knocked Long sideways, and Ross's shot went into the dirt. Avery capped his scope, stood up, and headed toward Virgil, who was running his way.

THE CROWD SCREAMED AND SCATTERED AT THE SOUND of the gunfire. Sandy ducked behind the podium. It wouldn't offer her any protection, but she'd be out of sight, at least from one direction. She turned and saw Virgil running across the grass, but he wasn't running toward her. When she looked where he was going, she saw a man walking toward him, his rifle held at port arms. Then suddenly the man dropped the rifle, and pulled out a handgun.

Murton ran toward the tent and grabbed Sandy. "Where's your car and driver?" he asked.

"Third in line," Sandy said.

Murton reached into his boot and pulled out his backup gun. "Remember how to use this?"

"Are you going to cover me, or insult me now?"

Murton winked at her. "Stay low, and stay with me. Let's go."

Murton ran along the side of the tent, with Sandy right behind him. When they got to the car, Linda already had the door open. Murton took a half-second to look for the medallion—saw it—then nodded at the driver. She ran to the other side, climbed in and started the car. Murton practically shoved Sandy into the back seat. "Love you, Small. Now beat it." He slammed the door and turned back toward the gravesite. He saw Virgil and Avery standing ten feet apart, Virgil in a shooter's stance, his weapon pointed straight at Avery.

Murton ran that way.

"I don't suppose I'm walking away from any of this, am I?" Avery said. "Don't bother to answer, Jonesy. If I were walking away, you wouldn't have your gun pointed at me, would you?"

"I've got my gun pointed at you because you're still holding yours. How about you set it down in the grass and we'll figure all this out?"

Avery looked at the gun in his hand like he didn't realize he was holding it. "I don't know if I should do that or not." Then, as if Virgil might have just arrived, Avery said, "I saved your wife's life. You do realize that, don't you?"

Virgil nodded. "I'm grateful for that, Ave, you know I am. I'll be forever in your debt. But I'm not asking, I'm ordering you. Set that weapon down. I'll do everything in my power to see that you're treated fairly."

"Will you?"

"You know I will. We were friends once. I believe we still are. I'm really trying here, Ave. Look, I'm holstering my weapon. I'm not a threat. We'll figure this out together. Now please, put the gun down."

Avery looked at Virgil for a few seconds and Virgil saw a light come into his eyes...one he hadn't seen since they'd fought together in the Gulf before Avery had been burned. He thought he had him. He thought no matter the past, no matter the crimes Avery had committed, he finally saw there was no other way...that it was finally over.

As it turned out, Virgil was right.

Avery smiled at him and said, “I used to think that no one ever gave my old man a break. That no one cared about him or what happened to him. But that’s not true. Your dad cared, didn’t he?”

“I’m certain of it, Ave. He treated everyone fairly and with respect.”

Avery nodded. “I suspect he did. That’s the story I tell myself anyway. People turn out the way they turn out, Jonesy.”

“What do you mean?”

“I mean that maybe the circle does close on this one, buddy. I don’t believe I’ve ever had a better friend than you, Virgil Jones.”

And Virgil suddenly knew he’d been wrong all along, because Avery raised his gun, pointed it at Virgil’s face and pulled the trigger.

ROSENCRANTZ HAD ROSS DIALED IN...ELEVATION, WIND direction, distance, and line of sight. Ross watched Avery through the scope and when he saw him raise the gun, he fired.

Virgil had his own weapon holstered and when he saw Avery bring his gun up, he had just enough time to whisper his wife's name before he heard the shot. He thought Avery had gotten a shot off, but he wasn't sure. He saw his head snap backward, and a spray of red mist seemed to hang in the air before landing on Avery's body.

Virgil looked to his left and saw Murton running his way, then slow, then finally stop. They were still on the tac comms.

"You okay, Virgil?"

Virgil walked over to Avery's body and sat down in the grass next to his friend. "No," was all he said. He took the gun from Avery's hand and ejected the magazine.

It was empty.

CHAPTER THIRTY-TWO

Sandy turned her phone on and saw that she had multiple voice messages from Virgil, and a single text from Murton, warning her of imminent danger. She tried to call Virgil, but didn't get an answer. When she tried Murton, he answered almost immediately.

"Murt, what's going on? Are you guys okay?"

Murton looked over at his brother sitting in the grass. Virgil had his hand resting on the chest of the man who'd saved their lives so many years ago...a man who paid the price with his own life. For the first time since he'd known her, Murton lied to Sandy. "Yeah, we're fine, Sandy. Everything is secure here. Virgil is a little tied up right now. I'll have him call you."

THE GOVERNOR HAD CHOSEN SANDY TO BE HIS lieutenant for any number of reasons, not the least of which was her intelligence. Maybe she was reading too much into the situation, but she knew Virgil and Murton better than anyone else in her life. Murton never called or even referred to Virgil by his proper name unless he needed his full and complete attention. And whenever she spoke to Murton he always called her Small. She wasn't exactly sure what was going on back at the cemetery, but something was wrong.

They were on 38th street, heading away from the cemetery and back toward the statehouse. She needed to be on the senate floor in less than an hour for the vote. She leaned forward and tapped her driver on the shoulder. "Turn the car around, if you would. We need to go back to the cemetery."

"Do not do it," Wu said.

Linda looked up and touched eyes with Sandy in the rearview mirror. "You'll have to forgive me, ma'am, but I don't think we should do that. I'm under orders to protect you and keep you safe while we are together. The safest place for you right now is back at the statehouse."

"I appreciate your position. I do. But we've got to go back."

"Ma'am, please. You're putting me in a difficult position."

"You're in no position at all. I'm the lieutenant governor. It's not a request. Either take me back to that cemetery or pull over and I'll walk back."

Linda kept driving and whispered, "Wu?"

"Wu not know what to do."

"What did you say?" Sandy said.

Linda glanced up at the mirror. "I said whew, as in I don't know what to do."

"Pull this vehicle over, right now. I won't ask again."

When Linda didn't pull over, Sandy played the only card left in her deck. She pulled out the gun Murton had given her and pointed it at the side of Linda's head. "Last chance."

VIRGIL WAS HAVING TROUBLE GETTING HIS THOUGHTS together. It felt like his brain was caught in a feedback loop. His father had arrested Joe Avery, taken part in his trial and subsequent conviction, and later watched him die in the electric chair. And now despite his best efforts, Joe Avery's son, Jacob, the man who'd saved Sandy's life and who'd also saved Virgil and Murton's life in the war, and paid the price with permanent disfigurement was dead. And all because Virgil couldn't prevent it.

Ross and Rosencrantz came down the hill next to Virgil, and Murton walked over as well.

"You okay, Jonesy?" Ross said.

Virgil stood up, Avery's gun still in his hand. "Do I look okay?" When he spoke he started loud and got louder as he went. He thrust Avery's gun into Ross's chest and started pushing him backward. "His fucking gun wasn't even loaded. He wasn't a threat. The man was not only a friend, he saved Murton's life, he saved my life, he saved Sandy's life, and you just killed him. Am I okay, you ask? No, I am not fucking okay. Anything else you need to know?" Spittle was flying from his mouth as he spoke and it ran down Ross's cheeks.

Murton rushed over and grabbed Virgil from behind and pulled him away from Ross. "Hey, hey, hey, easy Jonesman. Ross was only doing his job. I'm sorry about Ave, you know I am, but Ross had no way of knowing the gun wasn't loaded. You know that." Then he pulled him close and whispered in his ear, "Square your shit away, soldier. We're walking away. Again. Look at me. Count your blessings. One of them is standing right behind you."

VIRGIL SPUN AROUND AND SAW SANDY AND LINDA standing behind him. Sandy walked over and put her arms around her husband. Ross walked away, back up the hill without saying a word.

"Virgil, what happened?" Sandy said.

Virgil opened his mouth to speak, then not knowing exactly what to say, simply shook his head. Everyone was quiet for a few minutes, the grounds alive with the sounds of birds and other wildlife, the sky bright blue, a slight breeze in the air. In the distance they heard the sirens from the approaching squad cars. They were all standing in a little semi-circle.

Murton put his arm around Sandy and said, "Everything is going to be okay." Then, all of a sudden his expression changed. It happened so quickly it looked like he'd become a different person. He yelled, "Gun. Everybody down." Then he grabbed Linda with his other arm and pulled her to the ground, along with Sandy.

When the shot came, Virgil spun and saw Julie Long stumble down the hill, then fall face first into the grass. When he looked past her up the hill, he saw Ross, about two hundred yards away, his rifle still pointed at Long. Virgil ran over to Long and saw that she was dead, half her head gone. He also noticed that she had a shoulder wound, and a bad one at that. He waved his arm at Ross to let him know that she was no longer a threat.

Ross lowered his rifle, turned, and walked away.

WHEN THE CITY POLICE PULLED UP, EVERYONE WHO had a badge made sure it was visible. Sandy—with some discretion—handed Murton his backup weapon, and Linda stood next to Virgil, her hands in plain sight. Rosencrantz walked over and told the city cops that the entire area was considered a crime scene, that the MCU had the situation under control, and that there were two dead, both perpetrators.

One of the city cops looked at the casket and said, "Is that one of the perps?"

Rosencrantz thought about the question for a

moment, then said, “Yeah, I guess so. Make that three dead.” Then he walked away to go find his partner.

Sandy looked at Virgil. “You okay?”

Virgil sucked on his cheeks, then said, “No. But I will be.”

“Promise?”

“Promise. Go do your thing.”

One of the city cops overheard the exchange between Virgil and Sandy and said, “I’m going to need a statement from everyone before anyone is allowed to leave.”

Virgil started to say something but Sandy cut him off. “Here’s my statement. The man standing next to you is the head of the state’s Major Crimes Unit. His name is Detective Virgil Jones. Everyone calls him Jonesy, but you can call him sir. I’m his wife. I’m also the lieutenant governor of the State of Indiana, in that order, I might add. How’s that for a statement?”

The cop turned about four different shades of red, visibly swallowed and said, “That will do for now, I’m sure, ma’am.”

Sandy checked her watch, kissed Virgil goodbye, looked at Linda, and said, “Let’s go.”

Sandy and Linda got in the Town Car and drove

back to the statehouse. Sandy was in the front passenger seat this time, instead of the back. If the governor had chosen her for her intelligence, she was about to prove it. She leaned over, grabbed the earbud from Linda's ear, and said, "Wu, it's Sandy Jones. What the hell is going on?"

"Linda is safe, yes?" Wu said.

"Yes, Wu, she's fine."

"Tell Murton he no longer owe Wu."

Sandy didn't know what that meant, so she tucked it away. "I will. Now let's hear it."

Wu told her everything he knew, and the explanation took almost the entire trip back to the statehouse. When they turned into the parking garage, Sandy said, "I don't think that's ever happened before."

Linda pulled right up to the entrance and said, "What?"

"We hit every green light. Every single one."

Linda looked at her and turned her palms up.

Sandy got it. "Wu?"

She nodded. "We wanted to make sure you had enough time. But you should go now. Time is short."

Sandy opened the door. "Will I ever see you again?"

Linda shrugged. "Who knows what the future holds for any of us? For example, when I woke this morning, I never thought I'd wind up having a gun pointed at me...by the lieutenant governor, no less."

Sandy blushed. "Yeah, about that, I'm sorry."

"I think I peed a little," Linda said.

"Tell Nichole—"

"Yes, yes. Now go before it is too late."

SANDY RAN TO HER OFFICE AND TOOK A QUICK LOOK AT the board that her staff kept up to date, minute by minute, on the vote. It was a complete deadlock...a tie, right down the middle. As lieutenant governor, Sandy was also the president of the senate. She'd have the deciding vote.

She hurried down the hall and stuck her head into the outer chamber of the governor's office. Cora looked up and said, "What are you doing here? You're supposed to be on the floor of the senate."

"Where's Mac?"

"He's down there right now. I imagine he's praying to whatever God he believes in that you're about to show up."

Sandy left the office and ran toward the senate floor. She entered through the back, and took her seat in the large chair on the platform at the head of the chamber. When she looked at the board, she saw the vote was indeed tied. When she looked out at the members, she saw that all eyes were on her. The governor and Rick Said were standing next to each other at the far end of the chamber. Said looked nervous. The governor was smiling.

The vote on the floor was an open vote, which meant a fifteen minute time limit had been set. Sandy had taken her seat with less than eight minutes to go. After a few seconds she stood back up to make sure she had everyone's attention, especially the governor. Then she looked down at the panel in front of her. Everything was handled electronically. All she had to do was press a button. She could vote yes by pressing the green button, and the bill would pass, or she could vote no by pressing the red button and the bill would fail.

She reached up and put her hand over the buttons, then made her choice. When she pressed the button, a collective gasp was heard throughout the chamber. She'd pressed the white button, which cast her vote as neither yes or no, but as present. The vote remained tied, but five minutes still remained on the clock. She rapped her gavel a few times and leaned into the microphone and said, "Per the rules of the senate, the vote remains open. Everyone please remain in the chamber." Then, in a silly sort of way she added, "I'll be right back."

She stepped down from the platform, walked straight up the aisle to where Said and the governor were standing at the back. "Follow me, gentlemen."

They stepped into an anteroom outside the chamber and once the three of them were inside, Sandy closed the door, looked at both men, and said, "Who wants to go first? And remember, the clock is ticking out there."

"Mac went behind my back and made a deal with the Popes."

"What kind of deal?"

Mac shrugged. "A fine one, if you ask me. They're

going to put a little capital in Ar-Tell to provide the funding for the mobile voting."

Sandy turned to Said. "So you'll be able to do both at once. The platform and the AI boxes. Isn't that what you wanted?"

Said ignored her question and looked at the governor. "A fine one?" He looked at Sandy. "A fine one he says."

"What am I missing?" Sandy said.

"What you're missing is this: In return for their influx of capital, they get an ownership share of Ar-Tell, and they'll still get their share of royalties on not only the existing AI boxes for the drilling rigs, but all future boxes as well. I'd be trading fifty now for hundreds down the line."

This time Sandy didn't embarrass herself by asking if he meant millions. She knew he did. "Does it stabilize your house of cards, as you called it?"

Said told her, with more than a little regret, that it did.

Sandy turned to the governor. "Mac, would you excuse us for a minute?"

"Again?" He rolled his eyes and left the room.

"Rick, take the deal. Is it perfect? No. But it's better than what you had before. What's that saying? Better the devil you know..."

"Yeah, yeah, than the devil you don't. I get it. Except I don't like to be strong-armed."

"No one is strong-arming you, Rick. We're trying to help you."

"Sandy, I don't think—"

She grabbed him by the lapel and said, "I was shot at today." It was almost the truth, but she was out of time. "Virgil watched one of his friends die, and you're talking about money? Take the fucking deal."

Said pulled his chin back and said, "Are you...are you guys all okay?"

"No, but we will be. Now what's it gonna be?"

Said waved her off. "Yeah, yeah, I'll take it. But I needed Mac to know I couldn't be pushed around."

Sandy shook her head, said, "Jesus," and walked out of the room.

When she stepped back into the chamber, the governor looked at her and said, "He take it?"

Sandy didn't answer and walked back up to the platform. The vote had less than thirty seconds to go. It was still tied. She pressed the reset switch and then the green button. Half the chamber groaned, and the other half cheered. She banged the gavel and said, "By the rules of the senate, the measure is passed. We're adjourned." Then she looked up at the governor, leaned into the microphone and said, "And I'm going home."

It was decided that since no one could identify the young woman in the pictures who may or may not have been a minor child at the time, no charges would be filed against Senator Wright unless the girl came forward before the statute of limitations ran out. No one expected she would. It was also decided that the good senator would not be seeking reelection. Ever.

Julie Long was buried next to her husband and son. The only person in attendance was MCU Detective Andrew Ross.

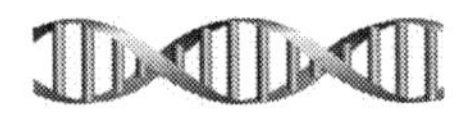

Jacob Avery was buried with full military honors. Virgil, Sandy, Murton, and Becky were all present. The flag that draped the coffin was folded into a triangle and presented to Virgil. Later that day, he took it to the US Army recruiting center. When he walked in, the people in the building looked at him, but no one said anything as he walked over to an empty desk near the back of the room and set the flag down right in the center of the desktop. He left the building without saying a word.

That night after everyone had gone to bed, Virgil was still thinking about the past...how he and Murton had been saved by Avery, and what it had cost his friend, how it had taken any chance of a normal life away from his old army buddy.

He knew sleep wouldn't come, so he climbed from the

bed and went into the kitchen and pulled his phone free of the charger. He dialed the number and when it was answered, he said, "I hope I'm not calling too late."

"Not at all. What's going on? Everything okay?"

"I'm hoping it will be," Virgil said. "Between us, I mean. I know I should be telling you this in person, but I'm sorry. No matter his misdeeds, he was my friend."

"I know he was," Ross said. Then after a moment, "So am I."

"That you are, young man. Thank you."

"For what?"

Virgil swallowed and managed to choke out the words. "For doing your job."

Ross was quiet on the other end of the line. During the pause, Virgil glanced out the window toward the pond and saw Delroy sitting next to Mason's cross. It looked like he was having a conversation.

"Listen, Ross..."

"Jonesy, I get it. Let it go. I have."

"Have a good night, kid. I'll catch you soon."

"You got it, boss." And then Ross was gone.

Virgil set his phone down and quietly stepped out on the back deck. The night was clear and calm, the moon reflecting off the black water of the pond. When it looked like Delroy was finished speaking, Virgil walked down to the cross, pulled a chair over next to his friend and sat down. Both men remained quiet for a long time.

Eventually Delroy looked at Virgil and said, "I speak to him, me, but I don't get an answer, no."

Despite the events that had played out over the past few days, Virgil let out a little chuckle. "That's not always a bad thing. Sometimes the answers can be pretty confusing."

"Delroy know you know about my past, me. The death of my baby girl."

Virgil nodded. "I do, and I'm so sorry."

Delroy turned his palms up. "It a long time ago now."

"What else has got you so upset, Delroy?"

"Delroy not upset."

"Then what is it?"

"Dat Huma Moon...she want to have a baby with me, mon. Delroy never been so scared in my whole entire life."

Virgil knew Delroy was one of the wisest people he'd ever known. What possible advice could he offer his friend in his time of need? He thought for a few minutes, then said, "You buried your daughter and planted a tree over her grave. Don't let your life be rooted in fear." When Delroy didn't respond, Virgil said, "Do you trust me?"

"You have to ask, you?"

"Wait right here. I'll be back in two minutes."

Virgil ran up to the house and made a phone call. When she answered, it was almost like she was expecting his call. "Hello, handsome."

"Hi Nichole. I'm sorry to get right to it, but I need a favor."

"Yes?"

"Have Wu and Linda left yet?"

"Not until tomorrow morning. Why?"

"Is there room for two more?"

"Of course. Are you and that beautiful woman of yours coming back to the island?"

"Not just yet. Then Virgil told her the story."

WHEN HE GOT BACK DOWN TO THE POND DELROY looked at him and said, "I don't have my watch with me, but dat longer dan two minutes, mon. More like two Jamaican minutes."

Virgil smiled at him. "Sorry. I had to make a call. You're taking some time off. As much as you need. Huma too. Nichole has a plane leaving tomorrow morning for Jamaica. You guys are going to be on it."

Delroy looked at him, his face a question.

"Don't you get it, Delroy? You're not getting any answers because you're talking to the wrong tree. Go be with your baby daughter. Take Huma with you. The answers you seek can't be found here. I promise you, there's nothing to fear. They say everything happens for a reason, and that may be true. But I also think everything happens all at once. If you close your eyes sometimes you can see it..."

EPILOGUE

AND THEN...

The hospital smelled of disinfectant and pee, the way most hospitals do. The rooms were small, the air circulation all but non-existent, and if ever a place existed where you could hang a sign that said *Death lives here,* Mason Jones thought this was it. He sat in a solid plastic chair next to the bed, his wife, Elizabeth, drifting in and out of consciousness. She was close to the end now, even though the doctors wouldn't actually say it out loud.

Murton stuck his head into the room and gave it a quick once over.

"Don't worry," Mason said. "He's not here."

"Expecting him anytime soon?"

"Probably not tonight. He had to work a double today.

He won't be done for another hour or so and I imagine it'll be right to bed for him after that."

Murton nodded and stepped closer to the bed. "How is she?"

"In and out. A lot of it is the meds, I'm sure, but listen, Murt..." Mason choked back a sob. "She isn't going to be leaving this time."

Murton didn't realize it, but he'd been holding his breath. Not from the smell, but from the news that he was about to lose one of the most important people in his life. Elizabeth Jones had raised him...saved him...from his abusive father, and maybe even himself. When he finally took a breath it was long and deep and loud.

The noise caused Elizabeth to stir. "Maybe we should step out into the hallway," Mason said.

"Don't you dare, either of you," Elizabeth said. "Murton Wheeler, get over here and give your mother a kiss." Murton walked over, bent down and kissed his adoptive mother on the forehead. When she reached up and put her arms around him, try as he might, he couldn't hold back the tears. He began to sob like a child.

"I'm sorry," he finally said.

"For what? I'm not. I'm the exact opposite of sorry, young man. I'm blessed and happy and honored that you walked into our lives that night, so long ago now. Oh Murton, the price you've paid to be a part of this family. If it were anyone else, I don't think they could have handled it."

"Anything for you, Mom. You know that."

"Do you mean that?"

"Of course I do."

"Then I'll ask two things of you."

"Okay," Murton said.

"I'll share this first, and I don't want any more tears when I do: I'm near my end, son. So very near."

Murton nodded, and despite his mother's request, the tears began to roll off his cheeks. "I know, Mom, I know. What do you need me to do? All you have to do is ask."

"The first one is easy," she said. It took some effort, but Elizabeth managed to scoot herself close to the edge of the bed. Then she patted the sheets next to her and said, "Lay down with me like you used to when you were a child."

Murton raised the back of the bed into more of an upright position, then sat down, put his arm around his mother and held her close.

"Mason, get the camera from my bag, would you, dear?"

"You bet," Mason said. He pulled out the camera and stood at the edge of the bed.

Elizabeth reached over and wiped the tears from Murton's face, then her own. "I know I don't look my best, but I want this to be a good picture. One with purpose."

"I don't think I've ever seen a more beautiful woman than you, Mom, as you are, right this moment." He was smiling when he said it, looking right at her. Elizabeth smiled right back and when she looked at Mason he caught it on camera. The Polaroid made a little whirring noise, and a few seconds later spit the picture out from the bottom of the unit. Mason walked over to the other side of the bed and held the picture out and together they all watched it develop, almost as if they were watching their family develop all over again.

Elizabeth held the photo for a long time then set it aside. "Mason, my bag, please."

Mason grabbed his wife's bag and handed it to her. She reached inside and pulled out an unsealed envelope. She put the picture inside then licked the edge of the flap to seal it up tight. That done, she looked at Murton and said, "Stand up, dear."

Murton gently removed his arm from around his mother's shoulders and stood next to the bed. "Here's the other thing I'm going to ask. You make sure Virgil gets this letter and picture. I don't care how you do it, or what you have to do to make it happen, but you find a way. Do you hear me? You find a way back to your brother. He needs you more than you know, and I think you need him more than you're willing to admit. The war is over, Murton."

Murton took the envelope and held it in his hand.

"Promise me."

"Mom..."

"Promise me Murton Wheeler or I'll haunt you the rest of your days."

Maybe that's what I want, Murton thought. "I promise."

"Good. Now kiss me good night. I'm so very tired."

Murton leaned down once again and kissed his mother. When she hugged him this time, he was surprised by the strength of her embrace.

"Never break a promise to your mother."

LATER THAT EVENING, EVEN THOUGH VIRGIL WAS exhausted from his double shift, he stopped in to see his mom. She was asleep, so he didn't disturb her. His father was sleeping on a cot next to the bed, so Virgil left him to rest as well.

When he walked out of the hospital that night, he saw a man sitting in a car, his hands gripping the top of the steering wheel, his head hanging down between his arms, his profile hidden from view. His whole body heaved and shuttered, probably with grief, Virgil thought. He considered going over and knocking on the window to make sure the man was okay, but ultimately decided no matter who it was, it wasn't his business to interfere.

If only he had.

MURTON FINALLY GOT HIMSELF TOGETHER. HE RAISED his head, and took his hands off the steering wheel. He wiped his face with both sleeves, started his car, then dropped it in gear. He held his foot on the brake for a moment, though if asked, he wouldn't have been able to say why. It felt as if something or someone wanted him to stay. But the hour was late, and it was time to go. He took his foot off the brake and drove away.

VIRGIL WAS ONLY A BLOCK AWAY FROM THE HOSPITAL, something chewing at the back of his brain. He didn't know why, but he felt an almost visceral compulsion to go back and offer any assistance he could to the grieving man. A kind word. Something. With little more forethought he turned his car around and went back to the hospital's parking lot.

When he got there, the man, whoever he'd been, was gone. Virgil pulled over and parked his squad car for a moment, wondering what, if anything, he'd missed. Ultimately he decided there was no way of knowing. He looked up at the hospital where his mother was slowly dying, and wondered about his future, what it would be like to continue on without her in his life...and what it'd be like for his father. He hoped Murton would come back to them someday, but he had his doubts.

Just then a car came screeching around the corner, the driver going much too fast to make the turn into the hospital's lot. The front tires lost their grip and the car plowed through a small row of bushes before the driver got it straightened out and back on the asphalt, his foot never letting off the gas pedal.

When the car finally skidded to a stop next to the entrance, the man ran around to the other side of the vehicle, screaming something unintelligible the entire time. He yanked the passenger side door open and pulled a young lady out. She was clearly pregnant and they were both panicked, shouting about bags and blankets and pillows and contractions, and what sounded like—though Virgil couldn't be sure—the moon. Then the woman doubled over in pain, the contraction dropping her to the ground. As Virgil ran that way, he let the odd moon thought go because the woman was on her hands and knees, and clearly in distress. Her hair was shock white, even though she couldn't have been more than twenty years old.

"I'm a police officer," Virgil said, as if his uniform and badge weren't capable of making it all clear to her. When she looked up, Virgil noticed she had a black eye.

"I walked into a door," she said.

Then the male driver was there, with a wheelchair, and two nurses. "Hey, get away from my wife. Let the nurses handle it." He was tall and broad through the shoulders, and his face had a hawk-shaped nose. He had a ridge line across his brow that, in the dim yellow light of the hospital's parking lot, made him look like a crazed caveman.

Virgil stepped back so the nurses could get the woman into the chair, but instead, the man grabbed her by the back of her neck and arm and practically tossed her in. "Hey, take it easy, there," Virgil said.

"Mind your own business," the man said. Then he spun the chair around and ran her inside.

One of the nurses followed, but the other walked over to Virgil and said, "Thanks."

"You're welcome, although I didn't really do anything. Might have a word with the father-to-be though. He was pretty rough with her, don't you think?"

The nurse put her hand on his arm. "How about we let this one go? I see it all the time...the panicked fathers."

"She's got a black eye. Said she walked into a door."

"Then maybe that's what happened," the nurse said. "We'll keep an eye on him."

Virgil thought for a moment about what to do. He was tired after the double shift, and he had to go out again first thing in the morning. He gave the nurse his card and said, "Call that number if you have any trouble. Or 911."

She took the card and said, "Or maybe I could just call sometime."

"That'd work too," Virgil said, a smile in his voice. A little brightness in an otherwise bleak moment of time.

After the nurse went inside, Virgil walked back to his squad car, an odd combination of thoughts running through his head. He often had a hard time understanding people...the good ones, the bad ones, and especially the ones that landed somewhere in the middle. Murton was in that category...the middle. It made him wonder not only about himself, his parents, and what he'd just witnessed, but also about the state of humanity.

ACKNOWLEDGMENTS

Thank you for reading this story. I maintain that it is an honor to write for each and every one of you. I hope that means something to you, because you have no idea how much it means to me.

I'd like to thank the following people for their help, support, and encouragement along the way:

My editor, Linda Heaton. Linda is a freelance editor with decades of experience and she runs her own shop at BluePenEdits.com. Her laughter is infectious, her eye is sharp, and her enthusiasm, dedication, attention to detail, and patience have proved absolutely invaluable. Any mistakes in this book are mine, not hers. As always, I couldn't have done it without you, Linda. I am so grateful to have you in my life and on my side. Thank you so much.

My wife, Debra: Every book is a contest with myself, and there is no one I'd rather have in my corner than you.

The way you encourage me, cheer me on, and understand why I'm always staring out the window is part of the magic that goes into each story. The excitement we share while working on a project is pure medicine for my soul.

My friend, Ted Butz, from Indianapolis. Ted is not only one heck of a good guy who helps me with all things firearms related, he is also one of the most enthusiastic and vocal supporters of my work. His generosity of time along with the wealth of knowledge he provides is immeasurable. Thank you so much, pal.

And speaking of thanks: To every single one of you who have taken the time to read my novels and leave reviews on Amazon: Thank you! Your endorsement of my work remains one of the highlights of my accomplishments. I am humbled by your trust, encouraged by your support, and in awe of your generosity during our continuing journey together. Thank you so much. Send me an email if you get the chance. I'd love to hear from you. I really would. Nothing lights up my day more than hearing from my readers. I wasn't kidding when I said it's the best part of the whole gig.

...and the story continues.

Virgil and the gang return in State of Humanity.

State of Humanity - Book 8 of the Virgil Jones Mystery, Thriller & Suspense series

Detective Virgil Jones thought he understood the Genesis of his past, but Humanity itself is about to show him he only had part of the story.

Six wealthy couples are taken from their homes, then

robbed of everything they own. The problem for the Major Crimes Unit is this: They have no evidence, no clues, and no idea if the victims are dead or alive. As Virgil Jones and the rest of the MCU investigates, the pressure mounts to find out who is committing the crimes, and more importantly, the location of the victims...

Huma Moon--Virgil and Sandy's live-in nanny has a secret--and she's kept it to herself for decades. Even her best friend and lover, Delroy Rouche doesn't know. But Delroy has a secret of his own, one that he's shared only with Virgil. And when Virgil sends Delroy and Huma to Jamaica to give them time to sort out their lives, he unknowingly sets off a chain of events that will either help them, or kill them...

The Pope twins are back with a problem of their own. Their neighbor in the hills of Hanover Parish in Jamaica isn't the type of person anyone would want living nearby. Roje Brenner owns one of the largest construction businesses on the island, one he uses to launder the profits from his international drug operation. And when Nichole and Nicky Pope discover Delroy's connection to Brenner, they have to make a choice, one that could cost them everything...

The past and present merge once again in the eighth installment of the Virgil Jones Mystery-Thriller Series.

You felt the Anger.

You experienced the Betrayal.

You took Control.
You faced the Deception.
You accepted the Exile.
You fought for Freedom.
You understood the Genesis. Now...
It's time to hold on to Humanity!

Get your copy of State of Genesis today!

ALSO BY THOMAS SCOTT

The Virgil Jones Mystery Series in order:

State of Anger - Book 1

State of Betrayal - Book 2

State of Control - Book 3

State of Deception - Book 4

State of Exile - Book 5

State of Freedom - Book 6

State of Genesis - Book 7

State of Humanity - Book 8

State of Impact - Book 9

And the story continues.

As Mason would say, "Stay tuned..."

Updates on future Virgil Jones novels available at:

ThomasScottBooks.com

ABOUT THE AUTHOR

Thomas Scott is the author of the Virgil Jones series of novels. He lives in northern Indiana with his lovely wife, Debra, his children, and his trusty sidekicks and writing buddies, Lucy, the cat, and Buster, the dog.

You may contact Thomas anytime via his website ThomasScottBooks.com where he personally answers every single email he receives. Be sure to sign up to be notified of the latest release information.

Also, if you enjoy the Virgil Jones series of books, leaving an honest review on Amazon.com helps others decide if a book is right for them. Just a sentence or two makes all the difference in the world. Plus, rumor has it that it's good for the soul!

For information on future books in the Virgil Jones series, or to connect with the author, please visit:

ThomasScottBooks.com

And remember:

Virgil and the gang are back in State of Humanity!

State of Humanity - Book 8 of the Virgil Jones Mystery Thriller Series

Grab your copy today!

Made in the USA
Coppell, TX
31 May 2020